PASSING
THROUGH
PARADISE

PASSING
THROUGH
PARADISE

John Schreiber

To order additional copies of this book, contact:
Xlibris Corporation
1-888-795-4274
www.Xlibris.com
Orders@Xlibris.com
20484

"Faith is part gift, part act,"
my father once said,
"part grace, part choice.
It's deciding to live,
confidently knowing that
God has been, is, and always will be in the future,
clearing the path before us."

—Angela Kiln

CHAPTER 1

"It looks the same, doesn't it, Angela?"

I don't reply.

Daddy has pulled over onto the shoulder of the highway. I stare at the new Paradise town sign, population 424, freshly peppered with buckshot. Across the highway, on our left, are the athletic fields. Beyond are tall, full cornfields, almost ready for the first frost. Looking north, down the highway, I see the town itself. Paradise looks like any other quiet small town, but I know better.

I shudder. Some memories just don't go away, even after ten years.

Just in front of us, the highway crosses the South Branch of Paradise Creek, the practical boundary to Paradise. To our right, an old, stone railroad bridge spans the creek. The water is low this late in the summer.

He drives north into town. Three blocks before Main Street he turns left, and we find ourselves passing the red brick, three-story school, its windows boarded up. Graffiti is scratched in the metal doors. Pigeons flutter around the bell steeple, its lightning rod askew. Weeds and tall grass cover the playground like a tattered, green shag carpet. Empty chains dangle from the rusted swing set. Several late-blooming, long-stemmed dandelions sprawl around the tire house.

Daddy next drives past the house where we lived for one year. It is still an attractive, early 1900's, two-story white house. The surrounding block, though seeming smaller, is just as quiet as I remember.

He turns west again and we pass Chelsea Turpin's house. Chelsea and I still write to each other. Across the street is the old Oatley house. Time and the new owners have not been kind to it. The roof is missing some shingles, and the paint on the siding is peeling like a bad case of sunburn.

Daddy drives down Main Street, or what is left of it. Except for a combined convenience store and gas station on the highway, businesses have completely deserted Paradise. The empty Main Street buildings are boarded up, even Miss Bloomsbury's corner thrift shop. The few brick buildings that aren't condemned have been converted into apartments. Compared to Paradise, Sinclair Lewis's Gopher Prairie was a cultural capital and an economic behemoth.

As Daddy turns north onto the highway, I twist in the seat, glancing back over my right shoulder. East of town stands the old depot—or what's left of it—a black scar of wood and a charred chimney reaching up awkwardly to a blue sky. Several years ago Daddy told me that unknown vandals had set it ablaze.

Vandals: perhaps. Unknown: no. Not in Paradise.

On the northeast edge of town, Daddy pulls off onto the shoulder of the highway. We look to our right, down the short street that ends at a cornfield, and see the dilapidated, rust-colored house that faces north. The house and the garage behind it still look the same, still needing paint, and the lawn still looks the same, still needing to be mowed. We don't have time to visit.

"I'll stop in on my way back," Daddy says.

Northeast of the rust-colored house stands Browner's Woods, dark green in the bright summer sun. The topmost, yellow-tipped leaves of the gnarled oak trees ripple slightly.

Just north of Browner's Woods is the gently rising ridge where a railroad line once headed off toward the Mississippi River. I wonder what is still in those woods.

"Ready to move on?" Daddy asks.

I nod and he drives north to my college orientation.

We cross the North Branch of Paradise Creek and, before we know it, Paradise is behind us, growing ever smaller in Daddy's rear view mirror, finally disappearing. Yet the year we spent in

Paradise won't disappear from my life so quickly. It never will. As we head down the highway, Daddy doesn't say anything and neither do I. At Paradise, our lives changed irreversibly.

After my time in Paradise, I came to expect death at any moment. "You got to have life to love life," Edgar Lee Masters wrote. I disagree. I think you've got to have death to love life.

In Paradise I stumbled onto a dead body, found my new mother, and was almost murdered.

The first time I saw a Paradise town sign, population 473, also pockmarked by buckshot, I had just sat up from sleeping in the front seat of our old Ford station wagon. We were heading south into town, from the opposite direction. We had just crossed the North Branch of Paradise Creek. I was nine years old.

"Here we are, Angel," Daddy said.

Rubbing my eyes, I looked around. Paradise lay in a wide, flat-bottomed valley, surrounded by fields almost as flat. Arching elm trees lined the highway, but they failed to break up or hide the town's dreary flatness or the absolute desolation. The only break from the monotonous bleakness was on our left: a ridge running east of town and a distant railroad trestle. Along the ridge's south side was a long stretch of woods also running east.

When I had told my best friend Becky back in St. Paul that we were moving to southern Minnesota, she had ooohed enviously. "It's so pretty," she had gushed. "You'll love the rolling hills and pretty streams."

Later I learned that she had only seen southern Minnesota along the Mississippi River. What I viewed was not river bluff country. No majestic stone bluffs rose toward the heavens. Paradise's part of Minnesota could easily be mistaken for North Dakota prairie.

My father, Jack Kiln, whom I still call Daddy, moved us to Paradise because his St. Paul teaching job had been cut after fifteen years. Paradise needed a teacher for one year, and, since the district was drowning in debt, thus consolidating, the school board felt that it could afford an experienced teacher. "What's an extra $2,000 now?" Mr. Cranberry had quipped to Daddy. They got more than experience in Daddy; they got one of the best.

"I'll need all the help you can give me," Daddy told me as we prepared for the move. He repeated that often during our year there. It was a tough time for Paradise, a tough time for Daddy, and a tough time for me.

Paradise was, I later learned, typical of many small towns in southern Minnesota, typical, that is, in its appearance. Most homes had been built between 1890 and 1930, in the L-shaped, two-story, prairie home style. A few notable exceptions were an impressive string of late Victorian homes that stood like majestic guardians on the west end of Main Street. Several blocks of houses on the town's south end were built right after World War II, Paradise's second period of growth. The third growth spurt showed itself in two blocks on the southwest edge of town. Here were the new homes built in the 1970's, Paradise's period of optimism. Several of those were for sale.

As we turned off the highway onto Main Street, I quickly saw that the business district was as bleak as the landscape.

"Paradise," Daddy said, "once had a thriving dairy business."

All I could think was that it must have been a very long time ago.

On the north side of the street, in rapidly deteriorating condition, stood three empty brick buildings. Warped plywood had been nailed over the windows. Still surviving on the street's north side was a brick post office, a small barbershop, a cluttered hardware store, a newspaper office (open two and a half days a week), and a café. On Main Street's south side, six brick store fronts stood vacant. Surviving was a second-hand store, a small office shared on alternating days by an accountant and a dentist, a movie theater that had been converted into a bowling alley (open only during the winter) and the town liquor store.

It was depressing to a nine-year-old girl who knew only the immensity and color and diversity of St. Paul.

I had not yet seen the house Daddy had rented. From the picture he had shown me, I knew it was a white, narrow, two-story house. Daddy had described the inside simply: a living room, large kitchen, open staircase, one main floor bedroom, and two bedrooms upstairs. "The backyard is large," he said, "compared to St. Paul, with a small garage that could maybe just hold our station wagon— oh, and two tall maple trees, either one of which could accommodate a tire swing."

I could only hope our house wasn't as bad as what I'd seen on Main Street.

Fortunately, my fears proved false. He stopped the car in front of a white house: tall and narrow, a large picture window, a beautiful flower garden in front, and a deep back yard.

"Is this it?"

"That's it," he smiled.

As soon as I crossed the front threshold, I knew that Daddy's description hadn't done it justice. The wallpapered dining room had a beautiful built-in oak hutch and an oak banister edging the open staircase. I ran upstairs and discovered two large bedrooms with hardwood floors, one with walls painted pink. I knew that Daddy would let me claim that one. It had plenty of space for my doll collection. Looking out the north window, I saw the street below and, to the northwest, the city park and playground. I dashed into the bathroom and found a massive, claw-foot bathtub, just like ones I'd seen in old movies. After using the bathroom, I ran downstairs and found Daddy lugging a box into the kitchen.

I followed him. The kitchen had tall cabinets and a table by the back windows.

"It's huge!" I exclaimed. Daddy raised his eyebrows at my exuberance.

Not everything was great, however. As I hurried through the dining room and into the living room, I came face to face with a dark green, upright piano.

"Joe Swanson, the owner, offered to move it out," Daddy said, "but I told him that it could stay."

He rested his hand on my shoulder, suddenly becoming enthusiastic; too enthusiastic, I thought.

"I'm sure we can find someone in town who gives lessons," he said. "I know you've always wanted to play the piano."

I did?

"The piano needs to be tuned, but it'll do the job."

Yeah, I thought. It'll do its job. That meant another job for me.

"Well, let's unpack," he said.

It didn't take us long, for we didn't have much: Daddy never liked to collect things except for model trains. Since the rented house came with appliances, Daddy had sold our stove and refrigerator before moving. We had, of course, some basic furniture, but none of it was as nice as Becky's. Her home, she once informed me, had colonial style furniture. After her comment, I asked Daddy what kind of furniture we had. He laughed and said, "Mid-twentieth century garage sale." At the time, I didn't see anything funny about it.

Daddy hauled in two large boxes marked with my name and set them in the center of my bedroom floor. Kneeling, I unpacked my carefully wrapped dolls. Daddy set up my shelves, and I neatly arranged my treasured friends.

Looking back, I must have been a terrible hindrance to him. While he moved in boxes of kitchen things and living room furniture and put together the beds and arranged the bathroom towels, I fussed over my dolls like a new mother over her baby's first public appearance. But patience was my doting father's strongest trait.

I never knew a girl who had a better father.

He would later retrieve his boxes of model train equipment that had been stored at Aunt Joan's in St. Paul. "The model railroad is my one vice, Angel," he would tell me on more than one occasion.

He only stood five feet, ten inches, but seemed tall to me, as all fathers seem to their children, and his black hair was thinning. "Thinner all the time," he'd moan in the morning as he shaved. He wore glasses and had gray eyes that, when he smiled, could seem as bright as the sun or, when he was angry, could turn as dark as thunderclouds and melt me to tears. His nose was straight and his chin was prominent and his jaw was square. He had a few freckles and a small scar on his forehead. I always thought he was the handsomest man in the world.

After my dolls were arranged to my satisfaction, I helped him in the kitchen. Silverware was my specialty. He scrubbed the kitchen cabinets while I organized the silverware in a drawer. When I was done, I helped Daddy clean the dark, musty cabinets below the counter. I never liked the lower cabinets. They smelled stuffy. I don't think Daddy liked those cabinets either, even after scrubbing them twice.

Maybe the bottom cabinets were like Paradise. Old. Too old. No matter how much we scrubbed them, they never got clean. They needed to be replaced.

"If you stay too long in Paradise," Mrs. Putnam would later tell Daddy, "you become just like it." We later moved to Hillcrest. You can only clean so much.

The next morning, a Saturday, I walked over to the town park.

Several small children were running around the rickety slide. One boy, instead of climbing the ladder, kept trying to walk up the shining metal slope but, like the mythical Sisyphus, slipped each time and slid back down on his stomach. On the other side of the playground, beyond the swings, was a wooden picnic shelter with low, fence-like walls and an attached stone chimney and fireplace. Inside the shelter were five red picnic tables.

I walked across the park, toward the shelter. I passed the teeter-totters. Three of the four teeter-totters had various names carved in the boards. The fourth had a new board, painted glossy blue. I kicked a ragged, dog-chewed tennis ball out of my way and strolled over to the animal springs on which younger children could sit and sway and bounce. One, an elephant, had a cracked trunk; another, a parrot, had a cracked tail. I walked past and stepped onto the concrete floor of the picnic shelter.

"You must be the new teacher's kid."

I jumped, startled by a girl's voice, apparently from nowhere.

Turning, I saw an older girl leaning against the side of the stone fireplace.

I blushed. "How did you know?"

She smiled. "No one moves into Purgatory without everyone else knowing it."

"Purgatory?"

"Oops. I meant Paradise."

I walked to one of the picnic table benches. Many names were carved into the wood. I picked out a name I liked and sat on it.

"My name's Angela. What's yours?"

"Jane Turpin."

I felt pretty special that a girl as old as Jane Turpin would take notice of me. I learned later that she was a junior in high school.

She stretched a grass blade between her fingers and leaned her head back against the stones of the fireplace, then tossed the blade into the black hearth by her side. She wore a simple white T-shirt and faded jeans, and she had a dark complexion with large brown eyes. I thought she was quite pretty. Her glistening black hair was tied back in a ponytail. I'd always wanted to have long hair, but it never grew right for me. Also, Daddy was quite hopeless in helping with my hair. So, caught between nature and Daddy, I always cut my dark hair short—like a mop, I thought.

"You see, Angela, everyone knows everything about everyone else in Paradise." She added, almost as an afterthought, "unless they want to ignore something."

"What else do you know about me?"

She rattled off facts quickly: "You don't have a mother. Your dad teaches English. I'll have him this year. You don't have much stuff because you shoved everything into that rusted-out blue station wagon, unless, of course, you're making another trip or two. You're from the Cities—"

"St. Paul."

"Whatever. You're going into the fourth grade and your teacher will be Mrs. Putnam. Want me to go on?"

"What's Mrs. Putnam like?"

"She's short with gray hair, about 200 years old. She doesn't yell much but makes it miserable for the whole class if anyone goofs off. You won't have parties like the other classes, and you'll work harder too."

"How do you know so much about her?"

"I had her. Everyone in Paradise has. Even my mother had her."

"Wow. She must be old!"

"I told you she was ancient."

A car drove by. Jane watched it closely.

"Someone you know?"

"Of course." She didn't say anything more, as if my question, like her answer, was obvious.

"What are you doing sitting here?"

She grabbed her knees, hugging them to herself. "Just sitting. It's quiet. Not too many quiet places in town."

I looked around. It did seem quiet. The kids by the slide were laughing and the boy was still slipping and thumping against the metal, but it was nothing like the continual hum and rattle of traffic in the city. In fact, it seemed too quiet.

Just then, Daddy called from our yard. I jumped up and waved. He spotted me and waved for me to come.

"See y'around," Jane said.

I said good-bye and ran across the park to Daddy who was ready to go to Rochester for groceries. As I hopped into our front seat, I glanced back at the park.

A boy with brown hair had just ridden up to the shelter on his bike. He got off and walked over to the fireplace.

Sunday we went to the nearby Lutheran church a block past the park and north of Main Street. The church was a large, truly impressive, steeple-crested brick building. Daddy didn't attend church very often, not since my mother died. He always sent me to Sunday school, though. I thought it was special that we were both going that morning: our first Sunday in our new home.

Daddy wore his blue sports coat, dark pants, and tie. I wore my white and lavender dress. It was my favorite.

We walked up the wide, cement steps. Twenty-five of them. I counted.

A wide-faced man with gray, crew-cut hair greeted us at the door.

"Morning," he boomed as he shook Daddy's hand.

"Morning," Daddy mumbled. Daddy wasn't very cordial with strangers, especially if he was a little nervous.

The man bent over and took my hand. "Morning, little lady."

I smiled, "Good morning."

His hand was wide, callused. He stood up, addressed Daddy. "You're the new teacher."

Daddy nodded. "And this is my daughter Angela."

"Pleased to meet you. I'm Larry Bates."

"Jack Kiln."

"I know. I read a little about you."

"Oh? The paper?"

Mr. Bates lifted his chin proudly. "Your personnel file. I'm on the school board."

Daddy smiled broadly, almost facetiously. "Well, then I am pleased to meet you. How is the consolidation coming?"

Mr. Bates stiffened, his face flushing. "We wouldn't 'a done it if we didn't have to. Towns need their schools. What's a town without a school? Hillcrest is already callin' the shots. They think they're so high and mighty. If I had two cents for every—"

Interrupting, Daddy nodded politely. "Well," he said, "glad to be here."

Mr. Bates blinked rapidly, no doubt remembering where he was. "Yes, we're glad to have you with us in Paradise."

"I hope that it will live up to its name."

"We sure think it does."

Daddy glanced at me. "Come on, Angel, we don't want to be late." He grabbed my hand and pulled me in.

The church's sanctuary was huge, with a high ceiling and tall, stained glass windows. The plaster walls were simple, undecorated, with the walls showing patches in numerous places, cracks in others.

On a recessed wall behind the pulpit was an elaborate painting of Jesus among a crowd. The beautifully painted people, gold glittering the edges of their ivory robes, looked truly somber and reverential. It reminded me of a picture from an old illustrated Bible my grandparents had, except that the people painted here looked more Scandinavian than Jewish.

The congregation was nice, I guess, though no one else really talked to us afterward. The service was too long, longer than the church we attended in St. Paul, at least the services I attended when Daddy would come with me. The singing was good, but the minister read his sermon in an only slightly varied monotone. I drew pictures on the church bulletin.

After the ordeal, the minister talked to us briefly at the door. "You'll be coming back next Sunday?"

I couldn't tell if he was asking or telling Daddy.

Daddy shifted his weight and I knew he was buying time. "Well, we just moved in and want to look around a bit."

"We're the largest church in town."

"I know. It's a big building."

"Built in 1893."

Daddy nodded in his politely uninterested way. "We might see you again." He grabbed my hand and we fled down the stairs.

"What did you think?" he asked when we got home.

I shrugged. "It is a pretty church. Big."

"But?"

"Lots of empty pews."

"Not many kids."

"No."

"I didn't like it either."

I hoped that we could find a church that both Daddy and I liked. He evidently didn't like the one we—or I—had gone to in St. Paul. I sure liked it better when he came with me, instead of dropping me off and picking me up.

I first met Becky at that church. I missed her.

On Monday we finished cleaning the house and arranging, then re-arranging things. Daddy usually placed things in three different spots before he settled on the one he liked, and once it was there, it was there for good, rooted like a tree. In my room, though, he let me arrange everything. And I knew exactly where I wanted my things. The first time. And that usually lasted at least a month.

I arranged my dolls so that they stood on their shelves across the room from my bed, placed so that when I lay in bed I could see them. When I woke up, they would be looking at me.

I don't know when I first started "collecting" dolls. I had kept every doll I'd ever been given. Daddy had bought stands a year ago so that they could stay neatly arranged on my shelves.

When I was six and a half, I first bought a doll with my own money, having saved the meager allowance that I regularly received for doing extra work—"chores," Daddy called them—around the house. It had taken me almost an entire year to save enough money for a doll, and then I found the perfect one in a catalogue. She had long brown hair, large brown eyes, and a matching brown dress.

I remember Daddy acting oddly when I showed him which doll I wanted to order. At first, I thought it was the doll's cost. Later, I discovered the reason for his hesitation.

One evening, a few months after I had bought her, I lay in bed while Daddy sat beside me, reading a story aloud. I could read almost anything by myself, but I always wanted him to read to me at bedtime. I think he wanted to read to me as well.

As he read, my gaze drifted across the room. The reading light, hitting my knees, cast a shadow across the room and onto the doll. I shifted, the shadow moved, and the light caught my doll's large brown eyes. It appeared to be looking directly at me, and it was if I suddenly saw the doll for the first time.

"Daddy," I said, interrupting his reading, "that doll looks like Mommy's picture."

Daddy stopped and took off his glasses and stared at the doll for a long moment.

"I know," he said softly.

He cleared his throat and continued reading and we never spoke of it again.

CHAPTER 2

"Schools must first be fiscally responsible. Schools must be run like a business."

—Superintendent J. Cranberry,
quoted in the *Paradise Post*, August 23, 1989

On Monday, a week and one day before school began, I went to school with Daddy to help him organize his room. He parked on the street so that I would get a feel for where I would enter the building on the first day of school. We walked along the sidewalk, stood by the yellow bus stop sign, and faced the narrow end of the red brick building. The year 1901 was engraved in the cornerstone. New windows had been added since then, but I saw no other improvements or additions.

"Do all the kids go here?" I asked.

"Uh-huh."

It was both exciting and frightening to think that I would be in the same building as high school seniors.

Left of the building, to the south, was the school playground with the usual swings, monkey bars, and merry-go-round. I ran over to see it better. Most unique was a tire house. Rising like a pyramid, the tire house was built from over twenty tractor tires bolted together at various angles, offering numerous places to climb, crawl, and hide. Behind the playground stretched a square grassy area, perfect for running games. I could just see the corner of a parking lot on the other side.

"You can check out the playground later," Daddy said.

"Where do the big kids play sports?"

"They play their football and baseball games on the south edge of town."

Daddy once said that the main door of a school tells you the most about a school. A welcome sign is nice. Or attractive colors. Something is needed which says that you are wanted, that school is exciting, that life offers great possibilities. As it was, there were two main doors, one near each corner of the building, with no indication of which door to enter.

Each main door was covered with a metal sheet, painted red. We chose the door on our left, near the playground. I ran up and gripped the door handle, but it wouldn't budge.

Daddy caught up to me and opened the door with a grunt. "Must've been installed in the 50's to withstand a nuclear blast."

The entryway was dark. It smelled of dust and old wood. A flight of steps led down to a musty basement. We chose the other flight that brought us to the corner of the classroom hallways. Ahead stretched a long, unlit corridor. On our immediate left was a classroom, and to our right ran a hallway, the far corner of which took us, no doubt, to the other outside doors. A hand-painted sign posted on the wall said, in gloss black letters: "Office—Upstairs."

The flight of stairs we were on continued up. We walked up the creaking, wooden steps to the second floor. Halfway up, before the steps turned back into the building's center, was a large window. I looked out the window, across the quiet houses and yards, and realized for the first time that this might be our home for a long time. I was scared and sad at the same time.

We reached the next dark floor and saw another sign: "Office—Upstairs." We continued up the next flight of creaking wooden stairs. Looking around at the open stairway, Daddy ran his hand along the wood banister. "All this wood makes for a poor fire exit."

I looked out the window between the second and third floors and could see the traffic on the highway, a semi and a car and a pickup and a van flowing past, people driving by without a glance to or a thought of Paradise.

"Come on, Angel."

At the top of the stairs on our left was a small corner room with a blood red sign over the door: "OFFICE". A bespectacled,

narrow-faced, gray-haired woman sat behind a long wooden desk,
typing. Papers were scattered all over her desk. I read her nameplate:
"Mrs. Thomas." She glanced up briefly and continued typing.

"Yes?"

"Jack Kiln. To see Mr. Cranberry."

"Other office."

"Other office?"

"Other office." Clearly frustrated, Mrs. Thomas stopped typing
and peered at us over her glasses. "We're above our elementary
wing and they're below their high school wing."

She didn't offer any directions.

Daddy nodded. "Oh."

He glanced down at me and shrugged.

We left and looked down the long, dark hall running west,
toward a far stairway. At the end of an equally dark yet shorter hall
heading north was another set of stairs.

"That must lead down to the other main door," Daddy said.

"Let's take that one," I said, and led the way.

We heard the secretary's rapid typing, its echoes sounding like
bullets.

"Daddy, didn't you visit the school before, when you first drove
to Paradise?"

"The school wasn't open then. I only needed to come here to
find a place to live."

"So you've never been in this building?"

"No. Mr. Cranberry, who's both superintendent and high
school principal, hired me over the phone. He said that he wanted
someone with a lot of teaching experience. Since this school is
consolidating with Hillcrest, they thought the students might cause
problems for a rookie teacher."

At the hall corner, I peered down the longer hall. Taller lockers
lined the walls, telling us that this, indeed, was the high school
wing. We walked down the steps, our footsteps echoing eerily.
"Do students cause problems for new teachers?"

"Sometimes. But experienced teachers can usually handle
problems better. Unfortunately, most school districts are financially

strapped, so they can rarely afford to take the financial risks to improve education by hiring experienced staff. Now, however, the district is so broke that a little more debt won't hurt them. What's a little more risk now?"

"Oh," I said.

We found the "other office" on the main floor along the west hall. The high school's office windows faced the paved parking lot. This office was more spacious and several landscape paintings hung on the walls. A secretary typed on the other side of a long, high counter that seemed almost like a barricade. I quickly and quietly sat on a cushioned bench. No one saw me.

Daddy introduced himself to the high school secretary who quit typing. She sighed at the interruption to her typing, then stood and stepped up to the counter. She said her name was Mrs. Benwick. She was a little younger than Daddy, I guessed, around thirty, and very short and plump. I'd almost call her "fat" but Daddy told me not to call people that. She had short dark hair and beady eyes that seemed most unfriendly. After her chilly greeting to Daddy, she waddled to a brightly-lit room to the right.

"Mr. Cranberry," she announced haughtily, "the new teacher is here."

Mrs. Benwick returned and looked Daddy up and down. The elementary secretary had been crabby, but Mrs. Benwick was snotty, with a superior air that I learned later in life only comes from a mistaken sense of one's own authority.

Mr. Cranberry emerged from his office. He was shorter than Daddy and stockier, with thick, wavy black hair and large jowls. His hair color looked fake, like a cheap doll's. Dyed, I thought.

When Mr. Cranberry ushered Daddy into his office, I was, for the moment, forgotten, which was fine with me. Mr. Cranberry didn't shut the door, so I heard their conversation. They discussed the school rules, schedules, and class lists. Daddy was surprised to learn that he'd be junior class advisor and direct a spring play.

"I don't know that much about theater."

Mr. Cranberry rustled some papers. "You are certified in English?"

"Yes."

"Good enough." Mr. Cranberry chuckled. "Even if you weren't, your room has two sinks and a mirror where students can get into make-up."

"Impeccable logic." I could recognize Daddy's sarcastic humor even at a distance. Fortunately, Mr. Cranberry didn't.

Mr. Cranberry then launched into a long discourse about his summer and the fish he had caught and what great fun he had had taking a couple of school board members to his cabin and what great morale the staff demonstrated. He went on and on and I began to doze off.

Daddy finally emerged, and Mr. Cranberry patted Daddy's back in what I think was meant to be a fatherly gesture. "Since this is the last year and so forth, the rest of the staff may become negative at times. Just remember that none of us likes change, so we grumble. But we can't let that affect our teaching."

"I'll always do my best," Daddy replied cheerfully.

"Fine. My door is always open." He handed Daddy a room key and returned to his office. He never noticed me. I quickly grabbed Daddy's hand and we left.

He led me back down the hall and up two flights of stairs to his room. Daddy turned on the lights. The room's walls were painted blue and a tall set of windows faced west, looking out over the parking lot. Below the windows, the plaster was cracked, and brown water stains marred the ceiling tiles. And, just as Mr. Cranberry had said, in the back were two sinks and a mirror. It wasn't nearly as nice as the classroom I had in St. Paul nor the one where Daddy had taught, but compared to everything else I'd seen in the building so far, it wasn't too bad. Of course, I was going to do everything I could to make it look better.

We went right to work. While he carried in his boxes of reference books from our car, I stapled blue paper to the bulletin boards. I had to stand on a desk to get to the top. While he sorted textbooks, I hung up posters.

During the morning I met two of Daddy's fellow teachers as they entered and introduced themselves.

The first one to walk in was Mr. Manitou. Daddy had gone to the office for more paper, and I was stapling a long blue sheet of paper onto the bulletin board when Mr. Manitou walked up behind me.

"Hello, little lady," came his deep, melodic voice.

Startled, I spun around, quite flustered. He was really tall, far taller than Daddy, with straight black hair, a dark complexion, and high cheekbones.

"You must be Mr. Kiln's daughter."

I nodded. He was the tallest Indian I'd ever seen.

"Is your father around?"

I swallowed. "He went to the office for some more paper."

Just then, Daddy entered. "Hello."

With the spotlight off me, I could compose myself. Usually, I am pretty good at meeting strangers, except when they come from behind and scare me.

Daddy set down his rolled-up sheet of white paper and they introduced themselves to each other. They talked about school details and then Daddy asked how Mr. Cranberry was to work with.

"As administrators go, he tends to be a bully. But since the consolidation went through, he's been very conciliatory. He talks about site-based management. Mentions getting our input. Not that he takes it, of course, but at least he mentions it. Most of us believe that he's hoping to be the superintendent of the new consolidated district. If he doesn't get it, watch out, because he hates being a principal. All of the work and none of the real power."

They talked awhile longer. I learned that Mr. Manitou taught high school mathematics as well as one history class, that he had three children, and that he lived near Hillcrest.

"And I teach next door," Mr. Manitou said. "If you need help with anything, just shout."

"Thanks."

He turned to go, then bent over and his dark eyes looked directly into mine. "A pleasure meeting you, quiet one."

He departed, leaving me speechless again.

Daddy smiled at me. "You've found yourself a friend."

Later, as I was cutting out large WELCOME letters, in came a man a little shorter than Daddy but seeming twice as tall. He had a big face, a thick neck, wide shoulders, and a large chest. Mostly bald, he combed long strands of hair from his temples over the top. If he was trying to hide his bald head, he wasn't succeeding.

"Hi there," he boomed. I learned later that Mr. Oldenburg rarely talked, he always boomed.

"Hi," Daddy said. "I'm Jack Kiln."

"Figured that. Leo Oldenburg. Social studies." They shook hands. "We're a pretty small faculty here, you know. In fact, I'll be bringing forms over for you to sign. Association stuff."

Daddy smiled knowingly. "Union dues."

Mr. Oldenburg grinned. "You got it."

"No. You'll get it."

Mr. Oldenburg laughed, deep and boisterous. "You'll fit in good."

You'll fit in *well*, I silently corrected.

"I hope so," Daddy said.

"Well, see you tomorrow at the faculty meeting." And out he went, without ever acknowledging me, which was just fine.

Toward the end of the day, Daddy and I wandered around the elementary's part of the building to see where my class would be. On our second trip through the school, I was even less impressed. Attempts at decorating the building had not been very successful. A short-beaked and small-eyed Big Bird had been painted outside the kindergarten room. Another door had a sun painted over it. But all the decorations in the world couldn't bring life into the poorly lit halls.

The dark wood doors were closed and locked, so we could only peer in the narrow glass windows beside the doors. On the second floor, we found a door with "Fourth Grade" above it in block letters. Through the glass I spied a large, imposing oak desk and slate chalkboard.

Suddenly, we heard piano music coming down the hall. We

followed the music past a few classrooms to an open door that led into a bright blue room.

Even though I had never taken piano lessons, nor, contrary to Daddy's opinion, did I have a desire to, I liked to listen to the piano if it was played well. I knew enough to realize that the pianist we heard was good. Very good.

We slipped in. Black notes and staffs had been painted on the wall above the slate chalkboard. In the center of the room, small chairs formed a semi-circle. In front of the chairs was a black upright piano. At the piano sat a slender brunette wearing a red silk blouse and black shorts. Her long and wavy hair accentuated her precise, petite features. Her long fingers danced over the keyboard like leaping ballerinas.

We waited until she finished playing the song.

"Hello," Daddy said.

Startled, as I had been earlier that day by Mr. Manitou, she stood quickly, looking momentarily flustered. She blushed and smiled beautifully.

"Please don't stop playing," Daddy said. "We enjoyed hearing your music, but we didn't want to be an audience without your knowing it."

Daddy stepped forward, shook her hand. "I'm Jack Kiln. This is my daughter, Angela."

She shook my hand too. Her hand was warm, slender, soft, and her dark blue eyes sparkled like a clear, deep, northern lake. She had very long eyelashes, longer than I'd ever seen.

"Linda O'Neil."

"Any relation to Eugene?" Daddy asked.

I rolled my eyes. Daddy was always making obscure jokes or pulling out some trivial literary connection.

After a puzzled second, she laughed. "Sorry, definitely not. You must be the new English teacher."

"Yes. And you're the grade school music—"

She cut him off. "Grade school *and* high school vocal *and* band."

Daddy whistled: "Quite a load."

"You get use to it at Paradise School. Everyone is overloaded."

"Is that why they're finally consolidating?"

"No. If they could afford it, they'd stay independent, no matter how much they pile on our backs. Just talk to Larry Bates, the school board chairman, or our superintendent, and you'll quickly see what I mean. Fortunately for the kids, the money can't stretch anymore."

Daddy looked around the room. "How is it that some elementary classrooms are on the second and third floors? Shouldn't they all be on the first?"

"Lots of things are backwards here," she said. "Did you know there are two faculty rooms? The high school faculty room is next to their office."

"Don't you mean to say 'the *other*' faculty room?"

She laughed, and her laughter was like fine crystal tinkling. "Yes. You catch on fast. You'll do well here."

"I hope so."

"And you, Angela," she said, bending over to face me, "I'll look forward to seeing you in music class. With your long fingers, I bet you play the piano and I'm sure that you have a gorgeous voice."

I blushed. "Well," I muttered.

Daddy put his arm on my shoulder, rescuing me. "She has a voice all right," he said. Before I could wonder what he meant, he gave my shoulder a squeeze. "And I love it."

Daddy was always like that.

As for Miss O'Neil, I knew then that I had found the perfect wife for Daddy and, of course, the perfect mother for me. I only had to learn how to play the piano and sing.

CHAPTER 3

School comes, as surely as death and taxes.
—from Mr. Cranberry's summer letter to teachers

The next day was the first official workshop day for teachers.

"I never know why they bother calling it a work day," Daddy muttered at breakfast. "The administration always packs these days full of meetings."

I asked if I could stay home by myself. In St. Paul, Daddy would never have let me. But this was Paradise: he said that I could. "But," he added, "I'll need your help around 10 o'clock."

Looking back, I'm not sure if he expected me to believe that he actually needed my help or not, other than in organizing his files. Our appointment did make me feel wanted, and it meant that we could eat lunch together, but it also prevented me from exploring the town all morning, which was probably his goal.

After he left for school, I watched cartoons for an hour, then walked to the post office. On my way along Main Street, I peered in the windows of the dark bowling alley. Past the small booths, I could see four narrow lanes. The sagging ceiling, just over the right lane, had two large water stains and a missing ceiling tile.

At the post office I bought some stamps. I still couldn't really understand why I had to walk to get the mail. I thought Daddy had been joking when he first told me that we would get our mail in a little post office box and that I would need to memorize our combination.

The day after we arrived in Paradise, Daddy had rented a box from the postmaster.

I was puzzled. "Daddy, how come you have to pay to pick up your mail?"

The gray-haired postmaster, leaning out his window, frowned at me over his half-glasses. "From the Cities, are you?"

Later, I tried to get Daddy to explain. It didn't help.

"But in St. Paul the mail was delivered to our house and we didn't pay."

"That's true."

"Do the people in the country get theirs delivered free?"

"Yes. It's called rural free delivery."

"Then how come we have to both walk and pay?"

"Politics."

Daddy always said that when something didn't make sense.

After I opened the box on the third try, I was able to reach in and pull the mail out.

In between two junk mail envelopes, I found a letter from Becky. I dashed home to read it.

> *Deer Angela,*
>
> *I miss you already. Schools almost hear and I have no one to walk with yet. My dad says he will drive me to school the first day on his way to work.*
>
> *My parents bought me a new blowse and two pears of jeens and a new dress for school. I'll have Mrs. Wallenberg this year. Yuch.*
>
> *Sunday I wanted to call you on the fone, but then I rememberd that it was long distinse. Dad says I can call you after school starts. If I had my way, I'd call you every day. Like I use to.*
>
> *Please write. I'll write you every week.*
>
> *Friends forever,*
>
> *Becky*

Her spelling hadn't improved, but that didn't matter: I read her letter four times. Folding her letter, I crammed it into my pocket.

She probably would be receiving my letter today. I sat down and wrote her another one, then ran back to the post office to mail it.

After jumping up and watching the envelope vanish in the slot, I went to the park. I saw no one else there, which was fine with me. I pulled myself onto a swing and swung awhile. The rhythmically squeaking chains irritated me, but the swinging motion made me feel happier somehow, lighter perhaps.

Over in the shelter, I glimpsed someone leaning against the fireplace. I guessed it was Jane.

I jumped off the swing and ran over.

I peeked around the corner.

"Hi, Jane." She still had her long dark hair in a ponytail and wore the same faded jeans but with a different T-shirt. It said "Paradise" on the front. She looked tired.

"How are you, Angela?"

"Pretty good. What're you doing?"

"Not much. Just sitting. Looking forward to school?"

I shrugged. "Guess so. I'm kinda bored without it."

"I know what you mean." She pulled her legs up, hugging her knees, and glanced back at the swings. "When I was your age, I'd spend hours on this playground."

"Do you come here a lot?"

"Sometimes. In the morning. Evenings I work over in Hillcrest."

I then remembered Daddy. "Do you know what time it is?"

She didn't have a watch. "About 10 o'clock, I'd say. Why?"

"I have to meet my dad at school."

"Is he a good teacher?"

Knowing I shouldn't brag, I gave an indecisive shrug and tried to act older. "I think so. Kids sometimes call him at home. They used to anyway, in St. Paul. He's a good dad."

Jane looked off again toward the empty swings, smiling rather wistfully. "That's nice." She glanced back abruptly: "Are you ready for Old Prune, Mrs. Putnam?"

I suddenly had a bad feeling in my tummy. "Is she that bad?"

"Terrible. But you better get going or you'll be late."

"See you later," I shouted, running toward home. When I came to the street, I stopped as a white convertible drove by. Two boys, one boy with a wide face and red hair, the other with a narrow face and curly blond hair, were looking at me. They slowed and laughed and I heard "teacher's kid." I glared at them, but they didn't notice. They were already driving past.

After I pulled my bike out of the garage, I glanced over at the park. The same brown-haired boy that I had seen the other day was just arriving, walking to the shelter. I hopped on my bike and rode to the corner. The white convertible was making another pass, this time on the other side of the park. The car slowed and stopped. The two boys were shouting something to the brown-haired boy and laughing. The boy ignored them and approached Jane. The two boys continued to laugh at them and whistle. Jane stood quickly, grabbed the boy's arm and turned my way. I spun my bike around before she noticed me.

I patted my pocket, making sure Becky's letter was securely there, and biked over to school.

I went straight to Daddy's room. The lights were on, but he wasn't there. I walked to the windows and looked across the school parking lot. Several young kids were riding their bikes around the lot as aimlessly as the two boys in the convertible had been riding around the streets of Paradise. Just then, Daddy came in. He looked irritated. He must have just come out of a meeting. He was always grumpy after a meeting and I knew that it would take him a few minutes to return to his normal self.

I wanted to tell him about what I had seen, to ask him why people liked to be mean to others, but I knew that this wasn't the time.

We worked together on reorganizing his files.

It was by sorting notes on Chaucer and Shakespeare and Milton and Keats that I learned about these men—or their names anyway.

"Didn't any women write in those days?" I asked.

Daddy, leaning over the bottom drawer of the filing cabinet, looked up. "Some did. Even Queen Elizabeth. Later, in America, Anne Bradstreet wrote many fine poems. And don't forget Jane Austen or the Brontë sisters. In the 1800's, George Eliot wrote some great novels."

"George was a woman?"

"It was a pseudonym—a pen name. Mary Ann Evans thought she'd be accepted better with a male name."

"So women weren't accepted then?"

"In Mary Ann Evans's day, most women wrote romantic novels, not the realistic books she wanted to write."

"But what about earlier? In Shakespeare's day?"

"Lots of people couldn't read or write. Many people assumed that women didn't need to."

"I'm glad I didn't live then."

Daddy reached over and gave me a hug. "Me too." He laughed. "No one would know what to do with all your questions."

He handed me a stack of folders. "These are student writing folders. Their names are on the tabs. Would you check to make sure they're all alphabetized?"

Daddy had taught me how to alphabetize at a very early age for just such occasions. In fact, I couldn't remember a time when I didn't know how to read. Reading was something I took for granted, like walking or breathing. He often told me about students who couldn't read, or wouldn't read, and I never understood that. How sad to be so limited in life, so crippled in perspective, with a silent imagination that only heard one point of view. The wordless person's inner world must be a dark and dreamless vacuum.

Around eleven, Daddy and I went to the faculty room. I had a donut and met Mr. Bakken, a heavy-set phy-ed teacher; Mr. Hanson, a short, mustached science teacher; Mrs. Walker, a short and very thin home ec and art teacher, and Mr. Wallace, a tall, athletic-looking special education and Spanish teacher. Mr. Manitou and Mr. Oldenburg were also there. Miss O'Neil wasn't.

"Is that all the teachers there are?" I asked when we left.

"That was most of the high school staff," Daddy said. "There are a few part-timers. Also Mrs. Peabody, a librarian from Hillcrest, comes over one day a week."

My school in St. Paul had about that many teachers for just the third grade. I was beginning to grasp just how small Paradise was.

For lunch we drove to the Paradise Café, the town restaurant.

Daddy held the restaurant's screen door open for me. Greasy smoke, like a fine mist, rose from the back kitchen. Behind the counter on my left, a chalkboard announced the specials. A long table was in the middle of the café, and chipped wooden booths ran along the other wall.

"Why don't we take someone with us to lunch tomorrow?" I asked. "Like Miss O'Neil?"

Daddy shrugged noncommittally. "I like to get away from school-talk for a few minutes. Besides," he smiled, "I can't let anyone else horn in on our date!"

Normally, I liked it when Daddy made me feel special. Not today. I realized how challenging it would be to get him to marry my future mother.

CHAPTER 4

Need clothes for school? Check the Paradise Thrift Shop!
Before you drive to Rochester, shop Paradise first!
—advertisement in *Paradise Post*

Daddy had workshop again the next day. For the second day in a row, he said that I could stay home by myself for a little while before joining him at school.

When we lived in St. Paul, he never let me stay home by myself, except for a few minutes when he had to dash to the store for some milk or something else we'd just run out of, and he certainly would never let me go by myself anywhere—except maybe up the block and across the alley to Becky's. Even then, he watched me until I arrived safely. He believed that Paradise was safe, and, since he did, I did too.

When the morning cartoons were over, I knew that the mail would be ready, so I ran to the post office, hoping that another letter from Becky would be waiting for me.

I turned the combination correctly on the first try. One junk mail flyer, a telephone bill, and a sweepstakes letter. Nothing for me.

I walked across the street toward home. On the other side of the street was the second-hand store. This morning, a plastic, red-lettered "Open" sign hung on the door. The normally dark interior was now lit.

I peered past the "Hours" sign posted on the large, dirt-streaked window. The inside was more cluttered than a badly organized, multi-family garage sale. A very fat—er, heavy-set—woman in a flowered print dress sat in the near corner. Her long gray hair was pulled back in a tight ponytail. She was engrossed in reading a science fiction paperback and didn't see me. Along one wall were several shelves heaped with porcelain animals, lava lamps, plant hangers, and faded wooden plaques. In the center of the store, five long clothes racks stretched toward the back wall. I shaded my eyes, trying to see farther into the store.

Out of the corner of her eye, the woman must've seen me, for she suddenly glanced over at me with her small eyes, smiled briefly, then returned to her book.

Beyond the long racks of clothes, in the darker recesses, I spied more shelves of discarded junk. Among the shadows and the clutter, I saw what appeared to be a doll.

Curious, I went to the door of the shop and opened it. A bell chimed.

The woman smiled at me and her wide cheeks dimpled.

"Feel free to look around." She paused, giving me a second look. "Are you visiting someone in town?"

I introduced myself.

Her small, dark eyes lit up and she swung her heavy arms out. "Oh, yes, the new teacher's daughter. I read about your father in the paper. Well, make yourself at home. I am Miss Bloomsbury, and this is Paradise's Time Machine, the store where you can see what people wore before they gained weight. What children once played with before they decided to grow up. What people received for wedding gifts before they were divorced. It's all here, for one man's past is another man's future."

She chuckled and I smiled at the woman's histrionics.

"Do you have any books or toys?" I was too shy to say "dolls." Some girls my age were abandoning them as quickly as adults dumped their trendy gadgets into landfills or thrift shops like this. But I wouldn't ever sell my dolls. They were more than toys to me, almost like family, but I could never explain that to a stranger.

"Check in the back."

I walked between two long racks of clothes: a musty menagerie of prom dresses, wool coats, stained children's shirts, and ski sweaters. Dust tickled my nose. I pinched off an impending sneeze.

Along the back wall were two long shelves. Miscellaneous

household paraphernalia like meat grinders, knife sharpeners, mugs, and dishes filled the upper shelf. The lower shelf held a few paperbacks ("trash romances," Daddy called them), mostly worn or coffee stained. On the floor sprawled a few games whose boxes had been crushed, ripped, or spilled on. In the center of the pile was the doll that I had seen from the window. She was propped up on top of several games. The doll's plastic chin was punched in, and its hair was mottled and stained. No doll deserved such a fate, but it was beyond my desire or ability to fix it.

I turned to leave, then spotted some model train cars in the corner. I walked closer, my feet creaking on the wooden floor.

I picked one up. From what Daddy had taught me, I knew what to look for. The brand of these model train cars was good and the cars themselves appeared to be in excellent condition. All couplers were intact and the wheels weren't missing. I counted six cars in all. Five of the cars were in superb condition, one meticulously hand-painted. The sixth car had a crooked decal that would never do.

I looked them over again, then headed for the door.

"It's sad about that doll," Miss Bloomsbury said, looking truly grieved. "You could tell the girl who brought her in was treated as badly as she had treated the doll. I'm thinking I should take that doll home and fix her up."

I wasn't sure what to say. I just nodded.

I left quickly, rode my bike up to school, and told Daddy about the train cars. I didn't tell him about the doll.

"Really? I'll have to check it out."

I knew once autumn came, Daddy would make it a point of visiting the store. I was glad to help him with his hobby. My favorite part was setting up the tiny people.

A short time later, on the pretense of becoming more familiar with the school, I went to find Miss O'Neil. I discovered her in the music room sitting on a folding chair in front of a cabinet. She wore black slacks and a royal blue blouse that matched her eyes. Immense piles of music surrounded her.

I patiently stood in the doorway until she noticed me. I didn't have to wait too long.

"Oh." She stood, smiled. "Miss Kiln, isn't it?"

I nodded, smiled too. Now that I had found her, I felt quite shy, awkward.

She gestured to the mounds of sheet music. "All this has accumulated over the years, long before I came here, and I finally decided to see what's here. But much of it is so old and dated, I can't use it. Most of it's heading for the trash."

I cleared my throat. "Do you need any help?"

Her large, dark blue eyes sparkled but she shook her head. "I'm afraid not, honey. It's the kind of job only I can do."

I shrugged, disappointed.

"But if I can use your help later, I'll call, okay?"

"I'll be in Daddy's room."

"Fine. I may just look you up."

I left, hoping she would. I needed to get her and Daddy together as much as possible.

The rest of the morning I helped Daddy put up bulletin boards, sort papers, and count textbooks.

I often glanced at the door, hoping Miss O'Neil would appear, but she didn't.

We ate lunch in his room: sandwiches that Daddy had made that morning.

In the afternoon, Miss O'Neil did appear in Daddy's classroom door just as we were finishing up his work.

She observed me moving some books. "You must appreciate your assistant."

"I sure do," Daddy replied. "Angela said that she had offered to help you. I wasn't sure if I wanted to subcontract her out."

"I'm afraid only someone who really knows music could've helped me with that mess."

I vowed instantly and fervently to work hard on my piano lessons, whenever they'd start.

"By the way," Daddy suddenly said, "we'll be having supper at the local café. Would you like to join us?"

Surprised and elated, I looked at Daddy: he was serious! All my prayers were answered in one split-second.

"Oh," she said, "I'd love to, but I'm leaving town in a few minutes. My parents live in Minnetonka, and I drive there every chance I get."

"Do you spend the summers there?"

"Oh, yes. Paradise is a nice place to teach, but it's not home."

Daddy nodded understandingly. I didn't.

She started to leave, but stopped in the doorway. "May I take a rain check?"

"You certainly may."

After she'd gone, I ran to Daddy, still dazed that he would seize the initiative like that. "How come you asked her?" Never in my wildest dreams did I imagine that Daddy could be so direct, so forthright, and so romantic.

He shrugged. "I don't know. I thought you'd like it. It must be boring to eat with me all the time."

I turned away, disappointed. He had asked her only for me.

"Didn't you want me to?"

I spun quickly, facing him. "Of course I did. I was just surprised, that's all."

Daddy nodded, uncertain, and, I think, perplexed at my behavior. He continued filling out a seating chart. "Almost done, then we'll be going."

I looked out the window, down on the small parking lot. I watched Miss O'Neil walk to a sparkling, red sports car. Seeing her car reaffirmed my course of action. If they married, the car would come with her.

A few minutes later, we walked to the parking lot. I climbed in the car and was painfully aware of our rusted station wagon's dusty interior. Yes, I had to get them together.

"You're very quiet. What are you thinking about?"

"Oh, nothing. Just dreaming."

When evening came, I met our first neighbor. The meeting

occurred as I was putting my bike in the garage. Daddy always insisted that I put my things away, even in Paradise. Nothing left out in the yard overnight was his standard rule. Because of all his years in St. Paul, he had grown skeptical—at times even cynical—of human nature. Maybe living in Paradise would change his viewpoint.

As I shut the garage's side door, I noticed a gray-haired woman watering the flowers on the other side of our narrow, gravel alley.

She stood up and looked at me just as I looked at her and our eyes met.

"Hello. You must be Angela Kiln."

"Yes," I said. I didn't think I'd ever get used to someone knowing who I was before we were introduced.

She had gray-blue hair, a wide, dimpled face, and faded green eyes. She had on a worn, flower-print dress that made her look a little plumper than she was, and her glasses had fallen down her nose. Her face reminded me of illustrations of Mother Goose.

Setting her watering can down, she walked over to me and pushed her glasses up.

"Have you settled in yet?"

"Pretty much," I said, somewhat guarded with a stranger.

"I thought about visiting earlier and welcoming you and your father to town, but then I remembered what it was like to have everything a mess and visitors show up. I finally decided to wait until you were unpacked and settled. How are you getting along?"

"We like it here."

"Do you? That's nice. Lots of nice people live in Paradise." She wiped her hands on her dress. "Are you looking forward to school?"

"Sort of."

She frowned in a good-natured, teasing manner. "Just 'sort of'?"

"Well, I've heard all about Mrs. Putnam, how she's just an old bear. And everyone's had her for a teacher, even parents of some of the kids, so she must be really old!"

I suddenly flushed, realizing that I might have offended her by talking about someone being "old."

She didn't seem to notice. "I've heard that too," she chuckled.

Phew, I thought. I hadn't offended her. I should have left it there, but I tried to cover my mistake. "I mean, she's old, old enough even to be your mother. They call her Old Prune."

"I know what you mean. My daughter had her, and she can be quite demanding."

"So you can see why I'm not looking forward to school."

"Maybe you'll like her once you get to know her. Some people have told me that they like her after a few weeks."

"I hope so," I groused.

Just then, Daddy opened the back door and called me in for bed.

"Good night," I said.

"Pleasant dreams," she winked.

Daddy waved to her and she waved back.

He held the storm door open for me. "I'm glad you got to know her," he said as he led me upstairs. "It'll be nice having Mrs. Putnam for a neighbor."

CHAPTER 5

On the trip to Owatonna, you'll pass the sleepy town of Paradise,
a town that grew along the old railroad line running from Des
Moines to St. Paul. The depot, a favorite of railroad buffs, can
still be seen on the east edge of Paradise.

—from Minnesota tourism brochure

Standing on a small stool, I studied myself in the bathroom mirror over the sink. I turned left, then right. I lifted a small hand mirror behind me and to the side and studied my profile.

Should I risk letting my hair grow long? My brown hair was as straight as straw. If I grew it long, it might look like a long broom.

Daddy would be no help to my decision. I could just hear him: "You look beautiful, no matter how you wear your hair." I didn't need a compliment. I needed the truth. I needed a female opinion. A reliable female. And in Paradise, I knew no one I could talk to about an issue so important, so personal.

Miss O'Neil, maybe.

But until she was my mother, she would give a teacher's answer: "That's a very personal decision. I'm sure that whatever you choose will be right for you."

Yeah.

I laid the small mirror on the sink's edge and sighed. I briefly combed my short mop of hair.

Maybe, if my hair were longer, it would develop some body, like Miss O'Neil's.

I doubted it.

I stepped off the stool, frustrated.

I returned the mirror to the drawer.

Trudging downstairs, I found Daddy sitting at the kitchen

table. He was eating Cheerios and reading the St. Paul morning paper.

I glanced at the green kitchen walls. Sometime during the last twenty years, the kitchen had been refinished with sheet rock, but instead of wallpapering to complement the rest of the house, someone had painted the walls a flat lime green. Of all possible colors, it was the ugliest. This morning, the green looked even uglier than ugliest.

"Morning, Angel," he said, setting the paper down. "What would you like to do this weekend?"

I shrugged and plopped down in the chair across from him and looked out the window onto our backyard. The morning sun was behind a bank of clouds, and a light breeze swayed the branches of our two maple trees.

"Got a bowl over on the counter ready for you."

"Thanks," I mumbled, watching four sparrows fight over the dry breadcrumbs I'd thrown out the night before. "I'm not hungry yet."

"It's the last weekend before school begins. Let's do something special."

I shrugged again. "I don't know."

"Well, if you think of something you'd like to do, just let me know." He picked up the morning paper again, turned a page.

I realized that I had nothing better to do, so I might as well eat. I got up and jerked the refrigerator's heavy door latch open, pulled out a half gallon of milk, poured it over my cereal, and joined Daddy at the table.

I stared out the window again. The clouds had moved and the sun shone brightly on the sidewalk and lawn. A blue jay came and frightened the sparrows away. It snatched the last breadcrumb and flew off.

The shades on Mrs. Putnam's house were pulled down. Her house might as well have been deserted. Most of the houses in the neighborhood looked that way: silent, lifeless.

I'd asked Daddy before going to bed if I should apologize to Mrs. Putnam. He laughed when I told him what I'd said. He was sure that Mrs. Putnam knew I'd only repeated rumors. "But," he added, "an apology never hurts."

I wasn't sure about that. It depends on which side of the apology you're on, and I was embarrassed enough already.

A squirrel scampered along our garage's peak. The squirrel slipped on a cedar shingle, quickly regained its balance, reached the edge, and leaped onto the telephone pole near the alley. So much for the morning's excitement.

"Are you going to eat, or just let your cereal grow milk-logged?"

Lethargic, I scooped a small mouthful.

"Maybe we should go to a park," Daddy suggested. "Rice Lake State Park is near Owatonna and might be very interesting."

"How about a picnic?" I grew a little animated.

"For lunch?"

I finally smiled. "Okay."

After breakfast, I got my bike out of the garage and rode around town. Everything seemed deserted, even more than usual. It was obvious that on Labor Day Weekend there wasn't much to do in Paradise.

As I rode around, I had to keep readjusting myself to Paradise: in St. Paul, streets just seemed to go on forever, but here, after a few blocks, the streets ended abruptly at the edge of corn fields. The only exception was Main Street. It became a county road heading both east and west.

As I rode through the west part of town, I noticed a young boy sitting on the steps of a run-down house. Most of the white paint had peeled off the narrow siding. Small concrete chunks were breaking away from the front steps. Large cracks also ran through the house's foundation.

The young boy on the steps looked not much older than I. His hair reminded me of a straw-colored bird's nest. He had a narrow face with a pointed chin, and his arms were bony-thin. What caught my attention most was the silver blade in his hand—he was whittling.

I slowed my bike a bit just as he glanced up. He had large, inquiring brown eyes that looked sad, wistful.

He quickly went back to his work, slicing into the wood block with greater intensity but with equal care.

Just then, the tall, brown-haired boy I'd seen talking with Jane at the park opened the front screen door—or tried to.

The screen door banged into the younger boy's back. His hands jerked with the impact.

"Sorry, Tom. Didn't see you there."

"Now it's wrecked." Tom glared up at the older boy.

I didn't want to slow further and appear to be listening, so I continued down the street, turned, and came back again.

"You can still fix it," the older boy was saying as he sat next to Tom on the cracked steps.

I could now see that the boy had been actually carving some shape, perhaps a human figure, out of the wood. I continued riding down the street, not daring to come back a third time.

I rode by the park and wondered if Jane might be there and if the older boy would be meeting her. I rode into the park and got off. I leaned my bike against the large elm tree by the swing set and walked toward the shelter.

As I had guessed, Jane was there, this time perched on a picnic table. Her dark hair was still tied back in a ponytail. She wore a white tank top and faded cut-off jeans that accentuated her figure and long legs. I wondered if I would ever have a shape like hers. My body showed as much hint of developing a figure as my broom hair did of developing body.

She saw me walking across the playground and put something down.

"Hi, Angela," she said as I stepped onto the shelter's concrete floor.

"Hi. What are you doing?"

"Just sitting. Thinking. And writing some in my diary." She kept her hand tightly on the small book beside her. "What about you?"

"Just riding my bike. Daddy and I are going to a state park in a little bit."

She pulled her legs up and hugged them, sighing slightly. She looked toward the swing set. "That would be fun."

"Oh, I don't know," I lied, trying to make conversation and hoping to sound more mature. "Trees can get boring."

"Not for me. I love being out in nature. The solitude, the birds, the wind in the trees."

I immediately felt bad that I hadn't been honest, for I knew exactly what she meant. Daddy had introduced me early to nature's wondrous diversity, regularly taking me on short day trips to parks. We avoided anything that hinted of commercialism, seeking out wilderness instead. When we hiked in the woods, he sometimes quoted Wordsworth or Thoreau or a Psalm from the Bible. I didn't always know what the words meant, but they sounded comforting.

I looked down and admitted the truth: "Actually, I do like the woods."

Jane smiled. "I thought you did. You should meet my younger sister. You'd like her, and maybe you could teach her to appreciate something other than television talk shows." She glanced up at the cobwebbed rafters overhead. "Not much to see here." Her brown eyes suddenly looked wistful. "I bet your father has taken you on lots of trips."

She looked back at me and seemed hungry in some way, for information perhaps.

"Some."

"I wish my father had taken me places."

"Why doesn't he?"

She let go of her legs, sat stiffly upright. Anger edged her voice. "He divorced my mom a couple of years ago. Now I only see him once or twice a year, usually around Thanksgiving and Christmas. Even that's too often."

Just then I heard a bike rattling across the gravel along the street's edge, then bump over the grass toward us.

I turned. It was the older brown-haired boy.

He saw Jane, smiled shyly.

Jane introduced me. "Robert, this is Angela Kiln. Angela, Robert Oatley."

He was tall, lanky, with a quick smile, blue eyes, and a cluster of pimples on his cheeks. "Oh, yeah, the new teacher's kid. How are you, Angela?"

"Fine." I noticed Jane's bike by the shelter wall.

"Well," Robert said, his blue eyes looking at Jane's bike, "want to go for a ride?"

Jane hopped gracefully off the picnic table. "Sure."

I took my cue and turned to go.

"Talk to you later, Angela." Jane got on her bike. "Have fun at the park."

"Sure." I watched them ride off, and I wondered if any boy would ever be interested in me. Not that I wanted them to yet, of course. I just wanted to know that it was someday possible.

When I got home, Daddy stood by the curb, talking to a man in a small green car idling in front of our house. The car had rusty doors and a bent fender. Daddy leaned in the passenger-side window.

I stopped my bike on the boulevard near the car. Daddy noticed me, stepped back, and introduced us.

The man in the car was Andrew Johanson, a ruddy and square-faced man. "Mr. Johanson is the town journalist who interviewed me over the phone three weeks ago. He wrote the newspaper article about us."

"I also serve Cherry Grove," Mr. Johanson added. He was very talkative by nature, I quickly discovered.

"So, have you met everyone yet?" he asked Daddy.

"Not quite. I think I missed several people on the west end of town."

"Give it another week. Are you ready for school?"

"Certainly. Angela helped me last week."

"What do you think of Superintendent Cranberry?"

Daddy was cautious in his reply. "He seems like a typical superintendent."

"He is going to have a tough time getting the superintendency of the new district." He gestured toward Main Street. "Businesses are depressed over the consolidation. Of course, how you can get more depressed than dead, I'll never know."

"But you're a businessman too."

He laughed sardonically. "That's how I know. You see, Paradise used to be a stable farm community. It weathered the Depression and even boomed with prosperity right after World War II. But times have passed Paradise by. Larger farms meant fewer people. The interstate missed us and the railroad pulled up its ties."

"That's true of many small towns."

"But Paradise is different. It hasn't yet accepted that we're not living in 1950. For example, we have the Morrison family here. The original two Morrison brothers who homesteaded in this area were dynamic entrepreneurs who influenced the railroad into laying tracks through Paradise." He chuckled cynically. "In other words, they bribed the management. Today the family still owns half of Main Street—empty though it is—and three big farms. Yet in no way do the Morrisons—or any of the other old families—want to transform the town into a bedroom community for Owatonna, or worse, Hillcrest. But if Paradise is going to be more than a staggering corpse, the town must actively attract new people. If they don't want to be a bedroom community, then they must attract small industry."

"Why don't they?"

"That would mean a new sewer system and improved roads. They're against anything that raises taxes today, even though it would lower taxes tomorrow."

"Those in power prefer a slow death to rapid change."

"It sounds as if you understand Paradise pretty well!"

"We're just talking about human nature."

They talked on and on. As for me, I was getting hungry. I finally tugged impatiently on Daddy's elbow.

Mr. Johanson was explaining to Daddy how the consolidation affected the school board. "Larry Bates is angry that he won't have control anymore. They may have to think about offering a real education for a change."

"Aren't they?"

"You've seen the school. Just like the town leaders, the board's interested in keeping things the way they are. School is seen as a custodian for the kids. Keep kids out of major trouble and don't raise taxes. 'Maintain' has been the unofficial motto ever since Bates was first elected to the school board and Cranberry was hired sixteen years ago."

I tugged again. Daddy finally got the hint. "Nice talking to you, Andy, but I have a picnic date with Angela."

"Sorry to keep you. Talk to you later."

As Mr. Johanson drove off, Daddy looked at me and raised his eyebrows. "Sorry, Angel, he just kept talking."

"I've heard you say that it takes two to talk."

He laughed, putting his hand on my shoulder. "You caught me there, Angel."

Rice Lake State Park wasn't too far away. The wooded park surrounded a shallow marshy lake where ducks were already gathering to migrate south. We sat on a blanket and had sandwiches, root beer, and chips beside the blue water, beneath the tall trees. After lunch we walked the park's groomed trails along the lake's edge and then hiked the winding paths which took us through the tall grass farther from the oak-rimmed lake.

I think, for once, that Daddy was tired of hiking before I was, and we headed back to our picnic site. Daddy then surprised me by having brought the food for supper too. He built a fire and we roasted hot dogs. We returned home in the evening, just as the sun was setting over the darkening lake. The clouds looked like pink rose petals. It was a still and beautiful end to a summer of change.

That night before falling asleep, after Daddy had read to me, I thought about Jane and her boyfriend Robert. I wondered if they would someday marry. And then I wondered if I would someday marry.

Daddy had recently explained in very general terms how God designed babies to be made. To me it seemed a rather crude design. I was glad that I wouldn't have to worry about it for a very long time.

Daddy had also explained that God wanted babies to be

brought into the world under the protection of a father and a mother.

That made sense to me.

What I didn't understand is why anyone would ever want to make a baby without a marriage first. Especially the woman. After all, it seemed that she was usually the one most responsible for the baby's care. It was a scary thought that some women could be so gullible and so dumb. And how could a man turn his back on his own child? It was an even scarier thought that some men could be so thoughtless, so selfish, so mean.

I fell asleep, thankful that Daddy was always watching over me.

CHAPTER 6

I know I'll never be strong like my brother. That's okay,
because he watches out for me. I enjoy carving wood, playing
solitaire, and working on puzzles. I don't have many friends. I
don't mind that. I like it.
—from Tom Oatley's 7th grade autobiographical essay

The first days of school flew by as fast as a dry maple leaf in a
stiff fall wind. Jane was right about Mrs. Putnam: she completely
controlled her class, showing no understanding or compassion for
misbehavior. I can still see her standing next to her lectern, and,
behind her, on an otherwise immaculately clean blackboard, her
name written in large, flowing letters. For Mrs. Putnam, teaching
was serious business, and it had better be serious business for any
student in her class. I saw no hint of the kind and friendly neighbor
who reminded me of Mother Goose. I can still hear her stern,
authoritative voice: "I know that you *can* do well, and that you
will do well, and you *will* prove me right."

I wanted to ask "or else what?" but, like everyone else, I didn't
dare.

After our placement tests during the first few days, she called
me up to her desk and handed me a list of books to read in my
spare time.

"You'll enjoy all of these books," she stated. Her green eyes
peered at me over her glasses. "The stories in the fourth grade
reading text won't be challenging for you. And I'm sure you want
to be challenged."

I stood before her desk, speechless, not sure if she was giving
me an actual assignment or if she was offering me extra credit. I
stared at the incredibly long list of books. I had read a few of them

already. I wanted to tell her that I didn't mind not being challenged, but I kept quiet.

I shuffled back to my desk, slid the list into it, and told myself that I would consider the list later. Maybe.

So this was my punishment for not apologizing to her.

During those first anxious days, I got to know the thirteen other students in my fourth grade class. Most of the boys seemed intent on showing off for each other and were certainly not interested in playing with the girls at recess.

The girls had a very strict hierarchy. It seemed so established, so inviolate, that it must have been set in kindergarten and hadn't changed since.

I don't think they knew how to handle a newcomer.

Was I to be on the bottom of the ladder, the girl everyone ignored at recess? Or, some girls must have wondered, would I strive for Margie Jones's leadership position?

This thought, this fear, must have occurred to Margie, for the first time we met, she sized me up like a butcher sizes up a prize blue-ribbon cow. Her gaze dropped to my feet, calculatingly strolled to my head, then plummeted back to my feet.

As for me, even if she hadn't been so cold, so cunning, I knew, even the first time we met, that we could never be friends. I didn't like her. I admit that. I knew instantly on some deep psychological level that we could never get along, not because she was the leader, but because she needed to lead. She was a bully, and I couldn't tolerate a bully.

She had shoulder-length blonde hair, the shade of blonde that reminded me of an old manila folder. She had a pug nose scattered with freckles, ice-blue eyes, a tight smile, and an even tighter voice when she wanted it to be.

In our first recess, she loudly informed me—as if I were hard of hearing—that I could play with her group . . . if I asked.

I chose not to ask. I chose to swing that morning.

The school's swings had long chains that allowed me to swing really high. But I stayed close to earth that day to hear what everyone else was talking about.

Without a doubt, Margie was strong. Solid as a brick. Anyone could tell by her thick arms and legs. Maybe that's what first attracted other girls to her; she could either be a motherly protector or a dangerous enemy, and other children, in pure self-preservation, did everything to keep her the former. She was quick to laugh in approval or quick to roll her cold blue eyes in disgust and turn her lips into a sneer of derision. Rather than allow a dictatorial bully in their ranks, the girls made her their protective leader.

In retrospect, maybe she was as much a victim of the group as Jane's younger sister, Chelsea Turpin, the frail, bespectacled, red-head who was always picked last during the recess games. She spent most of her energy trying desperately to fit in until she became a roaming leech, attaching herself to whoever would let her hang on. I think that I was the only one who saw the utter desperation in Chelsea's pallid, blue, almost always averted eyes.

What sort of future would Chelsea have? Would she run blindly from one person to the next, feverishly seeking reassurance of her worth, desperately clinging to anyone who appeared strong, hoping to find in others what she lacked in herself?

And what about Margie? She could never meet the high expectations that were now being formed in her imagination—limited though it was—by her powerful leadership role in our class.

By the end of the first week of school, the pattern was established. Chelsea Turpin and I sat on the top of the tire house while Margie and the other girls played Red Rover or some other game. Chelsea was an outcast by lot, and I, an outcast by choice.

I hated recess.

However, one thing I did like about our small school in our small town was that all students were housed in the same building. Yes, we were segregated from the "big kids," but after school I could go into their part of the building, observe their behavior, and find Daddy right away.

From seeing these older students in the hall and from persistently interrogating Daddy, I quickly learned their names as well as their social structure and who were friends with whom. For example, the boy I had seen whittling, Tom Oatley, was not, as I had guessed, near my age. He was actually a seventh grader. He had few friends, or, as Daddy explained, few true friends. The only ones who would let him hang around were the kids whose one goal in school lay in finding how many rules they could break.

"Calling them 'students' is a misnomer," Daddy said. I called them the future Stillwater Prison Chain Gang.

Within a few days, I saw Shawn Dixon, one of these students, in action. At the same time, I had a closer introduction to Tom Oatley.

During the end of the second week of school, as I entered the high school side of the building, I saw a group of students clustered in the hallway by the seventh grade lockers.

A boy angrily shouted something and I moved toward the wall of lockers, trying to see what was going on.

The cluster of bodies suddenly pulled in closer and then moved back as books slid across the floor like loose hockey pucks. Another voice shouted. A fight was beginning.

Like everyone else, I ran up to see.

I pushed my way between two older boys.

Surrounded by students, Tom Oatley was fighting Shawn Dixon, or, more accurately, Shawn was fighting Tom. Shawn Dixon was short and wiry, with long dishwater blond hair, a seventh grader whom Chelsea had just pointed out to me the other day as a boy everyone was afraid of.

Shawn, shuffling like a fighter and holding his fists close to his freckled nose, edged closer to Tom and violently kicked Tom's backpack out of the way. Two books and some playing cards spilled across the hall.

Cautiously peering at the scene between moving elbows, I quickly knew, just as everyone else watching knew, that Shawn Dixon would very soon have Tom's blood splattered across the floor. Tom swung wildly, almost spastically, and missed. Shawn held back, picked his moment, and jabbed, cleanly hitting Tom's chest. He could have easily punched Tom's nose, but Shawn's calculating stance told me that Shawn was prolonging the fight, probably waiting for a bigger crowd to appear before he issued the bloody coup de grâce to the head.

Spinning, I dashed up the stairs to Daddy's room.

He must have heard some of the shouting, for as I ran up the steps, he sprinted down past me.

Spinning again, I ran to catch up with him.

"Break it up," he shouted as he neared the fighters. He slowed his pace just a bit as he came to the crowd, giving students time to move back.

They did, hastily scattering like frightened sparrows: no one wanted to be called in as a witness.

Daddy deliberately stepped between the two fighters.

Daddy stiff-armed Shawn Dixon to hold him back while Tom collapsed against the wall, wiping his chin. Both boys turned to leave.

"Wait right here," Daddy commanded.

"What for?" Shawn Dixon snidely retorted, flipping his long hair back.

"What do you think?" Daddy snapped. He glanced at Tom over his shoulder. "Tom, are you okay?"

Quite pale, Tom nodded, his hands trembling. "Yeah. Sure." Sniffing, he hastily picked up his backpack and books. I stepped forward and gathered his cards, handing them to him. His blue eyes looked away.

"Thanks," he muttered softly and he blinked back tears.

"Both of you, let's go," Daddy said.

Daddy turned and led both Tom Oatley and Shawn Dixon downstairs to the office.

I went to Daddy's room and waited, my heart pounding.

In a few minutes, Daddy came in, bringing me a can of pop. I had never seen him break up a fight before. I was proud of his quick action and more than a little surprised at him for stepping between the fighters.

"Weren't you afraid?"

"In a situation like that, everyone is. But what would they do? They'd have no reason to hit me." He paused, reconsidering. "At least I hope not. Anyway, kids who are fighting usually want someone to stop them. They're afraid to stop it themselves, afraid they'll look weak, but if the fight continues, what then? When do they stop? How do they stop?"

Just then Mr. Manitou walked in. "Sorry I wasn't there to help you, Jack. I was in a special ed meeting in the office."

"Thanks anyway. It turned out fine. They'll both get three days suspension."

Mr. Manitou nodded thoughtfully. "Good. I'm glad to see Cranberry is showing some backbone. Sometimes he waffles terribly on discipline."

"I was surprised no one else showed up. I heard the noise way up here. Where were the second floor teachers?"

Mr. Manitou raised an eyebrow. "When a Dixon is involved, staff members have learned to be cautious."

"Why is that?"

"The Dixon family is notorious, not unlike some of the Morrisons we had a few years ago. Well, I'm off to volleyball practice." He turned to go, noticed me. "Good afternoon, quiet one."

I approached Daddy, worried. "He said the Dixons are notorious. Doesn't that word have to do with outlaws?'

Daddy laughed. "Outlaw is right. But don't worry. Shawn Dixon and his family are not outlaws."

I sipped my pop in silence while Daddy started correcting papers, little realizing that we would, indeed, eventually know what sort of outlaws the Dixons were.

That evening, Daddy began his fall running. Every evening when we could, Daddy ran and I rode my bike beside him. Earlier he had established a three-mile route around Paradise. First we went south out around the ballfield, then east across the highway to the old railroad bed where the stone railroad bridge crossed the South Branch of Paradise Creek, then north past the deserted depot to Browner's Woods, then west past a run-down, rust-colored house, across the highway, then back to Main Street, and south to our door.

He kept a steady pace. Sometimes I went ahead and waited, sometimes I stayed behind and then caught up. When we came to the gravel railroad bed, he ran along it while I rode on the parallel street.

"Why don't you run on the street?" I shouted. "It's smoother."

"Ah," he replied between breaths, "it's not as much fun. Here I can imagine the steam trains chugging into town."

Daddy always was a romantic.

As we neared the boarded-up depot on the east edge of town, Daddy slowed down to a fast walk.

His railroad bed and my street met at the depot. I stopped my bike and glanced up at the depot's steep roof. Most of the cedar shingles were still intact. The Paradise sign above the depot had faded and was almost indecipherable. Most of the paint on the depot itself had blistered away and the visible wood was severely weathered.

He caught his breath. "I wanted to see what this old thing looked like up close." He wiped sweat from his forehead.

Daddy pointed to a circle where the paint had lasted longer. "That's where the railroad herald hung."

We entered the shadow of the east side, what was once the track side. The main door had a big padlock on it. One of the two large windows wasn't boarded up, but the glass was dirty.

We wiped some of the dirt away and peered through the dingy window. Slivers of light from the setting sun shone between the boards that covered the opposite wall's windows. In the filtered light, we spied some dark wooden benches and a slate train schedule.

"See the ticket counter off to the side?" He lifted me so that I could see it too.

Daddy set me down and looked north and pointed along the railroad bed. "Look past Browner's Woods. Can you see the beginning of the ridge that heads east? That's where a track turned off to Red Wing."

Daddy and I walked around the depot, back into the fading sunlight, and waded through some knee-high grass. "You never know what you can find around these old places."

"Lots of junk."

"Remember the spikes I found in West Concord? Or the brick at Milaca?" He reached down, dug in the dirt an inch, and picked up a muddy pencil stub. He brushed it off and showed me the railroad name. "See?"

"Junk," I repeated.

We circled the depot, returning to the front. I absentmindedly rattled the padlock. He stood on the platform stones and studied where the railroad once ran. "Just think, though, how important the railroads were in settling America. They allowed the rapid transportation of raw materials, goods, and settlers. They were agents of change. And then think about how quickly they vanished from the countryside, leaving only a few buildings to be worn away by weather. They, too, became victims of change. Soon these old cuts and grades will be the only reminder that something once went through here."

Daddy stretched, then jogged in place for a moment. "Well, we better head north to Browner's Woods. You'll have to join me on the railroad for a little bit."

I hopped on my bike and followed him along the jarring gravel bed. I glanced back at the weatherworn depot. The sun was getting close to the horizon, and the depot cast a long shadow across the cornfield to the east. They were shadows that would grow longer.

CHAPTER 7

I remember roller-skating to the park. Apple tree blossoms
blew through the air. I saw my mother crying.

I remember when Jane and Robert were "married" in
kindergarten during recess, and I stood by the swings. It was
windy. I didn't smile.

I remember when Mrs. Putnam made Duane stand against
the chalkboard in fourth grade. For once, he had been caught.

I remember when my father walked away for the first time.
I didn't cry.

—from a poem by Tina Lewis

Daddy set aside Thursday evenings to correct papers. As usual, he had the students' papers sprawled across the dining room table, but he seemed unusually perplexed as he read through the papers.

I peered past his arm.

"Yes, Angel?" He was irritated at my interruption but was doing his best not to show it.

"Just wondering what you're reading. Something wrong?"

He sighed. "No. Well, actually, I don't know. I've been giving creative writing exercises to the juniors and seniors, and I've been getting some rather unusual responses. So many troubled kids."

"Troubled about what?"

He pulled me to his side, hugging me. "Lots of kids go through tough times, as we did when your mother died. But these students don't seem to have a good grasp on life. It's as if they're walking through a foggy maze, bumping into walls, taking the nearest way, not caring whether or not it's the best way."

He lifted the paper he had just finished, a wide-lined notebook page containing a large, flowing script. "Look at this one by Tina

Lewis. You don't know her, but she's brilliant. She remembers everything she reads and she has great insight. She could easily be accepted into any college she wants, but will she? She has no plans for the future. Most of these students, almost by default, will stay in the area, raise families here, grow old here, and die here. Unless parents show them the world out there, kids in Paradise don't realize the possibilities in life. Here."

He handed me Tina's poem. I read it. I didn't understand everything, but I liked it.

"Do you see her anger? She's boiling with resentments she doesn't recognize, much less understand."

I thought Daddy was smart to detect Tina's anger, but at that age I didn't realize that Daddy was waging his own battle with bitterness and could readily spot others' unresolved anger.

He handed me another paper. "Look at Chet Kelley's. He's not really bright, but he works hard."

I read it and didn't think much of it. "Is he that boy you were talking to after class yesterday? Tall, with curly blond hair?" It was the same boy I'd seen driving around Paradise in the white convertible on one of our first days in town.

"That's Chet. If he'd give himself a chance, he would do just fine in life, but instead he tries to imitate Duane Johnson."

When Chet had been riding around town harassing Robert and Jane, he had been with a big, red-haired, mean-looking boy.

"Does Duane Johnson have red hair?"

"Yes, and he's the football quarterback. He seems to go to school only because he can play football. Coach Oldenburg thinks the team is going far this year, but I doubt it. Because of players like Duane, the team will lose its big games. Over the years, I've never seen a team do well on the field that didn't do better in the classroom. The players will get into a tough spot, not be able to think their way out, not even believe that they can get out, and fold."

I looked through the sheets and saw Robert Oatley's paper. "May I see Robert's?"

Daddy rubbed his forehead. "I'm sorry, Angel, I shouldn't have told you about other students. I forget that we're in a small school now."

I put my arm around his waist. "I like hearing about other kids."

He handed me Robert's paper. "Since you've seen this much, you might as well see one more."

Beneath it was Jane Turpin's. "And that one too?"

I read Robert's poem. It was nostalgic and mildly interesting.

"He still misses his father," Daddy said.

I read Jane's but didn't understand it.

"What's her poem mean?"

"Lots of girls write poems about unrequited love."

"What's unre—unrequi—whatever—mean?"

"'Unrequited' means that you love someone but that person doesn't love you back."

I handed the two papers back to him, puzzled. Her poem seemed to describe Robert and herself, but did her poem mean that he didn't like her anymore?

I had the chance to find out the next week during Paradise's homecoming activities. In such a small school, even the elementary grades were invited to get involved with homecoming. All elementary students made signs about homecoming that were then taped to the walls in the high school side of the building. As a class, we made a long banner that we were to carry in the parade.

"Parade?"

"Yes," Mrs. Putnam explained to me. "There will be a homecoming parade on Friday."

Parade.

The word ignited hundreds of colorful sights and myriad sounds. Daddy had sometimes taken me to see St. Paul's Winter Carnival Parade. I envisioned floats and clowns and fancy cars from all over Minnesota descending on Paradise's Main Street.

But I had no idea what Mrs. Putnam meant when she talked about the homecoming coronation.

Margie Jones, amazed at my ignorance about homecoming, informed me, in tones so loud that everyone could hear, that the real highlight was Thursday evening's coronation. The other kids' excitement about the candidates was contagious. I didn't know exactly what this coronation involved, but I knew that it was going to be big.

"Daddy, do you know who the king and queen will be?" I asked as we drove home on Tuesday.

"I only know what you know: who the candidates are. Do you want my prediction?"

"Sure!" His hunches were usually good. I could share his— now my—reliable hunches with my classmates the next day and show Margie what I knew.

"I think Duane Johnson will be king and Mary Oldenburg will be queen."

"But they don't go out together or anything."

"No, but from what I've seen, Duane doesn't date any girl very long. Mary's a nice girl, is well-respected, and happens to be the coach's daughter." He smiled, shrugging. "That's just my guess."

"Margie Jones thinks Tina Lewis is going to get it." I had since learned what Tina Lewis looked like. She was a tall, natural blonde; thin, with long legs; and very athletic. She was the volleyball team captain. With her expressive blue eyes and lithe figure, I thought she could immediately land any modeling job just by walking into an agency.

"Tina is prettier than Mary," Daddy said, "but Tina won't ever be homecoming queen or receive any of these strange accolades that high school students bestow on themselves. A girl who aspires to such honors must be attractive but must also fit in with her peers." He parked the car outside the post office. "She must know how to play the game. Tina's admired, but is a threat to the group. She doesn't care what others think. She's too independent."

"It sounds like you admire her."

"Do you mean *as if*?"

I rolled my eyes. "It sounds *as if* you admire her."

"I admire her independence, and I hope she'll do something beneficial to others with her life."

"What about the other candidates?"

"The other two have wild reputations. That makes them popular at parties, but works against them at voting time."

He looked directly into my eyes. "I hope you don't ever get homecoming queen aspirations," he winked. "Work at developing that kind heart instead." He patted my arm softly. "It'll get you lots farther in life."

He got out of the car to get the mail. "I'll be back in a second."

I thought about what he had said and wondered just how kind my heart was.

He returned with the mail and I was getting hungry. "What's for supper?"

"Macaroni hotdish." He started the car.

I said nothing. That meal was one of my least favorites, but I had learned, over the years, not to complain. If I did, I would be the main cook the next night. Sometimes, when Daddy got tired of cooking, I suspected him of slipping in some of my hated meals, hoping that I'd complain.

"Oh, by the way," he said as he parked the car outside our house. "I'm helping with the coronation decorations in the gym Thursday after school. Would you like to come and help?"

He got out of the car.

My heart practically leaped out of my body. I got out and caught up with him.

"Would I like to help?" I imagined myself working beside the older kids and knew that the kids in my class would be envious. And I knew that Margie would simmer in a slow, jealous rage. "Of course I would!" I walked up our steps behind him.

The next day I waited until we lined up for recess, then I turned to Chelsea Turpin and mentioned, very casually, "I hope that I can be free after school on Thursday."

Chelsea, adjusting her glasses, replied, just as I had expected, "Why?"

"Oh, I have to help the juniors with their homecoming decorations."

By now, the whole line was looking back toward me.

"Really?" asked Chelsea. "My sister's going to be there."

"Some seniors will probably be helping too," I replied.

Recess, at least for one day, was now under my control. At first I chose to hang around Chelsea who was thrilled, not by my attention, but by the other girls who came over and asked what game I was going to play.

"Oh, we're just playing 'Guess the King and Queen.' Would you like to join us?"

Most of the girls did. Margie and a few friends ambled over to the swings and kicked some gravel. Margie didn't ask to join us, but then, I didn't expect that she would.

Thursday came quickly, but the day dragged on forever. Fortunately, we had no homework from Mrs. Putnam. She knew that most of us would be at coronation that evening. Assigning homework would have been assigning failure.

I ran to the gym after school and found Daddy stringing some high wires across the gym. Students were draping colorful crepe paper streamers over the wires.

"You could help with the balloons," Daddy suggested.

I went to the stage where several students were using an air compressor to blow up balloons. They then used paperclips to attach the balloons to wires that would then be hoisted upright into columns.

Jane worked the compressor. "Here, Angela, please help me attach these balloons." She showed me how. It was easy. I said little, but attended to my work—all ears.

Shelley Loone, a good friend of Jane's, worked beside me. I had never met her before. Shelley had bright red hair, clear blue eyes and very pale skin. Her hair must have been hard to manage, for she kept it short and teased it.

I watched her attach the balloons to the wire and noticed that she didn't do it very well.

"I think we can get the balloons closer together," I suggested.

"Oh." She laughed lightly. She didn't seem very bright.

Jane noticed Shelley's inadequate job. "Yes, Shelley, we want it to look like a solid balloon column."

Just then, Duane Johnson walked in and sauntered over our way. Duane had been to the barber, for he sported a fresh crew cut. His large hands swayed at his sides and he stuck out his chest. He was shorter than Daddy, but his wide shoulders and thick neck made him look bigger.

"Hi Jane. Hey, Looney, how's it going?" He ran his hand over his red crew cut.

Shelley flushed.

Jane snapped: "We're doing just fine, Duane." She spit out his name as if it were a dirty word. "Want to help?"

He shrugged condescendingly, shoved his hands in his pockets, and turned, surveying the stage and gym. He threw his shoulders back, sticking out his chest. "Naw. Just seeing how everything's coming." He popped a stick of gum into his mouth.

He strutted off, hands swaying again, to pester another group that was decorating a balloon-covered, freestanding arch. They ignored him, so he followed some other football players into the locker room.

"He makes me so mad," Jane said furiously. She looked at Shelley, and her voice softened. "I'm sorry." She lightly touched Shelley's shoulder.

Shelly hadn't looked up, ever since Duane had called her "Looney." She didn't look up now.

Shelley left another large gap between balloons, but I didn't say anything.

The junior class phoned Hillcrest Pizza and ordered pizza and pop to be delivered to the school so that everyone could work through supper. Robert Oatley and a few other football players showed up after practice and helped Jane and Shelley and some other girls tie and lift the balloon columns.

Everyone assembled on the gym floor and watched the stage while Robert and Daddy raised the four white and blue balloon columns and the arch. Then Robert jumped down onto the gym floor as Daddy turned off the gym lights and directed small spotlights that he called fresnels onto the balloons. They cast a blue light over the decorations. I think everyone was impressed with the romantic effect. At least I sure was.

In the dimmed light, Jane moved next to Robert and grabbed his hand. He stiffened a bit, then pulled away and hastily jumped onto the stage and adjusted the center arch.

"Is that better?" he asked.

"Sure," Daddy said, not sure what had been wrong with it before.

But I knew. Jane crossed her arms and walked over to Shelley. She looked toward the dark end of the gym.

CHAPTER 8

You kissed me, then went away.
I don't know why.
You left a key to our special place.
But not to your heart.

—a poem by Jane Turpin

I was very tired when coronation finally came. Adults and young children partially filled the folding chairs on the gym floor, and school-age kids sat in the bleachers.

An usher from the junior class handed me a program, then Daddy and I headed backstage.

The mimeographed program, printed crookedly on the page, had a picture of the school crest. Above the crest, bold letters proclaimed "The Last Paradise Homecoming."

I pointed out the cover to Daddy as we climbed the steps leading backstage. "They make it sound so sad."

"Change is very difficult for some people."

Precisely at 8 o'clock, the band under Miss O'Neil's direction played the school song. I peeked through a hole in the heavy stage curtain at the small band. Miss O'Neil wore a blue pleated skirt, a matching silk blouse, and a white scarf. The school colors looked better on her than on anyone else. Her wavy dark hair glistened under the gym lights. I hoped Daddy had seen her. I fervently hoped that she would come backstage and help after the band finished so that they could talk, but she never did.

When the band finished, Daddy pulled on the frayed curtain rope, opening the curtain, and he turned off the gym lights. Everything was dark except for one white spotlight on the student announcers, and then, as the first couple was introduced, Daddy turned on the blue fresnels. We heard the crowd's *oohing* approval of the blue wash over the balloon columns and crepe paper streamers and decorated chairs on stage. Evidently, no one had ever taken the time to work with the lights before.

Two by two, the candidates walked slowly down the gym floor. As the couples arrived at the foot of the stage in front of the audience, their names were announced, then the two candidates split and walked up the steps on opposite sides of the stage.

Backstage I soon found myself surrounded by the female candidates. Across the stage, I could see the dark shapes of the boys' tuxedoes. As for the girls, they wore beautiful gowns which, depending on the girl, either showed off her legs or shoulders.

While the girls clustered together, Daddy set up a folding chair by the curtains and sat down. I half-sat on his leg. He put his arm around me.

I stared at the girls who seemed to have been momentarily and magically transformed from everyday, blue-jeaned teenagers into fashion dolls, and I wondered if I'd ever have a figure like them. The candidates then paraded across the stage, the girls walking elegantly, the boys looking nervous. Duane was chewing gum like a cow chewing its cud. They finally sat down on the chairs on stage.

After all the candidates had been properly displayed, Coach Oldenburg went up to the microphone. "I'm really proud of the boys—" he stopped, for his deep voice sent the amplifier squealing. He moved the microphone farther from his mouth and began again. He then highlighted their football season so far, described the grueling challenge of this week's game, and urged everyone to support Paradise's fine young men at the game.

"Tonight," he concluded, "is Paradise's last homecoming." A somber, fog-like stillness descended on the gathering. "Some of you may think that just because we'll be consolidated next year that we're going quietly into that good night. Well, you're wrong. We're going to show the rest of Minnesota what Paradise is made of."

Everyone cheered.

Daddy chuckled.

"Why does he hate the consolidation?" I asked.

"He won't be head coach anymore. I suspect that we'll hear many more funeral orations before this year is over." At that time, neither of us realized just how ironic Daddy's observation would turn out to be.

Later, when the king and queen were announced, Daddy's homecoming predictions proved right. Duane Johnson and Mary Oldenburg were the king and queen. Tina Lewis and Chet Kelley were their attendants.

As camera flashes lit the stage like lightning, Chet put his arm around Tina's waist and pulled her closer to him. She smoothly reached behind, pried his hand loose, then gracefully lifted her high heel and planted it firmly on the toe of his shoe. She shifted her weight onto his toe, all the time smiling.

He winced and pried his foot loose. She glanced at him, coolly apologizing for the accident. The cameras kept flashing.

I told Daddy about it as he began putting microphone cords away.

"Good for Tina," he said, but he was too busy taking things down to really pay attention.

Robert came backstage and helped Daddy put equipment away. Some people were clustering around the homecoming court; the rest were streaming toward the cafeteria where refreshments were being served.

"What did you think, Robert?" Daddy asked.

"I think the cheerleaders might want the balloons for the football game."

"No, I mean what did you think about the coronation?"

"Oh, it was one of our best coronations." Shrugging, he looked away. "But I feel odd. This is the last Paradise homecoming."

"You'll have another homecoming next year. You'll just be part of a bigger production, part of Hillcrest."

He turned to Daddy, his blue eyes troubled. "But it'll never be the same."

Daddy finished rolling up a cord and handed it to me.

"Nothing ever is. We just fool ourselves into thinking that next year will be like this one."

"But why can't things stay as they are?"

Daddy crossed his arms and studied the royalty, now moving onto the stage in front of the balloon columns for more pictures. Cameras flashed. "Nothing stays the same. Even memories fade." He paused and looked off to a dark corner of the stage. "It forces us to treasure the moments we have with those we love."

I yawned and Daddy noticed.

"Come on, Angel, time to get you to bed."

"I'm not tired."

"Tell me that in the morning." He grabbed the last cords and locked them in the backstage cabinet. By then the picture-taking crowd had moved off. "See you tomorrow, Robert."

"Yeah." Robert grabbed the ropes and closed the stage curtain, darkening the stage, while Daddy took my hand and led me to the car.

Friday was cold. Daddy ordered me to put on my winter coat and insisted that I wear my gloves and hat to school. As we prepared to walk to the parade's starting spot outside the school, I noticed that other students weren't wearing hats or gloves. Daddy was sure going to hear about that.

As we lined up, I discovered that the parade would be nothing like what I'd envisioned: no out-of-town floats. No out-of-town dignitaries. No out-of-town clowns. The parade would consist of each elementary class walking through town, carrying a banner, followed by the band, weakly playing and poorly marching, followed by the homecoming court riding in convertibles. That was it. Not only was I the only one wearing a hat, I had to walk in a procession that was as far from a parade as a snowflake is from a blizzard.

I felt silly carrying the banner. On our route's first corner stood three elderly people shivering in the wind. They smiled encouragingly at us and pointed out several individuals, probably grandchildren. On the second corner, a mother and two small children waved at us. On Main Street, the high school students who weren't in the band were conversing and didn't even look at us. In the middle of a cluster of junior high students, Shawn Dixon was jostled, and he pushed another boy in retaliation. Some parents stood along the curb. A few of them took pictures.

Miss Bloomsbury from the thrift shop sat on a chair on the sidewalk outside her store. She had a ragged scarf wrapped around her neck. She held a book in one hand and waved at the youngest children with the other. No one stood near her.

Daddy watched at the end of the route, next to the pick-up truck where Coach Oldenburg was going to speak.

He spotted me, and, seeing my sullen scowl, winked and pointed to his own hat and gloves.

The elementary grades, our banners beginning to rip in the wind, formed a circle around the truck. In the shuffling, Margie moved next to me. She didn't look at me, but held her head high, as if posing for a picture. She didn't wear a hat or gloves and her shoulder-length hair blew ever so slightly in the wind.

Margie suddenly smiled and ran a hand through her hair, as if she were a model. Puzzled by her weird behavior, I frowned and was going to say something when suddenly I noticed Mr. Johanson pointing a camera our way. Before I could smile, his camera flash went off.

Oh well, I thought, let Margie look cute in the paper while I'm frowning. Yeah. Frowning and wearing a hat. Great. That will make her day.

We shuffled forward as the band moved behind us. The two convertibles drove up.

The crowd quieted as Coach Oldenburg talked, essentially repeating what he had said the previous evening. Then Duane Johnson, his blue crown slightly crooked, spoke. He was chomping gum again. I wondered if it was the same piece, then I began to laugh at the thought, and Margie poked me in the ribs.

"Quiet!" she barked.

"We hope to play good today," he stammered. "We're going to show them who's boss." A mild cheer. Some clapping. "Thanks for coming. We hope to put on a good show for Paradise's last homecoming."

The drummer beat his drum three times. Margie shrieked, "Go Paradise!" in my ear.

Mary Oldenburg, wearing her queen's white robe over her blue cheerleader's uniform took the microphone. "We want to thank everyone for their support over the years. The cheerleaders really appreciate your help in shouting Paradise's team on to victory." As I watched her light brown hair and direct brown eyes and ready smile, I found myself relax: only then did I realize how listening to Duane had made me nervous. When he talked, I didn't know or trust what he was going to say next. Maybe he didn't either.

Mary pulled her robe tightly around herself. She maintained her composure even while her legs trembled from the cold. I could see why she had won.

I suddenly shivered and was glad that I had worn my hat.

I glanced at Margie. She was completely enthralled by the event.

Our banner ripped into several pieces. Chelsea vainly tried to hold the banner together, but the center section pulled loose and flew off, tumbling down Main Street like a huge white leaf. I was ready to go back to the warm school.

I didn't understand football, but Daddy interpreted that afternoon's game for me as I sat beside him, a blanket wrapped around my shoulders. Paradise scored first, but then lost the lead. They never really had control for the rest of the game. During the last two minutes, they had a chance to come back, but Duane Johnson fumbled the ball on the fifteen-yard line, ending their drive, ending their game. Paradise lost its last homecoming game.

That evening, Daddy began working on his train set in the basement. He threw himself into the task, earnestly, passionately, as he always did in the fall. I knew, in a few weeks, that he would come out of his obsession and we would do all sorts of things together again. Not that he didn't want me to work with him on the train set—he did, but I always lost interest after I had arranged the little people and I saw the train go around the track a few times.

Saturday, he slipped out to the thrift shop and bought those train cars, all except one.

"Miss Bloombury said hello."

"She remembered me?"

"Of course. She told me that she's fixing a doll, so I told her that you collected them. She would like us to see the doll when she is done with it. I'm sure that it'll be for sale."

I groaned. I didn't want someone else's rejected, beat-up doll.

Later, as I finished rearranging my dolls and dressing several in their autumn clothes, I heard Daddy on the phone. My heart leaped. Was he calling Miss O'Neil?

I ran downstairs. "Who're you calling?"

"Just Robert Oatley. I asked if he could come over for a minute and help me with some wiring."

"Why him?"

Daddy was excited and didn't notice my disappointment. "Look." He showed me one of the boxes of the train cars he had purchased at the thrift shop. Robert's name was written on the bottom of the box. "It turns out that Robert is quite a model train hobbyist. He said that he'll be glad to give me a hand." Finally noticing my downcast expression, Daddy added, "I'm sure he won't stay long."

That wasn't the point. I wanted Miss O'Neil to come over.

"Oh," I said.

"What's the matter? I'm sorry I didn't ask you, but I need to lift the board and run wire at the same time. I just thought Robert could help more quickly."

"That's not it."

"What is it?"

I couldn't tell him. "I don't know."

"Maybe there's something good on television this evening. Let's make popcorn tonight."

I perked up. "Maybe we could ask someone over!"

"Sure. One of your friends? You like Chelsea Turpin, don't you?"

I looked down. "Yes, she's a friend, but, no, I don't feel like having her over."

"I've seen you talk to Margie Jones."

"Definitely not!"

"Well?"

"Maybe you want to invite one of your friends."

Daddy rubbed his chin. "I don't know. Rick Manitou is married and has several little children. Do we want his whole family over?"

"Don't adults have friends like kids have friends?"

He looked puzzled. "I guess I don't."

I knew then that I would have to take control of the situation. "How about Miss O'Neil?"

Daddy, quite surprised, adjusted his glasses and cleared his throat. "I suppose we could."

"Well?"

"Well, okay."

He found her number in the phone book and called her. I went upstairs. The last thing he needed was my standing at his elbow.

In a few minutes, I heard him hang up. I ran downstairs as quickly as if it were Christmas morning.

"Sorry, Angel, but she can't tonight. She's really tired from the coronation and chaperoning the dance last night and she's singing in church tomorrow."

I wasn't about to be deterred. "Which church?"

"Hillcrest Community Church," he replied. "I understand it's a merging of several smaller congregations."

"Well?"

He looked away for a moment, thoughtful, then knelt, looking into my eyes. "You want to go tomorrow, I assume?"

"We haven't gone in a while."

"You're right," he admitted. "We haven't found a church that we like yet." He sighed and spoke, as if to himself: "I guess it's been a convenient excuse." Brightening, he put his hands on my shoulders: "Tomorrow, we check out Hillcrest."

Robert came a short time later and helped him set up the train. While they were working in the basement, I studied my hair in the bathroom mirror again. It was long enough that I either needed to get a haircut or I should let it grow out . . . . Maybe long hair would work, after all.

After Robert left, I told Daddy that I wanted to let my hair grow long.

"Fine."

Maybe he hadn't been listening to me. "I said that I was going to grow my hair long."

"Whatever you want."

Hmm. That was simple enough.

That evening we watched a Disney video and I ate too much popcorn.

As Daddy tucked me into bed that night, he mentioned that we would stop in at the Oatley's on Sunday afternoon.

"Robert invited us over to see his model train layout," he explained.

"That's okay," I said. "Just so we don't stay too long."

"We won't," he promised.

After all, I thought, my future mother just might invite us over for Sunday supper.

CHAPTER 9

I remember reading Sherlock Holmes in my 10th grade study hall and thinking how interesting it would be to solve a crime.

I remember a young co-ed with long brown hair in the student union cafeteria. She was eating a dish of cherry ice cream. She became my wife.

—from a creative writing example by Jack Kiln

Sunday was much warmer. I put on my pink dress with the large bow in the back. While Daddy put on his blue tie that went with his tan sport coat and navy blue pants, I studied my hair in the mirror: straight as ever. Maybe, in another few weeks, my hair would be long enough that I could wear a headband. That would give it a semblance of shape.

Daddy drove us to Hillcrest. The church was very friendly, so much so that I soon forgot about my depressing mop of hair. An older woman warmly greeted us at the door. The minister, before the service began, walked into the congregation and introduced himself to us.

"We hope to meet more people because of the school consolidation," Pastor Jim Thorsen said when he heard that Daddy was a teacher. "Do you know Linda O'Neil? She's been attending for a couple of years."

I smiled and nodded while Daddy calmly replied, "Yes. We've met."

"Rick Manitou and his family also attend here."

"He's been a big help at school."

Shortly before the service began, I spotted the Manitou family hurrying in. Mr. Manitou was carrying a small, dark-haired girl. They sat toward the back. I couldn't see his wife very well.

In the pew right behind them, the Oatleys slipped in.

Daddy poked me in the ribs. "Face front," he whispered.

I did and looked around. It was a high-ceilinged church with a simply decorated sanctuary—a large wooden cross hung over the choir loft behind the pulpit. Two large black speakers were suspended from the ceiling near the front. Other than that, there wasn't much to look at.

The choir then walked in. Miss O'Neil stood in the front row behind a small wall. She wore a simple, straight, royal blue dress. Later, I noticed her matching blue shoes.

The service was much better than the Paradise church we had visited. I liked their song choices, and when Miss O'Neil sang her solo, I knew more than ever that I wanted a voice like hers.

And she noticed us, too. When she finished singing, she looked right at me and smiled.

Before the sermon, a tall and very pretty girl—a senior at Hillcrest High School named Amy Wilson—stepped up to the pulpit and thanked everyone for praying for her during her high school years. She nodded toward one family in particular: her older brother (I assumed) and her mother and father. She sang "In His Time" beautifully—not as professionally as Miss O'Neil could've sung it, but I glanced around and most in the church were wiping their eyes. Her father stared straight ahead, stone-faced. He scratched his nose several times and sniffed. He appeared to be struggling against his own emotions.

I looked at Daddy. He was smiling through some tears. I leaned into his arm and he patted my knee. I'm glad he was freer with his emotions than Amy's father.

I drew pictures in the church bulletin during the sermon, but I know that the minister delivered a good message: Daddy listened the whole time.

As the service ended, Daddy leaned over and whispered, "Do you mind if we take Miss O'Neil out for lunch?"

My heart skipped a beat. I didn't know what to say. Events

had transpired without any action on my part, and, for the first time, I realized that sometimes things move more quickly when I don't push them.

"I wouldn't mind."

I never did learn when he had asked her.

After church, we drove her to the nearby Bill's Café. It was a nicer restaurant than Paradise's, decorated in a country decor with old-fashioned pictures on the walls, paintings of things like sleighs on a farm in winter and children swimming in a pond on a hot summer day.

We sat in a booth, toward the back corner. I had a hamburger and french fries. I tried not to smile at Miss O'Neil too much during the meal.

She and Daddy talked about all sorts of things—Paradise, the Hillcrest church, her family's home on Lake Minnetonka, his family in North Dakota.

"And the young girl who sang," Daddy said. "I assume she's had some struggles."

"Years ago, I understand. But she's become a real leader in the youth group."

Daddy nodded. He wasn't one to gossip.

"She's a good example of how God doesn't let us go, even when we forget Him," Miss O'Neil added.

Daddy adjusted his glasses and looked thoughtful.

Toward the end of the meal, their conversation returned to Paradise.

"People in Paradise certainly resist change," Daddy said.

"They truly believe it *is* paradise, so it shouldn't change."

"The first settlers believed in change. They came here through various hardships."

"Paradise's resistance to change is ironic because the original town site lies to the east. They called it Paradise Valley. They had to move because of seasonal flooding in the valley."

Daddy nodded. "Interesting possibility for a metaphor. If we don't change and grow, we drown." Daddy suddenly turned to me. "I'm sorry, Angel, we've been leaving you out of the conversation."

"That's okay," I said, "I was listening."

Miss O'Neil laughed lightly, like Christmas chimes. "She doesn't miss a thing, does she?"

"No," Daddy smiled, "she doesn't. Angela keeps me on my toes."

My heart felt warm. God was answering my prayers.

After dinner, we dropped Miss O'Neil off at her red sports car, still parked outside church. For the first time, I was actually embarrassed by our old station wagon. Daddy didn't say much on the drive back to Paradise.

As we pulled up to our house, Daddy looked thoughtful. "Miss O'Neil seems very nice."

"Yes," I agreed enthusiastically.

He turned off the engine. "Very nice."

Yes, God was definitely answering my prayers.

At three o'clock, we visited Robert's house on the edge of town. Close up, the peeling paint on the house looked even worse. Flowers grew between the house and the sidewalk, but they didn't grow high enough to hide the cracks in the foundation.

Robert came to the door, opening the aluminum screen door for us. The hinge was broken, so the door didn't close properly behind us.

He led us through the living room. Although the furniture was old and the carpet was worn, the room was very clean and orderly. Every item of furniture, every picture on the wall, was placed in its best location.

Entering the kitchen, we met his mother. She was stirring something in a mixing bowl. Robert introduced us.

Mrs. Oatley had short and wavy auburn hair, and was almost as tall as Daddy. She wore a simple flowered dress, and her eyes, like Robert's, were bright blue. I suppose she was attractive, as older women go.

"How nice to meet one of Robert's teachers." She had a pretty smile. I didn't trust her. "It's great that you take an interest in your students." She looked flustered. "That is, of course you are interested in them. I mean, outside of school."

"Thanks," Daddy said diplomatically. "I appreciated Robert's help yesterday. We share a fascination with model trains."

Robert stood to the side, by the basement door, shifting his weight and looking uncomfortable.

He cleared his throat. "It's downstairs."

"Nice to meet you," Daddy said as he passed her.

"These muffins will be done shortly," she called after us.

Narrow wooden stairs led down into the basement. Robert turned on the light.

I caught my breath. I think Daddy did too. In the basement corner, in a space about 8 feet by 10, reproduced in HO scale, was an accurate replica of the eastern half of Paradise.

The water tower was authentically placed north of Main Street. From the south, the tracks neared the town, passed the depot, and headed north of Browner's Woods. Just north of the woods, he even had a spur to represent the eastbound tracks. On Robert's layout, of course, all tracks circled the town.

"I want to eventually send the main line around the basement, bringing it back into town again."

I studied the little people who stood along Main Street. Some were facing store windows; others were talking on street corners.

"Amazing," Daddy said.

"Paradise once looked like this. Well," he laughed, "I did add a few more people."

"You remember it?"

"Of course." He pointed to the ridge just north of the woods. "Here I used to sit and watch the trains. I was in fourth grade when they pulled up the tracks in 1984, about Angela's age."

While Daddy and Robert talked about the layout, I snooped around the rest of the basement.

In the far corner stood a small, neat stack of pine blocks. I walked over, then noticed a shelf above me that held several carved figures, about six inches high. I stood on my tiptoes but couldn't quite make them out.

Off to the side was a stepstool. I slid it over and stood on it.

On the shelf were nine figures, each finely detailed. Five were animals. Of the four people, one was clearly Robert, holding a model train, and I recognized Mrs. Oatley, sitting on a chair. Two were men I didn't know: one figure carried a suitcase; the other, a longhaired, bearded man, held a rifle.

I heard soft footsteps on the stairs. It was Mrs. Oatley coming down.

She approached Robert, proudly resting her hands on his shoulders. "Robert takes a lot of pride in his train set."

"I can see why," Daddy said.

"The muffins are just about done. Can you stay and have some?"

"Well," Daddy hesitated, "we don't want to impose."

"My pleasure," she smiled. "Coffee too?"

Daddy acquiesced—too quickly, I thought. "Milk or water would be fine. Caffeine doesn't always agree with me."

"I know what you mean," she replied pleasantly. She spotted me by the shelf. "Those carvings are Tommy's. Aren't they exceptional?"

Daddy turned and spied me on the footstool. "Angela, you don't look at something without asking."

I stepped down, embarrassed. "I was just curious."

"She's not hurting anything, Mr. Kiln. Tommy wouldn't mind, especially since it's Angela."

She returned upstairs.

Daddy shot me a warning glance and admired the train set again.

Later, I had two blueberry muffins. They were delicious, without the box taste we usually got from our instant mixes.

Although she could cook, I still didn't trust Mrs. Oatley. She was too kind to us, kinder than anyone else we had yet met in Paradise. Except for Miss O'Neil, of course.

The next few weeks were uneventful.

In school, I finally started to read some of the books from Mrs. Putnam's list. Her reading requirement wasn't anything close to what I'd feared. I had feared that these books were extra assignments, but she let me read her suggested books in place of the class's regular reading texts. Reading was now as much fun as when Daddy read to me. I always hated worksheets that came with textbooks. They were so boring that they drained the enjoyment out of reading.

In Daddy's classes, he continued to assign weekly compositions. He kept all student papers in folders, and it was my job to file them. I didn't mind. I often took my time filing them and even read a few.

Tina's papers always impressed me and I liked reading Jane's. Robert's papers usually confused me. Daddy always wrote lots of suggestions on Duane's.

"It would be interesting to see what Duane could do if he ever tried to be original," Daddy said.

"Maybe he can't."

"Can't what?"

"Be original."

Daddy glanced at me oddly, as if the thought had never occurred to him. "Maybe you're right."

Often I would find Daddy after school in animated discussions with students, usually Tina and Jane, and sometimes Mary and Robert. They would be arguing the merits of different stories they had read. Daddy loved it when students were interested enough to debate. Shelley sometimes waited in the hallway with me.

"But it just isn't fair," Tina would often remark about some story's ending.

"Of course not," Daddy would reply. "That's what the author wanted you to see. You can't fight injustice with more injustice."

Tina would arch her back and shake her head. "That makes me so mad."

"You should be a lawyer," he told her on more than one occasion.

On the weekends, Daddy continued to work on his train set.

Robert stopped in to see how Daddy's layout was progressing. Daddy returned the visit a time or two.

We saw little of Miss O'Neil, except on Sundays when we drove to Hillcrest for church. Daddy seemed to like the services there more and more.

"The Hillcrest church reminds me of the church where I met your mother," he said one Sunday. "People seem to genuinely care about each other."

"You met Mommy in college, right?"

"You know that. How many times have I told you the story?"

"I know. But I always like to have you tell it to me again."

I started weekly piano lessons with Miss O'Neil. I was glad because I got to spend more time with her, but it didn't get Daddy and her together. When I was done with my lesson, I just went back to his classroom.

And then, one Sunday—I don't know when Daddy arranged it—we drove Miss O'Neil to church and she cooked Sunday dinner for us. I watched them closely. Daddy and my future mother talk quite well together, I thought. Events began looking very hopeful.

The October weather had turned unusually warm, so while Daddy ran in the evenings, I continued to ride my bike alongside him.

One evening, about a week before Halloween, Daddy decided to leave his normal route and jog over toward Browner's Woods. The oak and maple leaves were beginning to show their autumn colors, and each gust of wind shook gold and red and brown leaves loose to sail and tumble across the grass.

We both saw a well-worn path that cut through the tall grass and entered the western edge of Browner's Woods. The path appeared to run roughly parallel to the ridge to the north.

"Leave your bike by the tree," Daddy said. "Let's see where this path leads."

The path was easy to follow, almost wide enough for two persons to walk side-by-side. Once in Browner's Woods, the tall trees created a dark canopy. The thick underbrush of the summer was now dry and thinning out.

Daddy pointed out various trees to me: maple, oak, ash, walnut, and box elder. The farther we went, the darker the woods became. Eventually, we came to three fallen trees. The main path turned sharply to our right, southwest, back toward town, possibly toward the depot. Beyond the dead trees, a narrow, faintly discernable path continued on, northeast.

Daddy looked over the darkening woods. "Imagine: years ago a train whistle would have reverberated through these trees like a pipe organ in a cathedral."

We listened. The wind rustled the treetops. A few yellow leaves fluttered to our feet. Bird wings rustled in the dark branches overhead. I heard a bullfrog croak. Browner's Woods was eerie enough without a loud, piercing train whistle to make it even scarier. I grabbed his hand.

Daddy didn't seem the least bit frightened. He looked at the small path beyond the dead trees. It wound past maples and a large thistle patch.

"Come on," he said, "let's check out this path."

He helped me over the three dead trees. The path ran east for just a bit before ending in a tangle of small trees and weeds and thistles.

"Look." Daddy pointed to our left. The ground sloped down an eroded embankment into a small valley. On the other side was the ridge that marked the northern edge of the woods.

But Daddy wasn't pointing to the ridge. At the base of the little valley and built into the side of the ridge was an old shack. It appeared to be a hybrid of building materials. Logs formed the base, a few pieces of cut lumber shaped the corners, dented and warped paneling created the front wall, and corrugated metal shaped the sides.

Daddy slid down the embankment toward it, loosening lots of dirt, then caught me on my slide down. Two sawed-off tree stumps, looking as if they were used for stools, stood outside the shack. A rotted blanket covered the entrance. Daddy moved the musty blanket aside and we peered in.

The odd shack appeared to be roughly in the shape of an upside-down cross, and we stood at the top. We stepped in. In the room on our left was a battered white door that lay across four tall logs, forming a crude table. Two old wooden chairs were pulled up to this table. Warped playing cards lay on the top, arranged, it seemed, for a game of solitaire. A small and rusted Franklin stove stood in the far corner, piped to the ceiling.

Straight ahead in the shack—the foot of the cross—was a long and narrow room cut into the side of the hill. A sheet of paneling served as a back wall. Dirt was crumbling in around it. None of the dirt side walls looked safe.

To our right hung a rotted bedspread. Daddy pulled it aside. Beyond was a small room, almost like an alcove, with two candle stubs. Quite a few crushed pop cans lay half-covered with dirt.

I shuddered and stepped out of the shack. Daddy joined me.

He pointed to several boards along the stone foundation. "Do you see how this building had originally been built by experienced hands? Virtually everything above the foundation is a crude add-on."

"What was it built for?"

"I'd guess it's a relic from the 1930's, a hobo shack hidden in the woods, a way station for those waiting between trains. Later it was torn down, or fell down, and rebuilt by some town kids—perhaps in the 1960's."

Daddy looked in again. "What amazes me is the relative cleanliness of this hovel. I don't see piles of beer cans or graffiti. It almost shows the loving care of a clubhouse."

"But it hasn't been used for years."

Daddy's gaze swept over it. "Don't be too sure."

He helped me climb up the eroded embankment and we followed the path back to the three dead trees.

It was growing even darker in the woods.

"I wish we had a flashlight," I said.

"Me, too."

Just then we heard crunching footsteps along the main path, coming in our direction.

Terrified, I gripped Daddy's hand with all my strength.

Suddenly a longhaired, bearded man appeared along the path. He wore camouflaged hunting clothes and carried a rifle at his side.

Spotting us, he stopped abruptly. "Who're you?"

Daddy stepped forward while I hid behind him. "Jack Kiln. This is my daughter Angela."

"What're y'doin' in the woods?"

Daddy looked around nonchalantly. "We didn't mean to trespass, but I thought this was state or county land."

I peered around Daddy's elbow, getting another look at him. His beard was scraggly and thin. His narrow face was smeared with dirt. The man's bushy eyebrows furrowed. He snorted: "Sometimes kids are messin' around in here."

"As you can see, I'm hardly a kid. I've been jogging past the woods for a month or so and wanted to see where the path led."

"Nothing much here."

"No. I suppose not. And you are—?"

"Warren Gallagher."

The man turned abruptly and shuffled back toward town. Daddy and I followed.

Warren Gallagher. I tried to remember if I'd heard the name before. I wondered where I'd seen him and then recalled one of Tom Oatley's carved figures: the likeness was astounding.

Gallagher. Could he be the Dirtball Gallagher that the kids talked about?

Daddy tried to make conversation as we followed him. "Have you lived in Paradise long?"

"All my life." His words were more like grunts than speech.

We walked on a bit farther. Daddy asked, "Do you live near here?"

"Just across from Browner's Woods."

Daddy glanced back at me. I nodded. We both had noted the two-story, rust-colored house on this end of town, its lawn rarely mowed, its hedges never pruned, its paint mostly peeled away.

We reached the edge of Browner's Woods. My bike was still there. Dirtball Gallagher walked past it, toward his house.

"Nice to meet you, Mr. Gallagher," Daddy called after him.

"Sure." He shuffled on, then abruptly stopped and came back. "Kiln, wasn't it? You that new teacher?"

"Yes. English."

He pulled at his scraggly beard with his left hand, shifting his rifle with his right. "I had an English teacher once I liked. In college."

"College?"

"Yeah. One year. During the war." He turned, walked away, then stopped again. He glanced back at us. "Hope I didn't scare you. The rifle, it's my security. Saw the bike, thought maybe someone was in trouble. Or messin' around."

Daddy nodded. "Sure. Glad to have met you."

"Had an English teacher once," he muttered, walking on. "In college."

I quickly grabbed my bike. "Let's get out of here."

Daddy watched Dirtball Gallagher walk to his home. "Don't worry, Angel. He's harmless enough."

That evening the temperature dropped below freezing, and it stayed cold through Halloween. It was too cold for Daddy to run, but somehow I knew that we'd see more of Warren Gallagher.

CHAPTER 10

*In order to survive, women must band together in this
male-dominated world. After all, men have created their power
base. Most employers are men. Most executives are men. Most
politicians are men. Men prey on women. They drag them off
today, just as they did during the Trojan War, whether it's date
rape or wife beating.*

—from an essay by Tina Lewis

After school on Monday, Daddy took me to the high school
faculty room for a can of root beer. Entering the lounge, both of us
realized that a heated argument was reaching the boiling point.

Mr. Manitou, whom I'd never seen upset, sat at the long, center
table, frustrated. He was shaking his head vehemently. "That's not
my point."

Ted Hanson, the short, mustached science teacher, sat across
from him, his back to the windows, equally upset. "It's not fair!"

"Since when is life fair?"

Daddy and I approached the table, behind Rick Manitou. Daddy
tried to lighten things up, lightly patting Rick Manitou's shoulders
in a warm and friendly manner. "What's the debate about?"

Clearly angry, Ted Hanson grabbed his coffee cup and spun
away, facing the windows. Out in the parking lot, some girls were
talking by the student cars. Among them, I could see Tina, Shelley,
and Jane.

"Oh, nothing, really," Rick Manitou said. "A second-year music
teacher in Cherry Grove—a woman—was seen on a date with a
senior boy. Pressure is being put on her to resign, even though the
boy was 18. I said that teachers have to be careful of what they
do."

Mr. Hanson snapped. "As teachers we shouldn't need to be more accountable than others."

Rick Manitou looked squarely at the back of Mr. Hanson's head. "Maybe we all need to be more accountable to each other." He abruptly stood, towering over me. I got out of the way as he walked past me and left the faculty room.

Mr. Oldenburg, sitting at the end of the table, leaned back in his chair. "In the old days," he pontificated, breaking the tension, "we were clearly instructed not to be seen at the municipal liquor store. *Or else.* Remember?"

Mr. Bakken, the heavy phy-ed teacher, leaned forward and patted Mr. Oldenburg's forearm. "And remember when Hadley returned from Europe?"

They both laughed.

We had no idea what they were talking about. Daddy turned to me, a little embarrassed by the drift of the conversation. He pushed his glasses higher. "Ready for that root beer?"

We slid past Mr. Oldenburg to the pop machine in the corner. As Daddy dropped coins in the slot, I turned and noticed that Ted Hanson's hands trembled as he poured himself another cup of coffee.

After we left, Daddy and I stepped into Mr. Manitou's classroom. I sipped my root beer and held in a burp. Mr. Manitou was sitting at his desk, leaning forward thoughtfully, resting his chin on his hands. His dark eyes stared at the back wall. Noticing us, he sat up, smiling sheepishly. "Sorry for that little scene. I don't know what ignited Ted. Unfortunately, my pride and convictions weren't about to back down, and I knew I had to leave before I said too much."

"We all wear masks of different kinds. Maybe Ted's outburst erupted because his conscience wasn't allowing him to keep his mask on straight."

Rick Manitou raised his dark eyebrows but didn't reply.

That evening during supper, I asked Daddy about the faculty-room argument. "Chelsea Turpin said that her sister Jane had seen Mr. Hanson and Mrs. Walker holding hands after school."

Daddy looked down at his plate and didn't say anything for a moment, and I wondered if he had heard the same rumor.

"We have to be careful of gossip." He took off his glasses and massaged the bridge of his nose. "The more I think about the argument this afternoon, the more I know that Rick Manitou was right. The public expects teachers to be a cut above. We can't be, of course. No one can. And Ted would argue that America has corrupt politicians, dirty cops, inept physicians, abusive childcare workers, and greedy investors. The list goes on and on. Why should teachers be expected to be different?"

He put on his glasses and continued. "Yet unlike other professions, we're society's hope for a better tomorrow. We're guiding the future politicians, police, and doctors. We're the surrogate parents, like it or not, and paid to be. On the job, teachers are expected to be better than the parents. Off the job, those expectations are still there."

The next day we had a *small* Halloween party in Mrs. Putnam's class. We didn't dress up. We didn't bring candy.

What Mrs. Putnam did do was bring popcorn, suspend all homework, and show us a cartoon of "The Legend of Sleepy Hollow." By Mrs. Putnam's standards, it was a big party.

During our gym time we had to be careful where we ran because the gym was decorated for a high school dance that evening. I knew from past experiences that if Daddy had been forced to chaperone, he wouldn't take me and he wouldn't let me stay home by myself. I also knew, with convictions as strong as Mr. Manitou's, that I was too old to have a sitter. But, fortunately, Daddy didn't have to chaperone, so we were saved from a conflict of wills.

After school, on my way up to Daddy's room, I saw Jane Turpin crying by her locker. Tina Lewis had her arm around her.

They were right in my path and I didn't know what I should

do: stop in the middle of the hall? ignore them? Before I reached them, though, they turned and walked in the other direction.

A piece of paper lay on the floor by Jane's locker.

I picked it up and read it.

Dear Jane,

I'm sorry I haven't paid much attention to you lately. It isn't because I haven't been thinking about you. I have. Often. It isn't because I haven't been noticing you. I have. All the time.

It's because I'm afraid. I began having serious feelings about you, and it scared me.

I used to think my dad was the greatest guy in the world. My mom and dad got married right after high school. As you probably know, he left us eight years ago this spring.

If a person as smart as my dad did that, I'm afraid I might do the same. I think they had problems because they dated and married too young.

I wouldn't want to hurt you the way my dad hurt my mom.

I'm sorry. For now, let's just be friends.

Robert

I felt guilty for reading it, but what else was I supposed to do? I hadn't known that it was going to be a personal note: at least, that's what I told myself. If I had known—well, I probably would have read it anyway.

Her locker was ajar. I slipped the note in and shut the door.

I was going to tell Daddy about Jane's crying, but before I could say anything, he walked out of his room toward the stairway and right past me. I knew something was wrong: his lips were pursed and his gray eyes glared directly ahead.

"Where're you going?"

"The office," he replied curtly. "I'll be back."

"Can I come too?" I asked quickly before he vanished down the steps.

His voice echoed up the stairwell. "You mean *May I.* Sure."

I caught up with him in the office. He was sitting at the secretary's desk, dialing a number.

"Who're you calling?"

He glanced at me briefly, sternly, then away. "Not now, Angel." He spoke into the phone: "Mrs. Dixon, please." He began tapping his fingers, something he rarely did.

I walked over to the chairs across from the counter and sat down. Some Halloween this was turning out to be. Just then, Mr. Cranberry's short, plump secretary, Mrs. Benwick, came out of his office. She looked irritated when she saw Daddy there, but—for once—she didn't say anything. She took some papers off her desk and loitered around the filing cabinet. It was obvious that she was eavesdropping.

"Hello, Mrs. Dixon," he said into the receiver. "This is Mr. Kiln, Shawn's English teacher. Yes, I know you're at work, but I couldn't reach your husband earlier. Oh, he's on the road? Yes, yes, I know you're at work, but I needed to let you know right away that Shawn is going to be serving detention. Yes, I know you're at work, but you need to know that if detention isn't effective, school will become progressively more difficult for him. Yes, but you need to know, and I would appreciate some help from your end. Do you have any questions?"

He listened to the phone for a moment, frowning. He raised his eyebrows abruptly, then slowly hung up the phone.

"Well?" I asked.

"She doesn't want to be disturbed at work. She said any discipline problems with Shawn have to be taken up with his father." Daddy stood and we left. I glanced back at Mrs. Benwick. She was resuming her normal sitting position and a smirk—ever so slight—crossed her plump face.

We ate an early supper and I hurried into my costume: a fairy princess.

"This is no disguise for you," Daddy said.

"What do you mean?"

"Masks are designed to hide the inner person. You already are a princess."

I smiled. "Oh, Daddy, you're so silly."

"No, I mean it. People wear masks and disguises all the time. Sometimes the most honorable and decent mask hides the most horrible and disgusting person. And sometimes the most unappealing mask hides the most beautiful person." He grabbed me and hugged me. "But with you, you're pretty inside and out."

I never felt pretty but I sure liked to hear him say it.

"How do you know what's behind a person's mask?"

"It takes time. Families keep us honest: among family members, you can't keep the mask on all the time."

The doorbell rang. It was Chelsea. She was wearing a plastic Darth Vader mask. I didn't go into Daddy's philosophical treatise on disguises.

Chelsea and I covered most of the town in an hour and a half. We ran from house to house, skipping the ones that didn't have any lights on. Because Chelsea didn't wear her glasses, I had to direct her most of the time.

It's funny what masks and costumes do for us, how they can give us extra courage. Normally I would never run across yards and would be terrified to go up to a stranger's door, but when I donned a costume, I could do it. More than that: I wanted to do it. For that short time, Chelsea and I reveled in the sheer fun of unbridled freedom.

When we came to the northeast edge of town, we both looked across the highway and spotted Dirtball Gallagher's front light on. I glanced at her. Her eyes shone behind her dark mask's twin holes. She knew where we were.

"Maybe we'll skip that one," I said.

"Fine with me." Chelsea's voice was muffled by her mask. "His candy's probably laced with drugs."

I pushed her arm, laughing.

"No, really," she said, quite offended that I didn't believe her. She lifted her mask. "He's the supplier for the county."

I laughed again. Yet her face was so sincere and she looked so hurt at my disbelief that I wondered if I should believe her.

We dashed back toward Main Street, having discovered the limits of our freedom and courage.

"By the way," I asked, "how's your sister?"

She shrugged. "Fine, I guess. She's always out with Tina and Shelley. I don't see her much. Why?"

I still felt bad about reading that note. I wished I hadn't known. I wondered if I should tell Chelsea about it. I took a deep breath of cool, October night air and decided against it. Maybe a person's sadness should remain private until that person wanted to share it.

"Just wondering," I replied. "Race you back!"

"No fair!" she shouted. "I can't tell shadows from real bushes."

"Tough!"

She and I sprinted to my house, cutting across yards and even leaping low bushes until we finally burst through our front door.

Breathless, we both laughed. "You ran fast for being blind."

"Yeah, I did," she said, amazed at herself.

We dumped our loot onto the floor where the multi-colored candy spilled into small mountains on the carpet.

Chelsea admired our sprawling twin piles "Pretty good haul."

"We had to run a lot, but it was worth it."

Daddy came in from the kitchen and stood over us, shaking his head. "I hope you both ration that sugar." He added: "And don't keep anything that looks as if it had been opened."

"Don't worry," Chelsea said. "We didn't go to Dirtball Gallagher's house. He's the drug dealer, you know. He's really weird."

Daddy raised his eyebrows skeptically. "There's an old adage: 'Believe none of what you hear and half of what you see.' Mr. Gallagher may have his own reasons for behaving differently."

"Like what?" I asked.

"Until you spend enough time with him to see behind his mask, you don't know."

Chelsea sneered. "Who'd want to spend time with him? No one wants to."

Daddy smiled. "Maybe that's the reason for his disguise."

Chelsea and I sampled our wares until we felt sick from too much sugar. Then, while Daddy drove Chelsea home, I divided my haul into various piles, one of which I tucked under my bed for emergency snacks, and brushed my teeth thoroughly.

Later, after Daddy had finished reading and praying, I said to him, "Do you know I once thought you were Superman?"

He laughed. "You never told me that."

"When I was really little, I saw Superman in a movie. He had glasses, just like you, and then he took them off and flew. I thought that maybe you were really Superman."

He continued to chuckle.

"I remember telling Mommy that in the hospital, and she laughed, too."

His laughter subsided and he grew thoughtful. "Yes, she would have found that funny."

"She agreed with me."

He looked at me over his glasses. "She did?"

"That's why I thought it was true."

He didn't laugh that time. He kissed me on the forehead and turned out the light. "It's late, Angel. Good night."

The next day in school, I almost fell asleep during reading time . . . and it was a really good part of *The Yearling*, too.

After school, Daddy said that Shawn had refused to come to detention. I went with him to the office as he called Mrs. Dixon at work.

He asked for her but then he hung up almost immediately. "Her supervisor says she can't come to the phone now."

That night, Daddy called her at home. No one answered the phone. He tried until 10 o'clock, then gave up.

The next day Shawn skipped detention for the second time. Again, Daddy called Mrs. Dixon at work. This time he got through.

"Hello, this is Jack Kiln, one of Shawn's teacher. I tried to call you last night at home—"

He laid the phone back on the receiver. "She hung up," he told me.

The next morning, as Daddy sat at his desk writing his notes for the day and I was gathering my books and folder in the back of the room, the classroom door opened.

In walked an unshaved man in a black leather jacket, about Daddy's height. He had long, stringy, rust-colored, greasy hair combed back, and a Fu Manchu mustache. It looked like an upside-down horseshoe.

"Kiln?" The man's harsh voice bristled with rage.

"Yes," Daddy answered, glancing up. Startled at first by the stranger's appearance, Daddy took a deep breath, adjusted his glasses and put on his most docile mask. "I'm Jack Kiln."

The ominous stranger strode to Daddy's desk and leaned across it, blocking my view. I could read the back of his jacket: Dixon Trucking.

"Quit bothering my wife at work," the man snarled.

Daddy's voice didn't change. "I didn't mean to bother her. I needed to contact either you or her, and I was told that you were out of town."

"So what? You don't bother her at work."

Daddy wasn't backing down. "I needed to contact you as Shawn's parents."

Cowering in my desk, I swallowed hard and leaned to my left so that I could see Daddy.

"What for?"

"Shawn wasn't following directions. You needed to know."

"Why?"

A moment's pause. Daddy was puzzled: he leaned back in his chair. "Well, you're his parents, his guardians, his legal supervisors. You have the right to know."

"We don't want to know. He'll do whatever he damn well pleases."

Daddy remained sitting. I thought he should have stood, should have stood to face this ignorant, belligerent, evil Mr. Dixon. Instead, he maintained a completely calm composure.

"You have the responsibility to know," Daddy stated firmly, "whether you want that obligation or not. You will be notified if Shawn doesn't follow directions, doesn't abide by the rules, or doesn't finish his work. This is my standard procedure. I do this with all my students."

Dixon stood up straight, blocking my view again, and crossed his arms. His leather jacket creaked. "You quit bothering my wife at work or I'll come back and kill you."

Daddy cleared his throat. Dixon just stood there.

"You hear me?" he snarled.

"I hear you."

I silently crept near the door of the classroom, ready to run for help. Daddy looked pale. He showed no sign of seeing me. He was staring down at his desk.

Suddenly he looked up at Mr. Dixon. His gray eyes grew more determined, his voice stronger. "Yes, I do hear you. Have you ever been in prison, Mr. Dixon?"

Daddy and I both knew that he had.

The man lifted his chin, looking proud.

"Well, consider carefully if I am worth your return visit, because either you or Mrs. Dixon will be notified if and when Shawn decides to cause other students not to learn. That is my procedure. Educating is my job. If you feel my procedure is inappropriate, you may talk to the administration or to the school board."

Mr. Dixon lowered his arms, confused by Daddy's unruffled response.

Daddy finally stood. "I will, until I hear otherwise from the administration, continue to do my job."

Suddenly exploding, Dixon swore at Daddy. He knocked Daddy's books off his desk, sending them flying onto the floor, and repeated his threat, yet this time his words seemed to carry less weight.

Daddy remained calm and didn't take his gaze off Dixon. "Perhaps you should try talking to Shawn about his problems in my class. I would be glad to sit down with both of you to see if we could reach some sort of understanding."

Dixon put his hands on his hips, and the third time snarled, "If you bother my wife at work again, I'll kill you."

Daddy nodded patiently, as if talking to a small child. "Yes, Mr. Dixon, I am not hearing impaired: I heard you the first time. And I will continue to notify you or Mrs. Dixon until all of us can have a conference with Shawn. Why don't you talk to Shawn about what he would like to do? As for me, I won't change my procedure."

Dixon sniffed loudly, spun on his heels, and strode to the door. He turned, not two feet from me. I could smell tobacco smoke on his jacket, see the grease on his knuckles.

"Kiln, you heard me," he bellowed, his voice echoing down the hall like a sick calf.

"I heard you," Daddy said calmly. "And I hope and pray, for your sake, that you heard me too."

Dixon was gone. The door slammed shut.

Daddy collapsed in his chair, and I ran to his side, trying desperately not to cry.

Daddy let out a long, slow sigh, then rubbed his forehead.

I put my hand on the back of his neck. He glanced up at me. "Oh, Angel, I forgot you were here." He reached around my waist and hugged me. "I'm sorry you saw that."

I finally burst out crying.

"What's wrong?" he asked softly.

"That was the bravest thing I ever saw!"

"I didn't feel very brave." He stared at the closed door. "Did you hear him shout at the end? That was so others could hear him."

The door suddenly opened and Mr. Manitou rushed in. "Jack, are you all right? What happened?"

"Nothing much."

"That evil man threatened Daddy!" I shouted in between sobs. "He told Daddy he'd kill him if he called about Shawn."

Mr. Manitou folded his arms: "Jack, should I call the sheriff?"

Daddy sighed. "No, I'll write up the incident for the office. I think he was all wind."

Mr. Manitou picked up Daddy's scattered books and set them on his desk. "Maybe you're right and maybe not. Let me take your first hour study hall while you write it up."

Daddy stood slowly, suddenly seeming unsteady on his feet. "That would be nice." He grabbed Mr. Manitou's arm. "Thanks."

"Anytime." Mr. Manitou smiled: "Though I hope it never has to happen again."

"Me, too." Daddy turned to me, touched my cheek, and then wiped my tears. "Angel, you better get your things together. You don't want to be late for Mrs. Putnam's class."

I hugged his waist. "Daddy, I was so scared."

He knelt, his gray eyes looking directly at mine. "For a moment, so was I."

"But you didn't seem to be."

"No, I put on a mask to counter Mr. Dixon's. He wore a bully's mask."

"What's behind his mask?"

"I don't know yet. We'll know in a day or two."

He laid his hands softly on my shoulders, and then he hugged me. After a moment, he stood. "I'll be in the office," he told Mr. Manitou.

After he left, Rick Manitou stared at the open door. "I'm beginning to think your father would rip the mask off the Devil himself."

Shawn Dixon wasn't in school that day.

The next day he returned, and he didn't cause any trouble, none at all.

But that's what I should have expected. You don't mess around with Superman.

CHAPTER 11

*I don't remember my father much. Robert does. They used to
do lots of things together. Especially watching trains come through
town. Stuff like that. Dad bought Robert his first train set. I
carved a statue of my father from an old picture. Mom still prays
for him. I don't understand that.*
—from Tom Oatley's autobiographical essay

Shortly after the Dixon incident, Daddy took me for a ride
after school. Before leaving, he grabbed his camera and put it in
the back seat.

"Where are we going?" I asked, surprised we weren't just heading
home.

"Out in the country. To see a home."

"We're not moving again, are we?"

He laughed. "No."

He turned off the highway and headed east of town. Except
for the ridge to the north that gradually rose higher than Browner's
Woods, the countryside continued to be very flat. The corn was
dry and brown and farmers were out in the fields with cornpickers.
From what I'd heard from kids at school, the crop was going to be
good.

We left Browner's Woods behind and the land grew hilly.
Daddy turned onto a narrow gravel road that wound around several
old home sites and groves. We crossed a stone bridge spanning the
North Branch of Prairie Creek. There were small arching trees near
the bridge, and I could see the ridge ahead and an old trestle that
was missing a few timbers.

"We're near the original town site of Paradise Valley," Daddy
said as he stopped the car.

"What're you doing?"

He pulled out his camera and took a picture of the trestle. "Might be a useful reference for a model train layout some day."

We then drove a little further northeast past a run-down, two-story farmhouse with a newer metal shed. He slowed the car almost to a stop.

"Take a good look," he said. From the decrepit house, large patches of paint peeled away like white leaves. Long patches of siding were missing, revealing torn tarpaper. There was no storm door and the main door's wood veneer was cracked and bubbled. Of the three windows facing us, only one had a combination window. One window had tarpaper stapled over the front and the other had no screen or glass but looked more like a square hole in the wall, a large yawn opening into nothing.

I turned in my seat to look longer as Daddy drove slowly on. Behind the house, garbage was thrown in a heap only a few feet from the back door. A rusted tractor stood nearby. The grass hadn't been mowed in a long time.

As for the newer metal shed, its wide, sliding door was open. It was empty except for refuse scattered on the dirt floor and a rusted tricycle near the door. The shed was large and long, long enough to hold a truck and a trailer.

It finally dawned on me.

"Is that where—?"

"That's the Dixon place."

I looked at the tranquil, rolling countryside around their house. Daddy seemed to read my mind. "Quite a contrast, isn't it, Angel?"

I said nothing as he drove back to town.

After school on Thursday, when I walked into his room, Daddy glanced at me in an unusual way: awkward and surprised. Then he quickly shuffled some papers. He was nervous about something, almost as if he were hiding something. I set my backpack on a front desk, sat down, and waited.

He glanced up at me a few times in between his paperwork. I

waited longer. Finally he walked over to me and sat beside me in another desk.

I bit my lower lip, suddenly worried. Maybe Mr. Dixon was returning.

"Angel, I know you don't like it, but I hired a sitter for this evening."

This was bad. Not in the realms of Mr. Dixon or death, but bad enough.

I moaned, rolled my eyes. "Who is it?"

"Jane Turpin. She's an older girl—"

"Yes," I pouted, "I know her. What meeting do you have to attend this time?"

Daddy shifted in the desk awkwardly, then stood, as if making a final decision. He nervously cleared his throat and adjusted his glasses. "I'm taking Miss O'Neil out for dinner."

"Why can't I come too?" I blurted, then I realized the full implication of his statement. My eyes narrowed skeptically. "Do you mean on a real, official date?"

He laughed. "On a real, official date?" He walked back to his desk. "I guess so."

For an official date, I could forgive him. After all, in order for her to become my future mother, he had to get to know her better. Yet, at the same time, I couldn't help feeling left out, maybe even a little jealous. Ashamed of my feelings, I pushed them aside.

"Well," I sighed dramatically, following him. "I'll overlook it this time."

He smiled. "Thank you, madam."

Within the hour, he was hastily giving directions to Jane in the kitchen while I watched TV in the living room.

"And here's the number I'll be at. If an emergency arises and you can't get me, do you have an adult to call? Mrs. Putnam lives across the alley."

"Relax, Mr. Kiln. I know what to do."

They walked into the living room.

"I haven't left her in some time," he said.

"We'll be fine. Is it still okay with you if Tina and Shelley come over and do homework?"

"Sure." He opened the front door. "I appreciate this, Jane." He came back into the living room. "How about a hug from my Angel?"

I ran to him and gave him the strongest hug I could.

"I know you'll be good for Jane," he whispered. "Go to bed on time."

"I will. Say 'hi' to my—to Miss O'Neil."

Blushing, Daddy stood and glanced awkwardly at Jane, embarrassed.

Whoops, I thought. Evidently, his date was a secret.

He smiled briefly, cleared his throat, then left. From the window, I watched him drive away in our rusted station wagon. If he hoped to make a favorable impression on my future mother, he needed to buy us a new car.

"Do you want to play any games?" Jane asked.

"Not yet." I started watching cartoons.

Jane went to the kitchen table and read a book.

After our frozen pizza supper, Jane and I played a game of Clue. I won. It was Miss Scarlet with the revolver.

Around 7 o'clock, Tina and Shelley came over. Both were dressed casually in blue jeans. Tina wore a white T-shirt under a cardigan sweater and her blonde hair was pulled back in a ponytail. Shelley had her red hair teased and pulled back and wore an extra large ski sweater. Jane came upstairs with me and helped me get started on my science homework, then she slipped downstairs and the three girls gathered around the kitchen table, listening to the radio and doing homework.

It didn't take me long to finish. I came down again and pulled out a coloring book and sat at the table with them, next to Shelley and across from Jane and Tina. The radio was playing some love song and they were humming to it. Their jackets and Tina's sweater were piled in the corner. Tina, sitting between the others, seemed to come up with most of the answers.

Suddenly Tina stopped humming and turned the radio down. "You know, there's a lot of junk we sing along with."

Jane and Shelly glanced at each other and appeared uncertain.

But they gave a half-smile to each other and let Tina find another radio station.

From watching them work, I learned that Tina and Jane shared classes and so worked on the same assignments, but Shelley had some special classes, easier ones it seemed.

Once, when Shelley looked frustrated and Tina was helping Jane, I glanced at Shelley's work.

"Those are fractions," I said. "I can help you." I showed her what to do.

Her eyes widened. "You're a really smart kid."

I beamed. "Daddy says so."

Tina glanced up from what she was showing Jane and stared at me thoughtfully with her large blue eyes. "You're a lucky girl." Tina returned to her work. I inwardly smiled, thinking she had complimented my intelligence, not realizing until much later that she meant something else entirely: my father.

Shelley, anxiously gripping her pencil with one hand and twirling a strand of hair with the other, completed her next problem.

"That's right," I encouraged, feeling important.

I looked across the table, surprised to see Jane struggling with her English poetry assignment. Tina helped her with practically every question.

I could see why Daddy found it easy to like Tina. She was smart, helpful, independent. And pretty. I wanted to be like her.

Shelley abruptly sat back and shut her notebook. "Done!"

Tina didn't look up from her work. "With everything?"

Shelley smiled meekly. "With math."

I noticed a design drawn on Shelley's notebook cover. It was a large letter "A" with a spear angled through it.

"What's that mean?"

She glanced quickly, almost fearfully, at Tina who was helping Jane again. Tina shrugged as if she didn't care.

"It's the Amazon sign," Shelley said.

"What's that? A rock band?"

"No," she smiled proudly. "Us."

I didn't understand.

"Tina and Jane and me," she explained. "We're the Amazons."

"Like a club?"

"Like a club."

"What do you do in the Amazons?"

"We get together, like now, and help each other. We—" she paused, seeming lost for words, "we just help each other. Show her, Tina."

Tina, not stopping her homework, just lifted the sleeve of her T-shirt. Tattooed on her shoulder was the same A and angled-spear emblem. I hadn't seen a tattoo on a girl before.

"Neat," I said, though I didn't really think so.

"We're going to get one too," Shelley said enthusiastically. "And when you get older, you can join."

"We'll be too old then," Jane pointed out.

Tina covered her shoulder suddenly. "The Amazons will always be needed."

Jane looked down sheepishly, almost embarrassed. "Maybe not someday."

Tina glanced at her, reconsidered. "Maybe not," she said softly.

At 8:30, I went upstairs and got ready for bed.

Jane came to see if I needed anything. I was already in bed with the night-light on.

"We usually have devotions and pray," I said.

"Oh. What are devotions?"

"We read Bible verses or stories."

She sat on the edge of the bed. It squeaked. "That's nice."

I leaned over and pointed at the book on the floor beside the bed. "That's what we use."

She picked it up, examined the cover. She looked hesitant, almost fearful.

"That's okay," I said quickly. "We can just pray. You go first, then I'll finish."

She bowed her head and recited a brief poem, then I launched in and thanked God for everything he'd given us and for Daddy and for Miss O'Neil and for my friends like Jane.

Afterwards, she tucked me in and went back downstairs.

I lay still for a while. I tried to fall asleep, but I didn't feel sleepy. I turned on my side. I could hear their muffled voices and the radio from the kitchen. I turned on my other side. It would be fun to have a club of girls. I turned again. I listed five school friends I'd allow in my group. I didn't include Margie. Somewhere, in the midst of those thoughts, I grew drowsy.

Almost asleep, I heard the phone ring and some quiet talking. I began drifting back to sleep, then suddenly feared the caller might be Daddy, feared that something might be wrong. I was instantly alert.

Slipping out of bed, I crept down the stairs, stopping halfway.

Jane was on the phone. "Oh, Duane," she said, disgusted, "don't be so crude." I heard her sigh. "Yes, she's here. You shouldn't call here. I'm babysitting. No, he doesn't have tests lying around. Don't be so dumb. Yes, but make it short."

She called Shelley to the phone.

Shelley talked more softly, so it was hard to hear, but it sounded as though he was asking her out for a date. She probably covered the phone then, because I could hear her whispering something to the other girls.

"All right." She sounded happy, almost giddy. "Yes, you can count on me. Right. After the game."

She hung up.

I crept back upstairs and crawled into bed. I pulled the blanket up to my chin: What would I do if a boy ever called me up on the phone? I wasn't sure if I ever wanted a boy to.

I was asleep when Daddy came home.

The next morning, he didn't say much about his evening, even when I hinted about it. Finally, I had to ask him directly.

"It went well. We had a nice meal. We were able to talk about a lot of things." That was all that he divulged.

That day in school, at the end of music class, I lingered by Miss O'Neil's desk until the other students headed back to the fourth grade classroom.

"Daddy said he enjoyed taking you out last night," I said.

Miss O'Neil smiled politely, formally. "Thank you, Angela. Next time, we'll include you."

I shook my head. "No, you two need to get to know each other better first."

"First?"

I nodded. "See you Sunday!" I hurried to get back to class before Mrs. Putnam marked me late.

Saturday afternoon found me defiantly blocking our back door. "No, we don't have to see her!"

"Yes, we do," Daddy stated. "If you don't want to come, you may stay here."

You could sooner stop the earth from spinning than stop me from being there if Daddy was going to visit Mrs. Putnam.

"It's the neighborly thing to do," he explained. "Besides, it gives me a chance to meet her on something other than a professional basis. It's important to be on friendly terms with your neighbors. You never know when you may need their help, and, more importantly, unless you leap over some fences, you never know when they might need your help."

I thought of our other neighbors. "We don't visit the Millers," I pointed out.

"The Millers both work odd shifts. You know they're never home."

"What about the Taylors?"

"They both work and their kids are always at day care. Besides, you complain about those kids being brats. Mrs. Putnam is the logical place to start."

He was right, but I wouldn't admit it. I begrudgingly put on my jacket, grumbling the whole time.

"Don't forget your hat," he said.

I held out my hand. He tossed me the stocking cap and I shoved it angrily onto my head so that it almost covered my eyes.

As he opened the back storm door, the wind caught it, jerking it completely open and nearly pulling the door off its hinges. Now that autumn had officially arrived, it always seemed to be windy in Paradise. In the back yard, the twin maple trees' branches were swaying, and some yellow leaves ripped loose, tumbling across the grass into the Taylors' yard and beyond.

Daddy pushed the door closed and put his arm over my shoulders. "Winter's coming quickly." He clutched the cookies with his other arm and together we ran down the sidewalk and across the alley.

The white paint on Mrs. Putnam's house was fading and becoming streaked with dirt. Leaves swirled around her house and were piling up by her stone foundation.

We ran across her yard to her wooden backdoor steps. The bottom step looked rotten, so Daddy quickly hoisted me to the second step. He knocked on the door.

Shivering, I looked back at our house and our tiny garage and our two yellow maple trees. I'd never seen our yard from this side. It looked smaller, but it also looked warm and safe. It looked like home.

With a loud whooshing noise, the inside door opened.

"Why, Mr. Kiln and Angela," she said. She opened the outside storm door. She didn't have her glasses on.

Daddy held out the paper plate piled with cookies. "We were doing some baking and wanted to share some cookies with you."

She looked at the full plate and, for the briefest moment, appeared uncertain, as if not sure how to respond. The wind lifted strands of her blue-gray hair.

"Why," she stammered, blinking quickly, "thank you. Angela, did you help your father bake them?"

I looked down. I now felt guilty that I hadn't helped much. "Some," I mumbled.

"She helped mix the dough," Daddy said.

"Won't you come in?" She stepped aside, straightened her hair, and led us through her immaculately clean kitchen toward the dining room. Her kitchen, like ours, was painted a pale green. The countertop was linoleum, and it was cracked, but, unlike ours, it was spill-less and crumb-less and no dishes were piled in the sink.

Entering the dining room, she turned on the overhead brass chandelier. She brought us to an oval table and four chairs made of very dark mahogany. A matching antique hutch with glass doors stood along the wall.

"Would you like some coffee? Some hot chocolate, Angela?"

"Oh no," Daddy said. "We came to treat you." He glanced at her dark, quiet home with its subdued print wallpaper and the short nap carpet which looked hardly worn yet freshly vacuumed, and the shades pulled down, even in the middle of the day. "On second thought, if you really mean it, some hot chocolate would be very nice on a cold day."

Mrs. Putnam smiled and patted him on his arm as if he were a small boy. "Of course I mean it. As Angela knows, I never say anything I don't mean."

I nodded begrudgingly. Unfortunately, that was quite true.

Daddy sat down and I perched on the chair next to him. I felt strange being in my teacher's home. I looked up and pointed to a dark metal grate in the ceiling. I could see into the room above. "There's a hole in the ceiling," I whispered.

"That's for gravity heat."

"What's that?"

"Older homes, before there was forced air heat, used the principle that heat rises. The grates allowed the heat to get to the upper rooms. They called it gravity heat."

"Oh." The principle made sense. The term didn't. Gravity goes down.

Mrs. Putnam, her glasses now on, returned carrying a silver tray with three cups of steaming hot chocolate. She set the tray before us. One cup clinked against another. I realized we were using real china dishes.

She left and quickly returned with the cookies neatly arranged on a china plate.

"We brought those cookies for you," Daddy protested.

"What good are cookies if you can't share them?"

He grinned. "I'm afraid you've caught us there."

She sat across from Daddy. "Did you hear how the football team did last night?"

"They lost."

She shook her head, sympathetically. "Poor Leo Oldenburg hasn't had a good year, has he?"

"No, he hasn't."

While I helped myself to two cookies, Daddy and Mrs. Putnam talked about all sorts of things. I ate my cookies, content to be ignored. I glanced up at her open stairway and wondered how many rooms she had, what she had in them, and what she did with all the space.

"My husband died almost 20 years ago," Mrs. Putnam said. "He was such a handyman. I'm afraid I don't keep up the house as he would've liked."

"It's still hard, isn't it?" Daddy was always so good at sounding empathetic. He was, of course, completely sincere. And people like Mrs. Putnam liked him because he was genuine.

"The pain has dulled to an ache. I still miss him."

Daddy nodded.

"When did your wife die?"

"When Angela was two." Daddy stared at the cookie in his hand and his gray eyes simmered. "It was at Thanksgiving." He ate the cookie. "Thanksgiving. Ironic." His bitter tone surprised me.

He sipped his hot chocolate.

Mrs. Putnam abruptly sat up, her stooped shoulders immediately straight as a board, and smiled, clasping her hands together. "If you don't have other plans, would you like to come here for Thanksgiving?"

I flushed and swallowed hard, desperately looking at Daddy to get his attention. He must certainly know that the last thing I wanted on vacation was to spend time with my teacher!

"That would be very nice. Very nice indeed."

Mrs. Putnam then talked about her husband, about her house,

about her years teaching in Paradise, about her interest in retirement. I tried my best to be patient. I really did, but I fidgeted more than I listened. Finally, I could tell from the way that Daddy cleared his throat that he was getting ready to leave. I perked up.

"So, might you take early retirement?" Daddy asked as she cleared our plates.

We followed her to the kitchen.

"I don't know." She stared out her kitchen window, toward our house. A fresh gust of wind pulled more leaves from our trees. "Some days I'm ready to. I'm tired. I can't keep up with the little ones' energy any longer. And yet—" She paused, took off her glasses, and looked at me with her green eyes. Her voice grew softer. "I'm afraid of not being needed anymore. Of not having a reason for getting up in the morning." She hastily put her glasses back on.

Daddy nodded understandingly. "Thank you for the hot chocolate."

She looked back at Daddy and I thought I saw a tear behind her glasses. "Thank you, Jack. Please come again."

"We will," he said. "Thanksgiving, if not sooner."

Shortly after supper that evening, the phone rang. Daddy answered it while I began clearing the table.

As he listened, he grew agitated: pacing, breathing rapidly, twisting the phone cord.

Then he stopped. "I'll be right over." He hung up the phone. "That was Robert Oatley. I'm needed over there. Can you stay by yourself for a little bit?"

"No, I'll come along."

He was in too big of a hurry to argue. He just rushed for the door. He grabbed his jacket, tossed me mine, and ran for the car.

I caught up as he opened the car door for me. He got in and started the engine. "Don't forget to buckle up."

Daddy, who always came to a full stop at stop signs, glided through the intersections and we were there in less than one minute.

He ran up to the house, didn't knock, went right in.

As I followed, I heard shouting from the house.

I opened the front door and entered. Daddy was already in the kitchen. Mrs. Oatley was saying "Settle down."

I heard a man's voice, one I didn't recognize.

I peered around the doorway into the kitchen. A man stood by the table and he held a shotgun and he was waving it like a baton to emphasize his points. The stranger was Robert's height with shiny dark brown hair parted on the side. He hadn't shaved for a few days and his brown eyes were bloodshot and he wore a rumpled gray sports coat with food stains on the lapels.

Just in front of me, Daddy stood, assessing the situation. Mrs. Oatley sat at the table, her trembling hands in front of her as if praying. She was biting her lip.

Robert stood against the far wall, near the door to the basement. Tom was nowhere to be seen.

"I'm taking these things," the man shouted.

"Fine," Mrs. Oatley said. "Just take them and go."

The man's bloodshot eyes turned to Daddy. "Who're you?"

Daddy's voice was extra calm. "Robert's teacher. I just came over to see him about his train set."

The man blinked twice. "His what?"

"His train set. The one you gave him years ago. It's grown quite a bit."

"Oh yeah? Well, stay out of my way."

"Fine." Daddy stepped back. I stepped back too. Then Daddy asked, "Anything I can help you with?"

"Nothing. Just get out of here!" The man spat.

Daddy didn't move, but the man didn't notice. He was now yelling at Mrs. Oatley. "You had no right to take my guns."

"I didn't want guns in the house with the boys."

"They're my boys, aren't they?" he bellowed.

I began shaking and gripped Daddy's coat. In the far corner, Robert was white and shaking too, but he didn't have anyone to hold onto.

"I think it's best if you'd leave," she stated.

Mr. Oatley swore with words that I'd never heard before,

then he lifted the shotgun. Whether he meant to shoot or not, I don't know, but the gun went off as he pointed it at the basement door.

I shut my eyes and screamed and heard wood chips flying and smelled smoke.

I screamed a second time when I realized that Daddy's jacket was no longer in my grasp. I opened my eyes and Daddy had grabbed the barrel of the shotgun, forcing it to point at the ceiling.

Robert leaped forward and grabbed his father by the back of the neck and slammed his head onto the table.

Daddy tried to wrestle the shotgun away, but Mr. Oatley wouldn't let go of it. Robert slammed his father's face down again and blood splattered across the table.

Daddy finally pulled the gun loose and stepped back and emptied the other chamber of the shotgun.

Mrs. Oatley was sobbing at the table, her hands covering her mouth.

Robert slammed his father's face down again and again. And again.

Daddy set the gun down and grabbed Robert's shoulder. That was all that was needed. Robert stopped and stared down at his father's bloody face, then he turned to Daddy and hugged him tightly and sobbed uncontrollably.

I was still shaking and I ran to Daddy and hugged him from behind. With one hand Daddy reached behind and gently touched my head.

Tom came up from the basement where he had been hiding, saw the shattered door, the bloody table, his unconscious father, and didn't say anything.

Everyone except Tom cried for a long time.

Two deputies came, took statements, and hauled Mr. Oatley away. Except for a badly broken nose and bruised forehead, he was okay, I guess.

Later, as we sat in the Oatley living room, Daddy took the initiative and made us all some hot chocolate.

"When I called you, I never thought it would get that bad," Robert said. "I would have called the sheriff if I'd known."

"You've now seen the side of your father that I had to deal with," Mrs. Oatley said, "a side I had hoped that you would never know." She turned to Daddy. "I'm sorry you had to be involved in this, but I can't tell you how much I appreciate your coming. Jeff was decent enough when sober, but when he wasn't, well, that's why I had to divorce him—"

"You don't have to explain anything."

"Yes, I do. You've seen, and I want you to understand. He wouldn't get help, and when he did, he only went to counseling under a court order, and that didn't do any good. The boys were in danger. I was in danger. This evening he showed up after all these years, drunk and looking for some old guns of his. You can pretty much figure out the rest."

We could.

We didn't stay much longer.

As far as I know, Robert never talked to Daddy about the incident, and Robert's train set never ran again.

CHAPTER 12

*Some liberal freaks don't like guns and want to outlaw
them. The gun isn't the problem, people are. I say if you train
kids early to handle guns right, there won't be accidents. Execute
all murderers and we won't have any problems.*
                              —from an essay by Duane Johnson

During the week, the cheerleaders taped painted banners in
the hallways, bright banners that proclaimed imminent victory in
Friday night's game against Cherry Grove. I wondered why the
girls' volleyball team that was doing better than the football team
didn't get much publicity.

I asked Daddy about it. "For most people," he explained,
"football is a greater spectator sport."

"I liked the volleyball game you took me to. Football is boring."

"But people don't see much volleyball on television. They're
not used to it. Maybe by the year 2000, people will be ready for
change."

I shrugged. It didn't make sense to me. It seemed to me that
change, like the seasons, keeps coming. You could accept it or not,
but change will always be there. If you walk outside in January
wearing a sundress, that is your choice, but ignoring the change
will surely end up giving you a serious case of frostbite.

My dislike for football grew that week, or at least my animosity
toward some of the football players. Wednesday after school, six
football players, Duane Johnson among them, were leaning against
the lockers near Daddy's room, three on each side of the hall.
Other students had to walk between them on their way out of
school. I didn't understand what they were doing.

"A seven," one boy commented as a girl walked past them.

The other boys nodded and laughed derisively. Duane Johnson wrote something in a notebook and snickered.

Another girl went by and they did the same thing, this time saying a lower number.

Then I understood. I stopped, shocked. I wouldn't pass through a human sale barn where people were rated like prize cattle.

Three girls, arms linked and glaring furiously at the boys, walked past them.

"Five, six, four," Duane said.

Another boy shook his head, disagreeing. "Make that four, five, three."

One the girls looked back, glaring. "Jerks!" she yelled.

Duane laughed. "Give them each a two."

Jane Turpin walked down the hall toward them, saw the gantlet of boys, stopped. She planted her hands on her hips. "Why don't you guys grow up?"

Duane glanced at the boys beside him. "Hey," he smirked, "we're tryin'."

She glared at him and spun around, walking the long way to the other staircase.

"Hey," Duane shouted, "afraid?"

She didn't look back. "Not of you."

The boys laughed. "Oo-oo-oo-oo," they intoned.

"A five," Duane said.

Just then Chet Kelley walked out of Daddy's room and joined them. Scratching his curly, blond hair, he studied Jane's departing figure. "Make it a six."

"All right." Duane snickered lecherously, changing his notation. "You always were an easy grader."

Daddy came out of his room and quickly sized up the situation.

"Move along, *gentlemen*," he ordered. Unfortunately, they didn't grasp his sarcasm.

"It's okay," Duane laughed, quite cocky, "I think we've got most of them rated anyway."

"How would you like it if the girls rated you?" Daddy asked.

Duane shrugged, strutting over to Daddy, puffing up his chest like a rooster. "I got nothin' to fear." He shifted his broad shoulders back, glanced back at the others and grinned.

The other boys walked past me. I'm glad they didn't notice me. I felt vulnerable, exposed. And if I had been old enough, I would've joined Tina's Amazons right then and there.

Duane, though, was still talking to Daddy who said, "Maybe the girls would rate boys on their kindness."

"Hey, I was plenty kind to them. Want to see my ratings?"

Daddy gritted his teeth, finally losing his temper. "Take the hint, Duane. Get out of here."

Duane turned, smirking, and caught up with the other boys as they tramped down the hall.

I looked at Daddy and saw the turbulent anger in his gray eyes, anger I rarely saw. If lightning could've exploded from the fury in his eyes, those boys would've been fried instantly.

Then he saw me. As the darkness vanishes when the sun comes out after a storm, so his anger evaporated.

I ran to him, and he hugged me.

That Friday night it was too cold to go to the football game. Instead we drove to Owatonna for groceries, then had popcorn at home and watched a video of *Little Women*. I cried.

I heard later that the boys won the football game. I was hoping that they would lose.

A frost lay on the grass Saturday morning, but the sun quickly melted it. Our two maple trees had finally shed their leaves except for a few stubborn and shriveled brown ones that hung defiantly onto otherwise bare branches.

I knew that it would be a leaf-raking morning.

After breakfast, Daddy stared at the trees, disgusted. "Look at those branches that are crossing each other. Those should be pruned. You'd think nature would be more efficient."

I wasn't really looking forward to raking, but I tried to have a good attitude, so I said, "That's why we're needed."

Daddy glanced down at me, surprised, and didn't say anything.

Had I said something funny? He patted my shoulder and smiled. "Angel, sometimes you are so profound."

A short time later, Daddy and I, wearing warm jackets, hats and gloves, were raking leaves on the side of the house when a rusted, olive green pickup with a bad muffler rattled by. The pickup stopped in front of our house.

Out stepped Dirtball Gallagher, still in camouflaged hunting clothes. To my utter shock, he began shuffling our way.

At that moment, Daddy was kneeling and shoving a pile of leaves into a black plastic bag. He didn't see Dirtball coming.

I touched Daddy's shoulder. "Someone's here."

Hiding his surprise, Daddy stood and walked over to him. "Hello, Mr. Gallagher." Daddy shifted his rake and offered his right hand.

Dirtball, as much as one could tell under his long hair and beard, was frowning. "Morning, Mr. Kiln." He evidently didn't notice Daddy's outstretched hand.

A long pause.

Daddy pulled his hand back, wiped his hand on his leg. "What can I do for you?"

Dirtball tugged at his beard. "Mr. Kiln, you know the kids in school nowadays."

Daddy nodded slowly, cautiously.

"Someone vandalized my garage last night."

"That's too bad."

"They spray-painted obscene words on the walls. Black spray paint. Gloss."

"I'm sorry. How can I help?"

Dirtball kicked aimlessly at our leaves. "I'd like to get those kids."

Daddy leaned on his rake. "What would you do with them?"

"Make them clean it up. We gotta teach these kids responsibility."

Daddy cleared his throat. "We certainly do." He shifted his weight. "If I hear anything, I'll let the police know."

Agitated, Dirtball shook his head. "Sheriff don't do no good. Tell me instead. I'll talk to those kids' parents myself."

Daddy ran his hands along the rake handle. "I'll listen for any news."

Dirtball nodded, seeming satisfied. "Thanks." He turned to go, then stopped and came back. "And I'd leave you out of it." He then shuffled to his pickup, muttering, "Had a good English teacher once. Taught me responsibility."

When Dirtball was out of hearing range, Daddy turned to me, rolled his eyes. "He is one strange character."

"Will you really tell him if you hear anything?"

Daddy knelt by the leaves again. "I'd call the sheriff. There are right and wrong ways to handle things like this. As for Mr. Gallagher—" He watched the pickup disappear around the corner. "I don't know." He shoved the last of the leaves from that pile into the bag. "Let's see about pruning the maple trees."

In the late afternoon, Daddy put on his sweat clothes and headband and began warming up in the living room.

"May I ride my bike with you?"

He stretched his legs. "It's getting cold. Sun's setting earlier."

"It's probably the last time I'll be able to ride my bike before winter."

He turned over and started his sit-ups. "Okay," he said between breaths, "but wear your hat and gloves."

When we came to the depot, I didn't want to ride past Dirtball's weathered house. "I'll wait by the depot and meet you as you come back into town," I said.

I was experimenting with giving statements instead of asking questions. It seemed to be a more efficient method of getting my way.

"Fine," he said, already jogging along the old railroad bed toward Browner's Woods. The autumn wind rippled the remaining gold and red leaves, making them shimmer in the final glow of the setting sun.

I got off my bike, put the kickstand down, and left it by the side of the depot.

I walked around the old building, aimlessly kicking the dry grass. The depot cast its shadow across the corn field to the east. The dry tassels swayed in the breeze.

I ambled to the front door. I looked through the dirty window. Faint sunlight streamed through cracks in the back boarded-up windows. I touched the lock, began to rattle it.

My heart skipped a beat.

The lock didn't rattle. It swung loose on the latch eye.

Not only was the padlock open, the latch was flipped back.

I lightly pushed the door. After a slight hesitation, it squeaked open about a foot. I knew that Daddy would like to see this. He hadn't yet reached Browner's Woods, but his back was to me. I waved, then jumped, but he didn't see me.

I pushed again and the door swung the rest of the way open.

Enough light streamed in for me to see the cracked plaster walls. I looked and felt for a light switch. I found one to my right, but it didn't work.

Inside was the old ticket counter. The slate arrival and departure board next to it had been erased but looked to be in perfect condition.

As my eyes adjusted to the dim light, I walked in farther. Pew-like seats were piled in the far-left corner. I looked behind me. Some graffiti, mostly graduation dates, had been painted on the inside of the front wall.

My feet were cold and my hands trembled. This must be a meeting spot for high school students over the years, I thought. A secret place. Forbidden ground.

I walked over to the counter. Behind it were many small wooden boxes on the wall. I imagined the women in their long dresses and the men in their high collar shirts coming here and buying tickets, maybe a ticket to St. Paul, and waiting for the train on a bench outside, finally hearing the whistle in the distance.

For the first time, I appreciated Daddy's interest in trains.

I walked past the ticket booth, toward the west side, toward the boarded up windows.

I stopped. My feet hit something soft.

I felt dizzy, panicky, as if I were suddenly plunged into a crazy and terrifying nightmare, trying desperately to wake up but couldn't.

I screamed, short, loud.

A body lay at my feet. It was a young man, or a tall boy. He lay on his stomach, a pistol in his right hand.

Dark blood was pooled beside his curly, blond head.

I shook, screamed again. Turning, I dashed out the door, screaming as loudly as I could for Daddy, hoping that I'd wake up.

CHAPTER 13

I remember being scared by all the desks in first grade.
I remember playing baseball with Duane.
I hit a triple and he struck out.
I remember giving a speech in fifth grade and
everyone laughed at me because my zipper was down.

—from a poem by Chet Kelley

Thankfully, Daddy heard me and sprinted like a lightning bolt back to me. He quickly checked the depot and saw what I had seen. I was shaking all over and didn't go back in. He took me home, then called the sheriff's department.

I was trembling for a long time.

I learned the facts later. The dead person was Chet Kelley. Daddy found a suicide note, written on a half-sheet of notebook paper, lying by his feet. His parents confirmed that the note's handwriting was Chet's. The sheriff's department determined that the pistol belonged to Duane Johnson's father. Evidently, it had been taken from the Johnson home on Friday evening, during a party that Duane had hosted. His parents weren't home during the party and didn't realize that the pistol was missing.

Based on the graffiti on the walls, the sheriff's department surmised that the depot had sometimes been a hangout for high school kids. They also assumed that some students had keys to the depot's padlock. In a small town, one key quickly multiplies. They further surmised that someone else had left the depot open, for no key was found on Chet.

Before I learned all these details, however, I was interviewed several times that night at my house as I sat on our living room sofa. First one deputy, a tall man named John Garrison, talked to me, then another came and asked more questions, and then Deputy Garrison came back and asked even more detailed questions.

Daddy brought me hot chocolate and some cookies on a tray. He didn't usually permit eating on the sofa unless I was sick. He was worried about me, but I felt fine: the initial shock had passed, and I wasn't about to turn down cookies and hot chocolate.

I was up until midnight.

Daddy took his time tucking me in. After devotions, he asked if I wanted to talk about anything.

"No," I said, yawning deeply. "I just want to sleep." I turned onto my tummy.

"I'm sorry that you had to be the one who found him," he said softly, rubbing my back.

I mumbled something before falling asleep.

We didn't go to church the next morning because Daddy let me sleep in. I had just gotten out of bed when someone rang our doorbell. I looked out my window and saw Miss O'Neil's red car. As Daddy let her in, I dashed to the bathroom, threw on my bathrobe, brushed my hair, and stuck in a hair bow to hold the longer sides back. Miss O'Neil and Daddy were sitting on the sofa when I came downstairs.

She smiled as I rushed in and hopped up on Daddy's lap. "I stopped by to see how you're feeling," she said.

"Thanks." I smiled back. "I feel okay." Then I realized how tired I felt and yawned.

"She held up great yesterday," Daddy said. "I was proud of her. Linda, can you stay for lunch? It won't be much, I'm afraid, but we'd like to have you stay."

She refused at first, but Daddy and I insisted until she relented. "Only if you let me help in the kitchen."

Daddy smiled. "Those are harsh conditions."

She stayed until mid-afternoon.

A short time after she left, Mrs. Putnam knocked on our back door. She was very kind, almost grandmotherly. She even hugged me. Was I surprised!

As she left, she turned to Daddy and, in the commanding voice I'd heard her use in school, barked: "Now, Jack, you take good care of her."

"Of course, Mrs. Putnam!" He saluted and winked.

Later, Mr. Manitou drove over from Hillcrest to visit us and brought us some blueberry muffins that his wife had baked.

"Why did they come over?" I asked Daddy when we were finally alone again.

"To see how you were." We waved out the window to Mr. Manitou as he drove away.

"But Chet is the one who died."

Looking exhausted, Daddy sat on the sofa. "Well, it can be hard on the person discovering the, uh, incident."

Feeling equally exhausted, I plopped on the sofa beside him. He put his arm around me.

"Are you sure you're okay?" he asked.

"Yes," I said, leaning against his chest. "Why did Chet kill himself?"

Daddy frowned and his gray eyes smoldered behind his glasses. For a moment, I thought he was angry. "I don't know. Life is hard sometimes. And often it looks even harder than it is."

"You told Miss O'Neil that you read his note. What did it say?"

Daddy stared off toward the piano. "It said that he'd had enough of life and couldn't measure up."

"Is that all?"

"He didn't want his mother to think badly of him, and he said he loved her."

"Did he say anything about his dad?"

"Nothing."

I studied Daddy's face. He was still staring at the piano, but his mind was focused on something else, somewhere else, and someone else.

I realized then that he was the one having a hard time with the suicide, not me.

I hugged him tightly. He sighed briefly, and hugged me back.

On Monday, everyone at school was subdued and somber. Before school began, older students clustered together and spoke in hushed voices.

Even the elementary students acted oddly. Other kids hung around me, but they didn't seem to want to talk to me or to anyone else. It was as if everyone just wanted to move through the building in groups, as if the presence of other bodies could push disturbing thoughts away.

We had a guest speaker come into our classroom, a psychologist named Mrs. Hill who talked to us about suicide. With her gray hair and bifocals, Mrs. Hill looked as old as Mrs. Putnam, but she dressed more stylishly, wearing a navy blue woman's suit. She smiled whenever she wasn't talking about suicide, and she talked to us as if she had been our friend for years.

I think if anyone had wanted to hire a professional grandmother, Mrs. Hill would be first on the list. As for me, I didn't want a professional grandmother; I wanted a real mother who would be there all the time.

I didn't listen much.

During art time, Mrs. Putnam called me up to her desk and told me to report to the grade school office to meet with Mrs. Hill.

"Do I have to?"

Mrs. Putnam peered over her glasses and lowered her voice. She dropped her stern classroom demeanor and looked as though she wanted to give me a hug. Her voice cracked just a bit: "I'm sure it would be best."

I shrugged and left.

Mrs. Thomas, our cranky elementary secretary, looked unusually sympathetic as she directed me into Mr. Allen's office. Calling it Mr. Allen's office was really only a formality. Mr. Allen filled the title of principal but taught sixth grade. Daddy said that Mr. Allen was a very good teacher, but he didn't do anything as a principal other than lead an occasional grade school faculty meeting or meet with a parent on a discipline issue. Mrs. Thomas did everything else.

Maybe that's why she was so crabby.

I entered Mr. Allen's office. He wasn't there: Mrs. Hill perched on the edge of his desk.

"Please sit down," she said. She had me tell her about what had happened (as if I hadn't told the story enough times already), and she wanted to know if I had any fears or questions.

"No."

"Nothing at all?"

I was wondering about something, though, that I hadn't asked Daddy last night.

"Did Chet know Jesus?"

Mrs. Hill's pleasant smile froze. "What?"

"Did Chet know Jesus?"

She blinked rapidly a few times. "Why do you ask that?"

"If he knew Jesus, why did he kill himself?" I shifted in my chair. "If he didn't know Jesus, I wish someone would've told him."

She grew animated, her direction evidently now clear.

"If you could've talked to him, what would you have told him?"

"That he needed to know Jesus. That because of Jesus' death on the cross, God would forgive him. That he could know that he was going to go to heaven."

Mrs. Hill nodded. "Are you worried about Chet?"

I crossed my arms, puzzled. I hadn't thought about that before. "I don't think so. It's like when my Daddy's correcting papers—I can't do anything about it." It was hard to put what I felt into words: "I don't know if I should be sad or not because I don't know if he knew Jesus."

"You need to focus on all the positive things you know about Chet, all the positive things you know about yourself." She told me a variety of encouraging things that I should think about, good things about myself, good things about others. Everything she said sounded nice but seemed empty, like an attractively wrapped present with nothing inside. By the time she was finished, I was sorry I had ever asked her the question.

Focusing on good things didn't change anything, anymore than doing good things earned a person a place in heaven. Everyone who had ever been in Sunday school knew that.

During supper that night, Daddy told me that Mrs. Hill had held an assembly in the gym for the entire high school. "She handled the big group pretty well."

"Daddy, do Christians ever kill themselves?"

He cleared his throat and seemed to choose his words carefully. "Some people, even Christians, may become so depressed that their minds become sick. Their sickness grows until they want to kill themselves. An illness in the mind can happen to a Christian, just like a physical illness. We're not immune to pain in this world."

"Was that what happened to Chet?"

"Maybe. But I think you're really wondering if Chet was a Christian. Remember, Angel, that only God can know a person's heart. Chet evidently attended a church, but from what I saw in Chet's behavior, I don't think that he had accepted Jesus."

"Why didn't someone tell him?"

Daddy put down his spoon, leaning on his elbows thoughtfully. "I've been asking myself that too. I fool myself into thinking that with young people, there's always time." He folded his arms. "But time ran out."

We stopped eating and prayed for Chet's family and for a greater ability to see those who are hurting.

Daddy didn't have all the answers, but he admitted it. I liked his honesty better than Mrs. Hill's solutions. He didn't tell me what I should think about.

During Tuesday's morning recess, while I perched on top of the tire house, I looked across the playground and saw a white van stop. As a man stepped from the driver's side, a well-dressed, petite woman in tennis shoes stepped out from the passenger's side and pointed in our direction. He pulled a large camera and tripod from the back of the van. They walked briskly toward the playground.

Suddenly, Mr. Cranberry sprinted from the building and intercepted them before they got to us. Wildly waving his arms and shouting at them, he chased them back to the van. The woman and man moved down the street and set up the camera. The woman held a microphone and soon was talking into it. Frustrated, Mr. Cranberry watched them from a distance and kicked the ground, disgusted.

After recess, I told Mrs. Putnam about it.

She shook her head sadly and glanced out the window. "They should let Chet rest in peace and let his family mourn with dignity."

School was closed at noon so students and teachers could attend the funeral.

As we drove the few blocks to Chet's church, I told Daddy about the reporter and cameraman. "Will they show the school on TV?"

"Maybe." The church parking lot was filled. Cars lined the streets. We had to park several blocks from the church, and we were actually closer to our house than to the church.

"Why are the reporters so interested?" I asked.

Daddy began parallel parking, something he had never had to do in Paradise before. "Teenage deaths are always news. Besides, they probably got word that the sheriff's department interviewed some students. They're trying to find the key to the depot."

"Why?"

"Either the place had been left open or someone else had been with him. So far, no student admits being there that night." He finished maneuvering the car into place and turned it off.

Stepping out of the car, I straightened my dress. "Do you think someone else was with him?"

Daddy came around the car and took my hand. "I don't think it matters. Chet's dead. All I know is, Paradise is closing ranks to the outsiders."

"Who's an outsider?"

"Anyone not born here."

"Even us?"

"Yes."

We walked to the church. The wind was cold. For once, Daddy didn't insist that I wear a hat. It was also cold when my mother died. I don't remember much else about my mother's funeral, just the flowers and her lying in the coffin. I wish I remembered more of her.

Chet's church was smaller and newer than others we had visited in the area. A few steps led up to glass entry doors. Much of the church's exterior was covered with small rocks and the wood that did show was painted brown. A copper-plated peak led up to a metal cross.

Entering the small church, Daddy took my hand. The church had a large foyer where people waited quietly in line. Daddy's hand felt warm. I felt cold.

The line gradually moved forward and we entered and walked down the aisle toward the coffin. I was afraid to see Chet's body. I only recalled a few dark images of what I'd seen in the depot.

The casket was dark brown. I stared at the shiny brass handles.

Daddy noticed my nervousness and whispered, "The casket is closed."

I looked up, relieved. They had a large picture of Chet on the lid. He was wearing a suit and smiling.

There wasn't much to say about the funeral: it was short. I didn't think the minister said anything particularly encouraging or enlightening or even significant.

Lots of high school kids were crying in the church, and, afterwards, groups clustered together outside, crying on each other's shoulders. I wondered briefly if some of the grief didn't seem overly dramatic. When he was alive, Chet hadn't seemed that popular.

As Daddy and I came out the church's front glass door, a television camera's large lens was pointing right at us from the center of the street. The cameraman then spun the camera, quickly panning to the side of the church, to the large cluster of girls sobbing uncontrollably against the rock-covered wall.

I wanted to watch, but Daddy grabbed my hand and walked rapidly to our car.

Before we crossed the street, a woman's voice called after us. "Mr. Kiln?"

Daddy pulled me briskly the rest of the way to our car. I glanced back, nearly stumbling.

Chasing us was the well-dressed, petite woman I'd seen near the playground. She carried a large bag over her shoulder and still wore tennis shoes.

Daddy helped me into the car, then ran around, got in, and quickly shut his door.

Catching up to us, she rapped on the window.

Daddy sighed and rolled it down.

"Mr. Kiln, you discovered the body. What do you know about the sheriff's investigation?"

"Nothing."

"How are the students taking this?"

"As well as can be expected."

"How about you? Is this your daughter? Is it true that she was with you at the time?"

"Yes, but—" The cameraman, now carrying his tripod, was running toward us down the middle of the street.

Daddy started the car.

"Was there any sign that someone had been with Chet?"

The cameraman set his tripod down in the center of the street and began taping us.

"It's a tragedy for the community, a tragedy of our society," Daddy stated quickly. He began to roll up the window, but her elbow rested on the glass.

"What do you mean?"

"Any man's death diminishes me," Daddy stated. He violently spun the wheel and drove ahead. She jumped back. The cameraman, startled, jerked his tripod and camera clear of our path.

"Why don't you want to be on TV?" I asked, looking back at the astonished cameraman.

Daddy drove the long way home, around town. "They're not

really interested in people. They want a sensational scoop or a maudlin story to advance their careers while we are supposed to provide interesting little shots to fill up their touching narrative. I won't play along with their games."

That evening, I saw myself twice on TV. First, when the reporter's voice was heard introducing the news story, I was shown on the playground at recess along with all the other kids. Next, the reporter, as she described the suicide, explained that we had discovered the body. That's when they showed a picture of Daddy and me in our car. They cut out Daddy's talking.

It was exciting to see myself on television and I wondered if the other kids had seen the report. I couldn't believe it: we were famous, but Daddy didn't care. He glanced at the TV only once.

The reporter said that Chet's blood showed a high concentration of alcohol. That was the first time I'd heard that information. It was also the last.

When the news was over, Daddy turned off the television. He was not in a good mood.

I stood and faced him. "Don't you ever want to do something great? Really great? And be famous? Like Lindbergh flying across the Atlantic or being a movie star?"

Daddy chuckled, his cloudy mood quickly breaking up. "Those are contrasting examples, Angel. Lindbergh actually accomplished something, and he spent much of his life trying to influence America. I suspect that many movie stars are driven to make money. The personalities we see are only images—and very superficial ones at that—which are produced by a company, itself interested in making money."

I groaned. Daddy could get hung up on some little detail to avoid a difficult discussion. "Daddy, you know what I mean. Don't you want people to know that you did something great? Look at your teaching. Don't you want people to know what a great teacher you are?"

He put his arm around me and pulled me up beside him on the sofa. As he did so, I remembered when he used to be able to lift me easily onto his lap. I missed that.

"I'm glad that you think I'm a good teacher, but one achieves greatness in teaching, not because others know it, but because you know, in the core of your being, that you face ignorance or prejudice or mediocrity, day after day, and you persevere. You check your life at the door and attack presuppositions and self-satisfaction, day after day, year after year; and, after it's all over, a few pearls that you scattered glisten in the dark night. You'll know that you did the right thing. No one else will know it, not even the pearls.

"And you know what, Angel? I think that's true for most of the really important tasks in life. To your mother, the most important thing she could do for you was to quit her job and do her best to raise you."

"I wish I could remember her."

"You do, in ways you don't even know. Sometimes it's in the way you think about people, it's in your confidence, it's in your ability to stand alone."

He grew quite somber. "Come here," he said. I didn't think he could do it anymore, but he hoisted me onto his lap. I leaned against him and could hear his heart as he put his arms around me. "Listen, Angel. A child's going to grow, no matter what. A parent can, at the most, only direct that growth, just as I pruned that tree in the back yard. And if a parent wants to direct that growth, then that parent must be there as much as he or she can, to catch the moments that need encouraging, and the ones that need pruning. Your mother felt that you were the most important thing in the world. No one will ever know that but you and me. And she believed that shaping one decent human being out of a baby that wants to grow wild is the greatest thing that anyone can ever do."

He rested his chin against my head. "And she succeeded," he whispered. "If she doesn't know it now, she will someday."

He hugged me tighter. I hugged him back. It was one of the few times I saw my Daddy cry.

CHAPTER 14

Dear Becky,

I haven't heard from you since Halloween. I went trick-or-treating with Chelsea Turpin. She bugs me sometimes, but she just needs a friend.

How is fourth grade? Did you like the last card I sent you? What do you want for your birthday?

As you can see, I'm still full of questions. Daddy says I never stop talking. Mrs. Putnam says I read well but I don't write enough. She told Daddy that I need to write more, so he bought me a bright pink notebook and said I should write my ideas down every day. I've been trying to do that. I've also written some stories. As you can see, my letters are getting longer.

We had some really weird things happen in Paradise. Maybe you saw it on the news. I don't like to think about some of it. I've been having nightmares lately about bad things happening to Daddy. He talks to me about them and has told me to give the dreams a happy ending. So I imagine the bad dream again and fix the ending. That helps a little.

I hope to hear from you soon. Please write.

Love, Angela

A few days later, as my fourth grade class left for recess, I asked Mrs. Putnam if I could stay in the room.

Looking concerned, she peered over her glasses. "Anything wrong?"

"I just don't feel like going outside."

"Fresh air is good for you."

"I'd like to be quiet for a little bit."

Her green eyes narrowing, she scrutinized me as intently as a cat studies its prey. She always insisted that all students go outside, regardless of their wishes, but this time she visibly softened.

"Very well. Just this once. But I won't be here. Please stay in the room."

I nodded. Soon I was alone in the room, appreciating the solitude after the emotionalism of the last few days. Since Chet's death, the other kids clustered around me at the beginning of each recess, prodding me for details of what I'd seen. They always shuffled away disappointed because what happened at the depot happened so quickly that I couldn't recall anything significant. What could I say? I saw. I screamed. I ran.

I moved to a back corner of the room and started reading *The Hobbit*.

I hadn't gone beyond the third page when in walked Tom Oatley carrying a small backpack. He didn't see me.

Methodically sliding a student desk next to the windows, he set the wastebasket beside the desk, then sat and pulled a wood block and jackknife from his back pack. Bending over the wastebasket, he began whittling.

I watched him, fascinated.

After every slice of wood, he held the block up to the window, turned the block around, then cut again.

Every muscle and fiber in his body was completely absorbed in his task.

I didn't say anything or make a noise, afraid that I'd destroy his concentration.

After fifteen minutes, I heard a tiny beeping noise. He looked at his digital watch, sat up straight, stretched, and stopped the alarm. Everything he did looked like a routine, almost like a sacred ritual.

He stood, put the wastebasket back, turned, then spotted me and jumped, quite startled.

His pale complexion blushed deep scarlet. "You—when did you come in?"

"I've been here the whole time. I didn't want to disturb you." I rose, held up my book. "I was reading."

He hastily shoved his knife and wood block into his backpack. "I . . . I come here during study hall." He sheepishly looked down. "Actually, I'm signed out to the library."

Though he wasn't doing anything wrong, we both knew that he could get into trouble for going to the wrong place.

"This is the only quiet spot that I know in school," he said. "During morning recess, Mrs. Putnam always goes to the lounge for coffee. She's as predictable as an old cat."

"What are you carving?"

He shrugged, embarrassed, and hoisted the backpack over his bony shoulder. "Nothing particular." His pale blue eyes glanced all over the room, anywhere but at me.

"I saw some of your work when my dad and I visited your home, the, uh, first time. The wood carvings were really good."

His face broke into a broad smile, displaying large white teeth, yet he still avoided looking at me. "Really?"

"Does Mrs. Putnam know you come here?"

"I've never asked, but she must see the shavings in her basket. It must be all right with her."

"You're right. She doesn't miss anything."

"No, not her." He headed to the door, then glanced back. He grinned and finally looked at me. "See y'later."

After school, I went up to Daddy's room as usual. He was sitting at his desk, talking to a visitor: a short man with dark hair, glasses, and a wide, square face.

"Angela, do you remember Andrew Johanson?"

He smiled. "Hi, Angela."

I smiled back, greeted him, and quietly sat in a corner desk and pulled out my work. They were discussing the suicide's effect on the students. However, the more they talked, the more their conversation turned to the town itself.

"Paradise prides itself as being a respectable community," Mr. Johanson remarked, "yet it's full of narrow-minded hypocrites. Paradise has walls around it: cultural and spiritual. Residents think that Paradise can go on and never change and the world will adapt to them."

Daddy leaned back in his chair. "I don't think that Paradise is any different than any other small town."

"No one here is interested in anything beyond the town borders. How many have been to a theater, or an art museum, or read any poetry since high school?"

"A few I've met."

"Ah, but they're imports, right? Like Linda O'Neil?"

"True, but I'd still guess that the percentage of people here who attend cultural events isn't that much different from the Cities. There the numbers are large because the base is large." Daddy leaned forward, planting his elbows on his desk. "Your complaints aren't about this town but about human nature. In the Cities, among all the frenetic movement, individuals hide within anonymous, crowded neighborhoods or drift to the bland, neatly spaced suburbs. Here, we can't hide. Everyone knows everyone else, so all the defects show."

Mr. Johanson closed his notebook and didn't look convinced. "Well, time will tell."

"Yes, as in all things."

Mr. Johanson walked to the door, then turned. "Thanks for taking the time. It's not often that I can engage in an intellectual discussion."

"I always like to talk."

"Don't we all," he said as he walked out the door.

Daddy went back to correcting papers and I finished my homework, then I read two chapters in *The Hobbit*. I was pulled from the book when I heard Daddy gathering his papers on his desk. "Hurry up, Angel. Let's go out to eat, I'm hungry."

I jumped up, shoving my books into my backpack. Eating out meant a hamburger and french fries with no dishes and no leftovers.

At the café, we sat in a booth near the back, as far away as possible from the center table where the most talkative people gathered. That table was the gossip hub of Paradise. If anyone believes that women gossip more than men, visit a small town café at 10:30 in the morning: men will cluster for coffee, donuts and gossip.

"Mr. Johanson sure likes to talk," I said.

"He's been coming to school during my prep time, looking for school news. I'm afraid this year he's gotten more than he wants."

"You like to talk to him."

"He's honest."

"But you don't agree with him."

"I do on many things. He's just very cynical."

"Why?"

"I don't know for sure. He doesn't seem very happy. And he certainly can't accept a compliment. When I commented that he was a good writer, he shrugged it off, almost acting as if I'd insulted him." Daddy saw our waiter coming. "Ready to order? Your usual?"

I looked up at our waiter, surprised to see that it was Robert Oatley. His hair was still wet from his shower after football practice. He took our order, then paused before leaving, as if he had something to say.

Daddy noticed too. "Working hard to save money for college?"

Robert stared at his pad, pursed his lips. "Actually, I'm getting money so I can paint the house for mom next year."

Daddy nodded. Robert said nothing more and went to the kitchen.

After we finished eating, Robert set the bill on our table. Again, he lingered a moment.

Daddy picked up the bill. "How are you, Robert?"

He hesitated. "Fine." He took a deep breath, then asked quickly: "How are you coming on your railroad layout?"

"Ever since—well, I haven't worked on it lately, but this week I hope to unpack the last of my buildings."

Robert nodded thoughtfully, as if he had more to say, but went back to the kitchen.

In school the next day, students and teachers returned to normal behaviors and regular schedules. Mrs. Hill was gone, her task in Paradise evidently accomplished, whatever that was. Mrs. Putnam was assigning homework again. I even saw Duane and some of the other boys huddled around a notebook. I assumed they were rating girls again.

My impression of Duane dropped even lower after an incident I witnessed Wednesday. After school, I went to Daddy's room as usual. As I walked to his open door, I heard Daddy discussing an English assignment with Shelley. He was trying to explain where to begin paragraphs. I was surprised to hear them talking about that—everyone knew where to start paragraphs, or so I thought.

At that point in my life I still lived under the delusion that because I knew something, everyone else did, and because I reacted to something a certain way, everyone else would, and because I believed a certain way, everyone else should. And if they didn't, then something was wrong with them.

Daddy was almost done explaining to Shelley what a topic sentence was, so I waited in the hall, set my backpack down, and leaned against the nearest locker.

Duane came sauntering out of Mr. Manitou's classroom with a supercilious smirk on his face. He walked to his locker a short distance beyond me.

Just then, Shelley came out. She started to walk in Duane's direction, then saw him and did a complete about face. Too late. He spotted her.

"Hey, Loony!"

She stopped dead in her tracks as if she had been shot, and she hugged her books to herself.

"Don't call me that." Tears brimmed her eyes.

He chuckled. "Okay, sorry. Say, Shell, there's a party at Morrisons' after the game on Friday."

Her chin quivered. "I have nothing to say to you."

Looking irritated, he threw his shoulders back and sauntered over to her. "What's the problem? I thought after our last date—"

She cut him off, her voice as cold and bitter as a January blizzard: "Aren't you late for practice?"

He stood behind her now and reached out to touch her shoulders. "Hey, coach bends the rules for me."

"Good for him." She started to walk away.

He grabbed her arm. "Hey, I wasn't going to ask you to go out with me. I was thinking that some of the guys from Oak Center would want to meet you."

She burst out crying and ran down the hall.

He watched her for less than a second. "Broads," he laughed.

The only reminder we had of Chet that week was during the all-school pep assembly on Friday. Everyone was called to the gym for the rally, and we sat on the bleachers according to grades. First Duane, the team captain, and Robert, the leading rusher, got pies in the face. Cheerleaders then led us in the school song. The elementary grades stood and sang loudly. The high school just stood.

Then Coach Oldenburg grabbed the microphone. He spoke one word, sending the speaker system squealing. I was beginning to think he liked the effect, for the squeal certainly demanded everyone's immediate attention. Moving the microphone farther away, he proceeded to pontificate in his deep bass voice about Paradise pride and the boys' dedication and what a courageous group of young men he had.

I recalled the gantlet of boys in the hallway, and to me the coach's words rang hollow, reminding me of Mrs. Hill's talks that sounded so good on the surface but were so empty underneath.

Mr. Oldenburg admitted that the play-offs were no longer a possibility. Daddy had been right about their chances. "But," Coach Oldenburg said as he launched into his new theme, "we want to remember Chet as we go into this game." He blinked rapidly and flushed. "We've cried over him, reminisced about him, fondly remembered him. As we go into tonight's game, let's win this season's final football game for Chet."

Almost everyone cheered.

It was a cold evening, but Daddy and I went to the game. The game was boring, yet I enjoyed sitting on the bleachers, wrapped in a plaid, wool stadium blanket and sipping hot chocolate from a silver thermos and watching all the bundled-up people.

At half time, Daddy commented that it was a slow game. I had known that after the first few minutes. I watched the cheerleaders a lot.

The boys lost.

Saturday afternoon Daddy went to school to get some papers he had forgotten. As long as he was going, he asked if I'd go along to file some other papers. I reluctantly agreed, but I was soon glad that I had, for in the parking lot was Miss O'Neil's red sports car. Daddy parked beside it.

As we walked down the hall, we heard Miss O'Neil playing the piano in the music room.

Knowing that they wouldn't talk adult-to-adult with me around, I cleverly asked if I could play outside on the playground.

Daddy grinned at me. "You didn't really want to file papers today, did you?"

"No."

"Go ahead, Angel. I won't be long. Keep your hat on."

A stiff wind was blowing across the playground and small flurries of snowflakes whipped across the grass. I grabbed a swing that was swaying in the wind and I hopped on. The chains squeaked and the seat was cold. I jumped off and ran to the tire house.

As I crawled into the dark center hole, I stopped and gasped. Someone was sitting hunched in the center of the four inner tire walls.

In the semi-darkness, the figure looked up at me and our surprised gazes met.

Shelley Loone's eyes glistened with tears. She sniffed.

"What's wrong?" I asked, squatting with my head against a tire rim. It was crowded with her in there. She didn't seem to mind.

"Nothing."

I didn't say anything.

She sniffed again and wiped her eyes with the back of her hand. "I suppose you think it's funny, me being here."

"Not really."

"I'm too old to play in here."

"Daddy once crawled in here."

She laughed briefly. "He did?"

I laughed too, remembering how he could barely get out. "He didn't stay long."

She didn't reply and I didn't know what to say.

Feeling awkward as well as cramped where I was, I started to leave, then stopped as she spoke again.

"I feel safe here."

"What's wrong?"

She wiped her eyes again. "Nothing is the same anymore."

I didn't know what to say, but I knew that she should talk to someone who could help her. "My dad's here. You could talk to him."

She shook her head. "I've talked all I want. I need to be quiet. When I was little, this was my favorite part of the playground. Here it was safe and secure. It's not changed since I was little." Her gaze wandered over the surrounding tires. "This tire house is still the same, but I'm not." She looked back at me. "Nothing is safe anymore."

Leaning forward, she rested her head on her knees and rocked slightly.

She said nothing more.

I crawled out and stood amid the swirling snowflakes.

I heard her sniffle again.

Daddy called and I ran to our car.

I told him about Shelley and he shook his head, perplexed, saddened, and, like me, unable to do a thing.

CHAPTER 15

Happiness is being chosen homecoming queen.
Happiness is a good marriage.
Happiness is a teddy bear.
Happiness is being with your friends.

—a poem by Shelley Loone

The next week dragged on and the Saturday I'd been looking forward to for a long time finally came. Daddy drove us to St. Paul, back to our old neighborhood for Becky's birthday party. I wore a new navy blue dress with white polka dots that Daddy had bought me in Rochester.

As I saw the stream of cars congested along the freeway, the tawdry billboards blocking the horizon, and, as we drove nearer, the compact houses built snuggly together with tiny matching yards, I felt grateful that I lived in a small town. The realization surprised me. Yes, I missed the museums and plays Daddy had taken me to, but I also liked the open and quiet surroundings, the walks to the playground, and the sense of freedom and safety.

But I did miss Becky.

As Daddy drove past our old home, he slowed the car to a crawl. The new owners had painted our white one-and-a-half-story house a light blue.

I was shocked. "It should be white."

"Our house changed with us. We went to the country, and our house went country blue."

I craned my head back as Daddy drove by.

"It looks smaller," I said.

Daddy drove up the block and turned toward Becky's. Several cars were parked in front of her house.

"I hope we're not late."

"No," Daddy reassured. "Right on time." He parked across the street from her house, a beige, stucco rambler. Her house, too, seemed to have shrunk.

Becky's dad, a Minnesota Twins baseball cap hiding his bald head, was in their narrow front yard, dragging a full leaf bag toward the back. A few brown leaves blew past his ankles and into another's yard.

He saw us, waved. "Party's inside!"

He shook hands with Daddy and they greeted each other like old buddies, even though they weren't. I always thought Becky's father was too friendly; that's not bad, of course, but his boisterous friendliness seemed almost aggressive. He sold insurance.

"So, d'ya miss St. Paul? Are you coming back to stay?"

"I don't know where we'll be heading after this school year, but we are getting to like small town life," Daddy said.

Becky's dad looked around proudly at his small front yard. "Ah, once you know city life, you can't go back to the sticks."

I left them to their conversation and went to the front door.

Becky's mother, still slender and artificially blonde, greeted me warmly at the door and helped me take my coat off, then she ushered me downstairs to their long basement.

Balloons and crepe paper hung from the ceiling. A big "Happy Birthday" banner was strung across the wall. Several decorated card tables, one piled high with presents, were set up. I placed my gift with the others.

Nine girls were clustered around a punch table. They all wore new fall dresses, and they all looked as if they had just stepped out of a catalogue. Becky always chose her friends carefully.

Just then Becky looked past Jenny Johnson and spied me. "Angela!" she cried, running to me. Her blonde hair curled beautifully along her shoulders.

We hugged and it seemed as if I'd never left.

"Oh," she squealed, "turn around. Look, mom, Angela's got long hair."

She flattered me, for it would take some time before it could be called long. Daddy continually needed to cut off the split ends, defeating some of my hair's progress.

The special moment of closeness between Becky and me quickly passed, however. Becky went to talk to others, and I realized that Becky and Jenny were the only other girls there that I knew.

"I wish you still lived here," Becky said to me later while we played pin the tail on the donkey. "I love fourth grade! I've made lots of new friends and we play together all the time."

It was my turn to be blindfolded. I was spun one way, then another. After stumbling in the wrong direction twice, I finally stuck the pin in the paper. Removing the blindfold, I saw the tail resting in the pony's eye.

"Ouch," I said.

Everyone laughed. I did too.

We had lots of fun but, in the quiet moments when I wasn't talking to anyone, I felt a little bit like crying. I wasn't Becky's special friend any more. And, somehow, she wasn't mine either. In a strange way, that change was okay with me, but knowing that the change was okay made me sad, and I couldn't understand it.

The late afternoon autumn shadows grew longer as Daddy helped me on with my coat. At the front door, I urged Becky to write to me.

"I'll try," she smiled, shrugging blithely. "But it's hard to find the time."

"I know," I said, lying.

As we drove down the car-lined, residential street, Daddy noticed my somber mood. "What's wrong?"

"Everything's changed."

He stopped at the traffic light. "I know. Sometimes we'd like to stop life, to hold it so tight that not a moment can escape us. Every day I see how fast you're growing. Your mother once said that she wished she could wrap you up and not let you grow, to keep you just the same."

A few minutes later he turned onto the freeway, heading south, heading back to Paradise. The sun was already setting behind violet-tinted thunderheads.

I looked out the window at the unending stream of cars and houses.

"Do you still miss Mommy?"

"All the time."

"I wish she were here right now."

"Me too."

He didn't say anything for a long time.

On Sunday it rained. We got up earlier to attend Sunday school for the first time at Hillcrest Community Church. To my surprise, Chelsea Turpin was there too.

She was thrilled to see me, just as much as I was to see her.

"I didn't know you went to church here," I said.

"I don't—or I didn't—or, I don't know." She took a deep breath. "Mrs. Oatley invited my mom. Jane and I came too."

My second surprise came when I learned that Mrs. Manitou was our teacher. She was tall and slender, with fair skin, jet-black hair and sky blue eyes. She seemed to know all about me. I was getting used to that feeling.

She told us to call her Joan.

After Sunday school, I found Daddy talking in the hallway with Mr. Manitou, Miss O'Neil, Mrs. Oatley, and a couple I didn't know. They were discussing something from their Sunday school class.

They were all friendly and pleasant, yet none of them seemed to be agreeing.

Mr. Manitou's deep voice grew more emotional. "But was my ancestors' idolatry any worse than the white man's greed—another from of idolatry? Both deserved punishment, yet only one culture was destroyed."

"For the moment," Mrs. Oatley said calmly.

Mr. Manitou smiled at her, almost as if he had wanted that response.

I pulled on Daddy's coat sleeve. I wanted to hurry so that we could sit by Chelsea during the service.

"That's exactly what we'll talk about next week," Richard Manitou said, his dark eyes twinkling.

They thanked him for leading the class. The couple—as the wife turned, I saw that she was pregnant—headed to the restrooms while Daddy started walking between Miss O'Neil and Mrs. Oatley. He looked a little uncomfortable between them; he dropped back to walk with me.

"The husband of that pregnant woman is David Browning. He teaches English in Hillcrest. His wife's name is Danielle."

I wasn't interested. "Can Chelsea sit with us?"

"*May* Chelsea?"

I groaned. "Yes, *may* Chelsea?

"Sure."

As it turned out, Jane, Mrs. Turpin, and the Oatleys sat behind us. Miss O'Neil sat on Daddy's left side in the same pew with us. I sat on his right and Chelsea sat beside me.

In St. Paul, the realization that Becky and I were moving apart had bothered me, but today letting go was suddenly easier. It was sort of like losing a favorite doll but having it replaced by a new, better one. Daddy once said that God is in the business of giving, not taking. We only have to be willing to see what he wants to give us. I peeked over at Miss O'Neil. Yes, things were going well.

During the sermon, I glanced back at Robert and Jane. They both sat stiffly and looked straight ahead.

On Tuesday morning of that week, Mrs. Putnam gave us a writing assignment. She explained that she was going to try a new method, something that she had read about in a teaching magazine. We were to write about a hobby or a favorite activity. We had twenty minutes to write, then we were to exchange papers and proof-read a partner's paper, then re-write our own paper, correcting any mistakes that the other person—or we—discovered.

I wrote quickly, easily, about my dolls, then Chelsea and I exchanged papers. I was surprised by her simple sentences, but many of them weren't sentences at all, and I wasn't sure how to fix them.

I raised my hand for help. Mrs. Putnam wasn't able to come and check Chelsea's paper because she was swamped with questions from everyone else. She never did make it over to me, so I did the best I could to correct Chelsea's paper and handed it back to her.

On my paper, Chelsea had corrected a few of my misspellings and had drawn a smiling face at the bottom. I wished I had thought to draw something nice on hers.

I rewrote my paper.

Mrs. Putnam next asked volunteers to read their papers to the class, yet she asked for readers in such a way that we knew that she assumed that we would all be eager volunteers. Belief in free will was not an option.

On my turn, I stood and read my paper confidently, for I was proud of my doll collection. I put a lot of enthusiasm into my voice as I'd always heard Daddy do when he read to me. Out of the corner of my eye, I saw Chelsea watching me enviously. When I finished, I was quite pleased with my performance, and I sat down. Mrs. Putnam's congratulated me for a fine paper.

As we lined up for recess, Margie poked me in the ribs.

I turned to face her and she smiled sweetly at me, too sweetly. "You read good, Angela."

I replied hesitantly, unsure what lay behind her sugar-frosted smile: "Thank you."

Her manner abruptly changed and she sneered. "Aren't you a little old for dolls?"

The other kids nearby spun to watch my reaction.

I felt my cheeks blush. "They're a collection."

She wrinkled her nose derisively as if I were a disgusting, too-many-legged crawling bug. "Dolls," she ridiculed, stretching out the vowel as if it were an ugly word.

We were released and, in the rush, I didn't have time to reply. Nor did I have a reply. I was stunned. Humiliated. It was as if something that I treasured in my heart had just been ripped up before my face and trampled on and I was powerless to prevent it.

I blinked back the tears as I ran to the tire house. I quickly climbed to the top before anyone could see my eyes.

I didn't care what Margie thought; I didn't care what anyone else thought. I knew that. But my heart still hurt, and I couldn't explain why.

Wednesday, the students didn't have school, but teachers had a day to coordinate curriculum prior to the next year's consolidation. In the morning, I went with Daddy to school. While he attended a faculty meeting, I changed his bulletin boards for him. It didn't take very long. When I was done, Daddy returned and asked if I'd get the school's video tape recorder from Mr. Hanson's room.

"It's on the cart," he said.

"Sure!" I dashed out the door.

The science room was at the end of the hall, on the other side of Mr. Manitou's room. Everyone knew where the science room was because every so often Mr. Hanson's sulfur experiments stunk up the entire school. Since no one else was around, I ran in the hall and my footsteps echoed down the empty hallway. I spun into Mr. Hanson's room, breathless.

The VCR cart was wedged between the chalkboard and the counter with the Bunsen burners. I wrinkled my nose: the room always smelled as if someone had mixed rubbing alcohol and vinegar.

I grabbed the cart, then noticed Mr. Hanson sitting at his desk, looking down.

"May I take it? Daddy wants the VCR."

"Sure." His flushed face was perspiring slightly. "Tell him I'm sorry that I forgot to bring it to him yesterday."

"I don't mind getting it." I pulled the cart toward the door.

Then I noticed someone else, a slender, short woman standing by the windows. Her back was to me. I wanted to say hello to Mrs. Walker, but I didn't because she never turned to face me and I felt awkward saying hello to a back. Also, something in their demeanors told me that I had interrupted an important conversation.

I got that VCR cart out of there as quickly as I could.

When I returned to Daddy's room, I told him about it in a

whisper. He sighed, leaned back in his chair and rested his hands across his stomach.

He spoke softly. "Troubles don't end when you get to be an adult, Angel. We can only pray that they'll jump off the merry-go-round soon and be able to face the right direction."

I didn't understand what was going on, but I knew it wasn't good.

After lunch, Daddy knew that I needed a diversion, so he said that I could go to the library. I had finished *The Hobbit* and I wanted a new book. I enjoyed browsing through the high school books. I liked the pictures in the grade school books, but the long words in the high school books were a lot more fun to read. They also made me feel more important, more grown-up.

At two o'clock the teaching staff had another faculty meeting in the library. Since I was sitting unobtrusively in the back corner behind a bookshelf reading *Anne of Green Gables*, Daddy said I could stay.

Both elementary and secondary teachers attended. No one seemed eager to meet. They all wanted to return to their rooms and finish writing curriculum.

I slid some books to the side and peered through the shelf. I could see most of the group. Mr. Cranberry was facing my direction. Daddy's back was to me, and I could see that his bald spot was growing larger. I hoped Miss O'Neil hadn't noticed.

Mr. Allen, my principal (of sorts), sat beside Mrs. Putnam and didn't say a word.

Mr. Cranberry stood up and cleared his throat. His jowls wiggled a bit. "Your general assignments are being drawn up for next year. Even in a normal year, we never know what everyone will teach the next year, and with this consolidation, it's even more difficult, but we can determine what general areas will need to be filled."

"And who'll be cut," Mr. Oldenburg snapped sarcastically.

Mr. Cranberry's cheeks turned red and he scratched his chin. "No one will be cut, at least for next year."

"Even Jack?"

Mr. Cranberry cleared his throat. "Except for Jack." He shuffled some papers on the table before him. "You understand, Jack, don't you?"

Daddy nodded. "I knew that was a possibility when I accepted the job."

"Of course, things could change."

"Better settle the coaching assignments soon," Mr. Oldenburg stated. "Athletics have broken consolidation agreements before. Remember when Hillcrest and Cherry Grove were considering it. Cherry Grove pulled out because they didn't want all the games played in Hillcrest."

"I think this consolidation is too far along for us to retreat now."

Mr. Oldenburg laughed sarcastically. "Retreat is right!"

Perspiration dotted Mr. Cranberry's upper lip. "A committee of board members is working on hiring procedures now."

Mr. Oldenburg spun his coffee cup with both hands. "What do board members know?"

Mr. Cranberry looked away, repeated, "They are handling it."

From what Daddy had told me, Mr. Cranberry was powerless in the whole process, as powerless as the teaching staff. I didn't know why Mr. Oldenburg couldn't see that Mr. Cranberry really couldn't do anything. Maybe Mr. Oldenburg was too worried about losing his coaching position to realize it.

Maybe he didn't care.

Nor was he about to be deterred. "We'll need to order new uniforms soon. We can't wait until the last minute. It's easy to shake hands on consolidating, but it's another to work out the details. Marriages, you know, don't always work out."

Mrs. Walker, sitting next to Mr. Oldenburg, suddenly looked down and blushed and adjusted the papers in front of her.

The meeting quickly degenerated into a babble of dissent and dissatisfaction which seemed to be exactly what Mr. Oldenburg wanted. Daddy had once told me that Mr. Oldenburg didn't like any opinions other than his own. Daddy also said the same thing about Mr. Cranberry. Maybe they didn't get along because they were too much alike.

Trying to be optimistic, Daddy spoke up. "Change is often good. It helps us keep our edge."

Mr. Manitou nodded, but Mr. Oldenburg leaned back. "Edge? We're people, not razors."

Daddy didn't reply, but I knew that Mr. Oldenburg was wrong. Some people *are* razors.

CHAPTER 16

I remember waiting at dad's elbow for the train on a summer evening,
hearing the whistle,
feeling the earth shake.
I remember my first train set on Christmas morning
and mom and dad looked happy.
I remember the railroad crew ripping up tracks by the depot,
ripping up my memories.
I remember designing a model train layout
that would make Paradise live again.
I remember dad's letter, saying he wouldn't be home.
I remember when I finally did see him again,
this fall
and I can't forget.

—a poem by Robert Oatley

I always enjoyed Thanksgiving vacation because it foreshadowed the longer Christmas vacation soon coming. I was not looking forward, though, to our visit to Mrs. Putnam's. Vacation was a way to get away from class, not spend extra time with my teacher, especially a stern teacher like Old Pr—I mean, Mrs. Putnam.

But I was surprised once we arrived at her home. She didn't look austerely over her glasses at me even once; in fact, she wasn't even wearing them, nor did she wear one of her dark dresses. Instead, she seemed relaxed in a pink blouse and slacks. Smiling often, she conversed openly, easily, as if we were family. After a while, I almost began to think of her as family. We ate turkey, potatoes, corn (which we brought) and pumpkin pie (my favorite) heaped with real whipped cream. Daddy always bought fake whipped cream.

I told Mrs. Putnam that.

"Well," she laughed, "I usually buy the artificial kind too. But Thanksgiving is a time to celebrate with friends."

Friends. I liked the sound of that. I'd never thought of a teacher as a friend, other than Daddy, of course. But then, now that I think of it, I'm not sure if I ever thought of Daddy as a friend either. He was Daddy. That was more than a friend. In those days, we were inseparable.

We stayed at her home the entire day, talking, playing card games that she taught us, and eating leftovers for supper.

I had brought over several dolls and was dressing them by the window when my ears perked up—they were talking about me. "You need to make sure she's writing even more, Jack," Mrs. Putnam said. "Do you know how quickly she read *The Yearling*? In a bigger school, she'd be in a special program."

"She's been through so much. She needs a sense of normalcy. Besides, I don't believe in special programs. All students deserve to be treated as individuals."

Just then I saw snow lightly drifting onto the grass. I jumped up, calling them to the window.

"Wait until you see a real country blizzard," Mrs. Putnam said. "We have no streetlights beyond town to help us. When the ditches fill and the wind whips over the roads—" She shuddered.

It sounded great.

"Have an emergency kit in your car at all times," she cautioned.

"Yes, ma'am!" Daddy replied.

When it was time to leave, I didn't want to go, and I think that made Mrs. Putnam pleased.

"You'll have to come to our home next time," Daddy told her as he helped me into my jacket.

On our walk home, I skipped through a half-inch of snow, but by the next morning, the snow had melted, leaving a dreary, soggy lawn behind.

The next week's gray, overcast sky promised snow, but it never came. I kept dreaming of the road ditches piled high with snow and the roads blocked by long, white drifts, but none of it materialized.

Daddy took me to the Paradise Café on Friday evening. I'd hoped Miss O'Neil would join us, but she was visiting her family in Minnetonka over the holiday weekend.

"She goes there a lot," I complained.

"She is quite close to them."

Robert Oatley waited on us. He seemed happy to see us.

"Are you glad football is over?" Daddy asked.

"Sort of. Now I can get caught up on my classes." He grinned as he pulled out his notepad: "Especially English."

I ordered my usual hamburger and french fries. Robert left and went to the kitchen.

"I still haven't heard from Becky," I complained. "Not since her dinky thank-you card."

"Maybe it's time to quit writing her. See if she finally initiates a letter."

After we ate, Robert gave us the bill, but then stood awkwardly by our table, shifting his weight. Daddy could see that Robert wanted to say something.

"So, Robert, how is everything? How's the model railroad layout?"

He cleared his throat. "Could you come over to my house tonight? About 7:30. That's when I get off work."

"Sure," Daddy replied quickly, and he glanced at me. I knew that he didn't really want to go over there. Maybe, like me, he remembered when we had last visited the Oatleys.

It was too cold for Daddy to run outside (or at least too cold for me to ride along, especially since my bike was hanging upside down in the garage), so he exercised in the living room. By the time he finished his shower, it was already 7:30.

Robert met us at the door.

"Sorry we're late," Daddy apologized.

"That's all right." He took our jackets and led us through the kitchen and immediately downstairs, as if he, too, didn't want to linger with us in the kitchen. The basement door had been replaced.

Mrs. Oatley, wearing a flowered peach blouse and jeans, was in the basement, sweeping a feather duster over the model railroad layout. None of the cars were running, nor did it look as if they would be. Mrs. Oatley must have been to the hairdresser, for her auburn hair had extra curl in it. I didn't like it.

She greeted us warmly. "Robert's quite talented, isn't he, Jack?"

I glanced up at her, shocked: Jack? She called him Jack?

Daddy nodded.

Robert moaned. "Aw, Mom."

Mrs. Oatley turned to me. Had she noticed my stunned expression? She smiled pleasantly at me. I grudgingly admitted to myself that she did have pretty blue eyes. "Angela, would you like a fresh chocolate chip cookie?"

For a homemade, hot-out-of-the-oven chocolate chip cookie, I could forgive her familiarity. I looked to Daddy and he nodded permission.

Once upstairs, she brought me into the living room and delivered the cookies on a tray. The cookies were warm, the oatmeal soft, and the chips were melted into chocolate fudge. I had three of them and a tall glass of milk.

Mrs. Oatley asked me about school, about how we liked Paradise, about church, even about when my mother died. She seemed very interested and sincere, and my impression of her improved.

After we talked awhile, she lowered her voice. "Thank you for talking to me," she said confidentially. "Robert needed to talk to your father."

"About what?"

Her blue eyes glanced toward the basement door. "I'm not sure. It might be about, well, it wasn't pleasant the last time you visited."

I had to agree.

"I think that Robert sees in your father what he wishes his father had been. It's not been easy raising two boys. Often hard. Very hard. Probably not unlike your father raising you."

I smiled and sipped my milk, but inwardly I fumed—a hard time raising me?

"We get along fine," I stated coolly.

Taken back by my frosty reply, she didn't say anything, but studied me for a moment, then reached forward and patted my shoulder. Her blue eyes looked envious, wistful perhaps.

"I'm sure you do," she said tenderly.

She abruptly changed subjects. "My former husband paid for the damages to the kitchen, then he went back to California where he doesn't have to be accountable to anyone. I don't know why he showed up again. I don't think he knows either."

Daddy came up in a few minutes and exchanged pleasantries with Mrs. Oatley. They seemed to talk easily together. For a moment, I became worried that he was starting to like her, but then he said that I needed to get to bed (our typical exit line). Robert brought us our jackets and we escaped out the front door, and none too soon for me. I was beginning to feel pulled in, trapped against my will.

As I crawled into the cold car, I glanced back at their house and all the work it required, and I decided that I needed to intensify my efforts to get Daddy together more often with Miss O'Neil.

Daddy was very quiet driving home.

"What's wrong?" I asked.

"I expected Robert to talk about his father, but he didn't. He told me that he was worried because he once had a copy of the key to the depot padlock. He wondered if he should tell the authorities. I told him he should, but he's afraid to. He also told me that several kids have keys."

"How did he get one?"

"Years ago his father left it."

"Where is that key now?"

"Robert said that he gave his copy to someone else. He didn't tell me who."

Daddy drove toward our house, then suddenly turned down the street toward the depot, parking on the road near it. In the crisp night air, under the soft blue moonlight, the depot looked serene.

Daddy kept the car running and opened his door. "Wait here," he stated and I wasn't about to disobey him. He grabbed the flashlight from the glove compartment.

I was nervous, even a little scared. "What is it?"

"I don't know. A hunch. A feeling." He glanced at me for a split-second and I saw worry in his gray eyes, and then he leaned over and quickly kissed my forehead. Just as abruptly, he stepped out and slammed the car door and walked through the fallen dry grass to the depot's front. He vanished from sight. My heart was pounding, remembering the last time I'd been in that depot, stumbling on the body, seeing the blood spilled like red milk.

I took a deep breath. The car was warming up, but I still felt cold.

Evidently, the depot was open because I saw his flashlight shine through the cracks between the window boards facing me.

Fear, like a long, cold icicle, began to creep up my back. I wasn't going to wait any longer. I grabbed the car door handle.

Just then Daddy came into view, walking slowly and thoughtfully. He returned to the car.

"It was open," he said as he got in, "but no one was inside. I don't like it." Pursing his lips, he started the car.

Just then, a tall, dark figure, waving its arms wildly, ran in front of our headlights.

Startled, I grabbed Daddy's arm off the wheel and uttered a brief scream. The dark figure ran forward, falling against the hood with a thud. The car lurched.

Daddy snapped an order: "Lock your door." I did, but my hands were shaking so badly, I almost missed the lock.

The face of the stranger swayed near our windshield. It was Dirtball Gallagher, disoriented and confused.

He must be on drugs, I thought.

Patting the car like a blind man, he stumbled to Daddy's side and feverishly knocked on the door.

Daddy lowered the window a crack.

"Who's in there?" he stammered. "I need help."

"Jack Kiln, Mr. Gallagher. What's wrong?"

"In the woods. In the shack. Please help." He moaned feverishly. "Come."

Daddy studied the wild, dark face outside his window for just a moment, then unlocked his door, and grabbed the flashlight.

"I'm coming," he said.

"I'm coming, too," I added.

Daddy looked at me, considered, decided. "Come on, but put on your hat and gloves."

I quickly pulled my hat and gloves from my pockets.

Dirtball stepped back so Daddy could get out of the car. As he moved back, Dirtball tripped on his own shoelace. Daddy caught his forearm, held it.

Daddy shined the flashlight into Dirtball's face. Dirtball winced, blinking, held up his hands. Sweat glistened on his face.

"I'm f-fine," he stuttered. Then, as if reading Daddy's thoughts, he added, "I'm clean. Been for years. Follow me. The other way's too slow."

"What other way?"

He didn't hear Daddy. He had already turned and was running down the gravel railroad bed like a lopsided dog. We followed, Daddy half-pulling me by my hand so that I would keep up. Daddy's flashlight bobbed along the gravel and dry weeds. Our breaths burst into the night air like tiny white clouds. It was growing windier, colder. I zipped my jacket up all the way to my chin.

We came to the edge of Browner's Woods.

"I left it somewhere," Gallagher mumbled, dropping to his knees.

Daddy directed his light onto another flashlight weakly shining in the tall grass. "There—"

Gallagher snatched up the flashlight. Beside it, half-hidden in the grass, lay a rifle. Daddy's light reflected on the dark barrel and I shivered. Dirtball left the rifle in the grass and lurched upright. Perspiration freely ran down his face, even in the cold.

He loped along the path ahead of us, knowing all the turns and low branches well. We followed his dim light that eerily bounced past trees and jumped past upper claw-like branches.

Daddy kept his light on the path.

We came to the three dead trees. Dirtball hurdled them as if he'd done it all his life. He headed to the eroded slope, sliding down on his feet, and disappeared from view. I heard gravel tumbling in the dark.

Daddy helped me over the trees. He handed the flashlight to me. "Wait here," he commanded.

"I'm coming too."

In the darkness, I could feel his intense gaze, hear his quick breathing. Dirtball was already at the shack.

"Come on." Daddy grabbed my hand and hoisted me up. He hadn't carried me in several years. He threw me over his shoulder like a large sack, forcing the air from my lungs, but I didn't complain.

He slid down the hill, trying to cushion the bumps for me.

Setting me on my feet, he ran to Dirtball's weak light that shone on the old blanket door. I followed, shining our bright beam on both of them.

Dirtball, leaning over, stepped into the shack and disappeared. Daddy followed.

I waited a moment, shining the flashlight around the outside of the shack, on the rustling and creaking trees around me, on the eroded hillside behind me. My white breath whisked across the flashlight beam. I glanced up. Faint, thin smoke rose from the shack's stovepipe and was quickly ripped away by the wind.

Afraid to go in, afraid to stay out, I took a deep breath and stepped forward.

Daddy and Dirtball were standing together, Dirtball's light shining down. Daddy knelt, reached out, stopped.

Dirtball's whole body began to shake, his legs swaying, and his flashlight's beam flickered over the shack's insides, making everything look like a scene from an old silent movie.

"Angel—the light," Daddy snapped.

I handed my flashlight to Daddy and then I saw what he saw. Duane Johnson's body lay in the center of the crude room, dark blood staining the left side of his half-open letterman's jacket. His right hand gripped a pistol. His left arm was stretched out, his hand in a fist.

Daddy grabbed his left wrist to feel his pulse. Duane's fingers opened slightly. A silver key glistened in the light.

I didn't scream, not until I turned and saw Dirtball Gallagher lying on his back, twisting like a snake, moaning, his flashlight's beam bouncing on the ceiling.

CHAPTER 17

My first touchdown for Paradise was the best part of ninth grade.
The first time I drove a car was a blast.
When it was finally legal, it wasn't as much fun
—from a poem by Duane Johnson

Daddy turned Dirtball onto his side. As the seizure passed, Dirtball lay still but was breathing heavily. Daddy put his arm around him and sat him up.

"Warren? Warren?"

"Is he okay?" I asked.

"He'll be fine in a bit. I need to get him conscious enough to get him home."

Dirtball gradually woke up but was so groggy he couldn't speak.

"Angel, you'll have to lead the way with your flashlight."

Daddy helped him up the hill, nearly carrying him along the path, back to his house. Dirtball fumbled with his key as he pulled it out of his pocket. Daddy grabbed the key and opened the door for him.

After passing a dark entryway, Dirtball felt around on the wall and flipped on a wall switch that turned on a floor lamp in the corner. The living room walls, a small stucco texture, were painted beige. A wide, black velvet painting of an Indian on horseback hung over his worn, brown sofa. An equally worn, leather easy chair, its stuffing flaking out of holes in the upholstery, sat next to a rickety end table. The chair faced a wide television console. The house smelled sweet, like really cheap perfume.

Daddy helped him to the sofa, turned him so that he could lie down, and lifted his feet.

"Do you need a doctor?"

Dirtball shook his head. "No," he whispered. "Help the boy." Dirtball pointed to the hallway with a trembling hand.

I followed close behind Daddy. In the hall hung a black wall phone. Daddy called the sheriff's office.

"Is Duane dead?" I whispered.

Daddy nodded. While he reported the death, I peeked into the nearest room off the hall. There was no curtain on the window and the shade was up, allowing moonlight to stream into the small bedroom. Along the paneled walls, above the unmade bed, hung wildly colored posters, like pictures I'd seen of the 1960's. One poster was of African lions, another was a sailing ship, another was the American flag, and another was the peace symbol. The posters' corners curled away from the wall.

I returned to Daddy as he hung up the phone. I took off my hat and gloves and stuffed them in my jacket.

Within a few minutes, a sheriff's deputy who had been patrolling Paradise knocked on the door. He was a barrel-chested man with long gray sideburns.

Daddy started to explain what he had seen, but the deputy nodded and cut him off: "Ambulance is on its way." He glanced at Dirtball, now sleeping on the sofa. Grunting his apparent disgust, he turned to Daddy. "Can you take me to this shack?"

Daddy reached out and took my hand. "I don't want to take Angela back there."

"She'll be okay here," said the deputy. "I know Gallagher from way back."

"Daddy, you can go," I said. "I'll wait here. Just hurry back." Dirtball's breathing was now slow and regular. In his soiled camouflage, he looked harmless, but I didn't want to be there by myself any longer than necessary.

Daddy studied me for a long moment, unsure, I think, if I really meant it. Looking back, I also think that he was as disoriented as I was, in a sort of walking shock, operating on a psychological autopilot and not sure what he was doing. I'm not sure why I was so calm, but I was somehow separated from my emotions, cocooned from danger, as if I were watching myself going through motions that I viewed from a distance.

"I won't be gone long," Daddy said as he headed out the door.

I peeked into the other rooms on the first floor. The bathroom was messy, but normal. Another small room was crammed with paperback books, some on shelves, others stacked in piles taller than I. His kitchen floor linoleum was cracked and his sink overflowed with dirty dishes. In the back entry hung two rifles and three handguns. The pistols were dusty and a spider had woven its web over them.

The ambulance arrived, and two EMT's came in. I explained what had happened to Dirt—Mr. Gallagher, and I told them how to get to the shack.

One man cursorily checked the sleeping Dirtball.

"Check on him later," said the other. "Let's find the shack." They ran out, driving over the grass to the edge of the woods.

As I waited there, my emotions returned slowly, like a foot that had fallen asleep and was now tingling as blood returned. A general eeriness crept up my spine, as if I were being watched. I turned on lights in the other rooms, but the creepy feeling remained. Walking over to the television console, I turned it on. It was an old television with a hard-turning knob, but I turned the dial until I found an old back-and-white comedy rerun. I sat in the worn chair by the end table.

My mind then began replaying the sight of Duane's body. Over and over. I couldn't make it stop. I shivered, but it wasn't from the cold. I kept my jacket zippered up. Dirtball began to snore, and I prayed that Daddy would return soon. I got up, turned the television louder, and sat down again. It didn't help. I kept seeing the body.

I turned down the TV, returned to the chair, pulled my legs up, put on my hat, and prayed again.

Just then there was a knock on the door and Mrs. Putnam walked in. Was I glad to see her!

"Oh my," she said. "The sheriff's department called me with a message from your dad to come over here."

She took off her gloves and coat. She looked over the room, doing a valiant job of hiding her displeasure at the general mess, and then looked directly at me and smiled as if nothing at all was the matter. She sat in the chair.

"Well," she said and smiled again. She held out her arms and I crawled up next to her and she put her arm around me. We were crunched together on that chair, but I didn't mind.

The next thing I knew, I was waking up in my own bed. A sliver of sunlight slipped past the window shade and curtain, hitting my dolls.

I stretched, feeling contented. What a terrible dream, I thought, until I saw Daddy sleeping on the floor beside my bed. I sat up, realizing that I'd slept in my clothes. Daddy, also still dressed, had my jacket over his shoulders like a short blanket.

I crept past Daddy, careful not to disturb him, went to the bathroom, then slipped downstairs to the kitchen and poured myself a bowl of corn flakes. I went back upstairs and ate beside Daddy who still slept soundly.

Later, while Daddy was eating breakfast, he filled me in on the details of the night before. Duane had been dead about an hour when we found him. The key in his hand fit the depot padlock. His blood showed a high concentration of alcohol. On the table, near the cards, was a note explaining that he and Chet had written a suicide pact.

"Did you read it?"

Daddy nodded. "It was short and addressed to Chet. He said he was sorry that he was late. He ended with 'Now I follow you.'"

Daddy stared out the window. "His punctuation was lousy," Daddy added.

The brisk November wind shook the bare branches of our maple trees. A few snowflakes blew across our yard.

I imagined Duane starting a fire in the small stove, steeling himself to his horrible task, loading the gun—

I shivered.

Daddy was still staring out the window.

"Why did they do it?"

He sighed sadly, looking back at me. His gray eyes were tired, bloodshot. "I don't know, Angel. It makes no sense to me. None of it. But then life sometimes seems like that." He ran a hand through his thinning hair.

I'd never heard Daddy sound so depressed, so discouraged.

The telephone rang. I ran to get it.

"Hello."

"Hello, Angela." Whoever it was talked as if we were old friends.

"This is Megan Warner-Winston with the *Rochester Post-Bulletin*. Would you tell us what you saw last night?"

"No," I shouted. "Leave us alone." I hung up.

"Who was that?"

"A newspaper reporter."

He chuckled. It was a good sound and I smiled.

Mrs. Putnam visited us that afternoon with some cookies.

"Thank you for coming over last night," I said. She looked at me for what seemed forever as if she wanted to say something. She finally said: "I'm glad that your dad had the good sense to have someone call me."

"That makes three of us," Daddy said.

She sat down at our kitchen table, and she and Daddy talked awhile. I sat in his lap until I got too heavy and then I got some dolls to dress.

"His death is such a shame," Mrs. Putnam said, shaking her head.

"I just don't understand it," Daddy said. "Chet and Duane weren't the types."

"You just never know what goes on inside young people's heads." Her green eyes blinking rapidly, she sighed, bewildered, and her expression was like a small child's lost in a busy shopping center.

Daddy stared out the window again, equally lost.

"Well," she said, rising, "I better get back to my baking. I hope—" she stopped and looked at Daddy, reconsidering. "If you ever want to visit and talk about it, please do. For my sake, as well. I remember Duane when he was young, so full of energy. Many days he wore me out with his antics."

Daddy glanced up, his gray eyes looking tired. "Thanks."

He stood and saw her to the back door.

Later, Mr. Manitou called on the phone, wondering how we were.

"I just happened to be there," Daddy said. "Duane's family is the one needing help." Daddy glanced over at me as I sat by the kitchen window, putting winter clothes on two more of my dolls.

"No, I'm fine," Daddy said, "a little shocked."

Mr. Manitou must've been insistent.

"No problem," Daddy said. "I just did what I could. Yes. It was Duane's pistol. Evidently, he and his dad were quite the collectors. We're both fine." Pause. "Really. Thanks for calling."

He hung up and stared at the phone for at least a minute without saying anything.

I asked hesitantly, afraid of his answer: "Are you okay?"

"Fine." His lips smiled, but his eyes didn't. "Fine."

That evening Miss O'Neil phoned us long distance. I answered the phone.

"I heard about it on television," she said to me. "How awful. They said Warren Gallagher and you found the body."

"He found the body then came and got us."

"Are you all right?"

I copied Daddy. "Fine."

"May I speak to your dad?"

I called him. He had been napping on the sofa. He scratched his chin as he took the phone from me. He hadn't shaved all day.

"Oh yeah. Fine, Linda." He repeated the story for her. "I don't know how his family's doing. Quite a shock for the school, too."

I wondered if I'd be seeing Mrs. Hill again.

That night, after we prayed, Daddy stayed by my bedside for several minutes. I turned over, looked at him in the glow of my night-light.

"What's wrong?" I asked.

"Just thinking how you've grown."

I smiled, reaching up to hug his neck. "I love you."

"I love you too, Angel."

Sunday we went to church in Hillcrest. My Sunday school lesson was about Moses and the Exodus. Mrs. Manitou taught us about how God provided manna for the Israelites every day, but if they collected extra and tried to keep it for the next day, it turned rotten.

"God gives us just what we need," Mrs. Manitou said. "We have to keep relying on Him each day."

After Sunday school, I found Daddy in the hallway outside his classroom. Mr. Manitou, Mrs. Oatley, and Daddy talked so long that we were late for the church service. We rushed in during the first hymn and had to sit in the front pew. Mrs. Oatley sat in the back with Robert. Tom wasn't in church.

After church, while Daddy was talking to Mr. Manitou, I went to the lobby for my coat. Joan Manitou was helping her three little children into their coats and mittens and hats and boots.

"I love having you in Sunday school," she said. "Not everyone listens as closely as you do." She wrestled a mitten onto her youngest child, a girl. I helped her get the other mitten on.

"Thanks," she said. "Richard respects your father very much. He really appreciates him at school."

She herded her children out the front door of the church, and I found myself envying them. I wished my mother were still alive. I seemed to be wishing that more lately.

Daddy finally came into the lobby, looking relieved to find me.

"You were talking forever," I complained.

He frowned and looked perturbed. "Sometimes adults need to talk."

That afternoon, Dirtball Gallagher knocked lightly on our back door, almost like a cat scratching. He was wearing clean camouflage clothes.

I refused to answer the door and called Daddy who let him in.

Dirtball shuffled into the kitchen near the table and looked down at the floor. He shoved his hands into his pockets.

"I wanted to come and thank you."

"No thanks are necessary," Daddy said. "Would you like to sit down?"

He scratched his beard and shook his head. "Naw, I can only stay a minute, but I wanted to thank you for helping me. Not everyone does that."

"I was glad to help."

Dirtball looked up at the ceiling. "The deputy found my rifle in the grass and took it, but they didn't have me call a lawyer or anything. I guess that's a good thing."

He stopped, sniffed, and picked his ear. Suddenly I found myself flushing, feeling almost faint, for I instantly realized that the two deaths weren't suicides. I grabbed Daddy's hand. He just patted it absent-mindedly and talked to Dirtball. Without any doubt, I knew that Dirtball had killed both Duane and Chet. They had probably vandalized his place and then he found out about it. After shooting them with his rifle, he stuck the pistols in their hands.

It was as if Dirtball had read my thoughts. He scratched his beard again. "My rifle was clean, they said." He wiped his nose on his sleeve. "I know I'm not popular in Paradise."

He didn't say anything more. Daddy stood there, not sure what to say. I stood there, knowing what I wanted to say and looking for some clear sign of his guilt.

Daddy cleared his throat. "Would you like to sit down?" he asked again.

Dirtball grabbed a kitchen chair and sat on the edge of it. Without encouragement, he told how he had been outside that night guarding his garage from vandals when he heard a noise come from the woods, a noise like a gunshot. He hurried back there, taking his rifle, checked the shack, and found Duane's body.

"I grew up in the house where I live now. My parents separated when I was in elementary school. Haven't seen my dad since I was a kid. My mother died a few years ago. Back when I was a kid, about your daughter's age, I fixed up that shack. It's not mine, of course, but I want to protect it, keep kids from getting into trouble, trouble like I sometimes did. I never expected to find—" He paused, swallowed, scratched his beard. "When I ran from the woods, I saw your headlights by the depot."

He took off his camouflage hat, scratched his straggly, oily brown hair. He reached his hand across the table. "Thanks."

Daddy shook his hand. "You're welcome."

Dirtball quickly stood and opened the back door, his back to us. "People say I take drugs. I don't take nothin' illegal, just drugs for my epilepsy. I'm usually okay, unless I get agitated." He glanced over his shoulder at us. "You've been a real help. Visit anytime."

Daddy watched him go, then shut the backdoor. "What a rotten life," he muttered.

Beyond any shadow of any doubt, I knew Dirtball had done it.

CHAPTER 18

I think we should change some laws. I don't think it's right
when a husband and wife get a divorse and the husband has to
pay money to his wife. Because she's usually got a job anyways
and if she don't she should get one. Anyways, after there divorced
she'll just move in with some other guy. Let the new guy pay the
bills.

—from an essay by Duane Johnson

Reporters descended on Paradise like crows to a road kill.
Camera crews were tramping over the school grounds, so Mr.
Cranberry gathered the reporters and gave a brief interview near
the swings before escorting them off school property. That happened
before school started. As we stood to say the morning Pledge of
Allegiance, Mrs. Putnam went over to the windows and jerked
down the shades with a previously unseen fury. Later I learned
that Megan Warner-Winston had tried to enter the building to
interview Daddy, but Mrs. Benwick, the high school secretary,
stopped her at the door.

During recess, Ms. Warner-Winston approached Mrs. Fisher,
the playground aide, but Mrs. Fisher chased her off. As we walked
inside, Mrs. Fisher informed me that the reporter had wanted to
talk to me.

I told Daddy about it that afternoon.

"Some reporters report the news," he explained, "some try to
sell the news, and some try to make the news."

"Don't you think they should be investigating Mr. Gallagher?"

"No, Angel," he said sternly, "and don't say anything like that
to your friends. We have already gone over that."

The evening before I had told Daddy about my belief in

Dirtball's guilt, but he didn't agree with me. I didn't know what it would take to convince him. I knew I was right.

I was also right about Mrs. Hill returning. She came the next day, looking and acting the same. She talked a long time with each class but I'm not sure what it accomplished. Yes, some kids had questions, but anyone could've answered those questions. She was, incidentally, prominently featured on the evening news, both out of Rochester and the Twin Cities.

The news also showed Duane's distraught parents and younger brothers tearfully consoling one another.

At that point, Daddy rose from the sofa, disgusted. "See what I mean about reporters?" He turned off the television. "They invade what should be private sorrow."

Daddy was very moody that evening, and he worked feverishly on his train set, painting a train car and assembling a building. I was worried. He normally worked on his trains in the fall, and as Christmas approached, his interest waned and he took the train set down after New Year's. This year his interest was increasing almost every evening.

The next day Daddy thought it was too cold to go outside for recess, but Mrs. Fisher brought us out anyway. Unless it was raining or snowing hard, we could always expect to get some fresh air, whether we wanted to breathe some or not. That day a light snow was falling. Chelsea and I tried to make snowballs, but the snow was too dry.

A few minutes into recess, Margie gathered the other girls by the slide. She ran to us and invited us to play with them.

"Sure!" Chelsea said immediately.

I went along.

Margie was unusually friendly. We hadn't talked since she had made fun of my doll collection.

Just before Mrs. Fisher rang her bell signaling us to go in, Margie tugged on my coat sleeve. "I'm going to visit my dad over Christmas," she grinned.

I smiled pleasantly. "Great."

"He's in California." She tossed her head back, like a model on a talk show, but, since she wore a stocking cap, it lost its effect. "I'll be going there for Christmas."

"That's nice."

"I may come back with a sun tan." She smiled smugly.

"Great."

Not sure what was going through her mind, I left her, caught up with Chelsea, and budged in line.

As our class came in from recess and climbed the stairs, I heard shouting in the hallway just down from our classroom. I recognized Mr. Cranberry's piercing voice.

The class, still in line, shifted toward the commotion.

Mrs. Putnam, hastening from the lounge, ran in front of us. Using her arm as a barricade, she held us at the door like a traffic cop, then, like an expert rancher, herded us into the classroom.

Risking her wrath, I lingered in the hall, letting others pass me.

From around the corner, Tom Oatley backed into view, an angry Mr. Cranberry pointing his finger at him. With his other hand, Mr. Cranberry shook a closed jackknife in front of Tom's nose.

Everyone was in the classroom except me.

"Angela." Mrs. Putnam only warned once.

"But look!"

She turned, saw. "Oh dear."

Mr. Cranberry was now yelling shrilly at Tom for carrying dangerous weapons in school. His face was red and his jowls shook. I thought his face was going to explode.

"Inside, Angela." Mrs. Putnam grabbed my shoulder, directing me in.

"But Mr. Cranberry shouldn't be angry at Tom. He carves with the knife."

Her grip was firm. She ushered me to my desk.

"He carves in here!"

Her hand forced me into my seat.

"Don't you know that?" I insisted. "Look in your wastebasket!"

She glanced in her wastebasket. She hesitated for a split-second, then sat down primly. For her, everything was back under her control and all was well with the world.

I fumed. Tears burned my eyes. She wasn't going to do anything to help Tom. In that moment, I hated her with a righteous, everlasting hate.

We began oral reading practice. Even under good circumstances, reading aloud irritated me. We each had to read a paragraph of a story, and that meant that I had to wait for slow readers. Whenever we read like that, I inevitably got bored and read ahead, and, when my turn came, I didn't know where the others were and I looked like a complete idiot. Today, I wasn't even trying to listen to what others read. I counted ahead, found my paragraph, and waited, practicing in my mind what I wanted to say to Mrs. Putnam. When my turn came, I read angrily, punching each word like a boxer hits a bag. When I finished, I glanced up to see if she had noticed my fury. She hadn't. She had slipped out of the class.

I swallowed hard, immediately embarrassed by my anger: maybe she was going to do something after all.

Within a minute or two, she glided back into class as if nothing had happened. Only a few noticed that she had even been gone.

At free time, I cautiously approached her desk.

I used my politest voice and sweetest smile: "What happened to Tom?"

She pursed her lips and spoke curtly: "That's between Mr. Cranberry and Thomas."

"But, Mrs. Putnam, he's been carving in your classroom for a long time! He hasn't hurt anything."

She peered at me over her glasses. "He's done it more than once?"

"Every day during recess!"

"How long has he done this?"

I shrugged. "All year, I guess. Maybe other years too."

Mrs. Putnam took a quick, sharp breath. "That doesn't excuse Thomas. Knives aren't allowed in school."

Fuming again, I returned to my seat, crossed my arms and pouted.

During lunch, I escaped from the cafeteria and sneaked up to Daddy's floor. Through the narrow window by the door, I saw him in front of the class. I could hear him lecturing about Henry David Thoreau. I gently rapped on his door like a shrub branch in the wind might tap a house before a storm.

He didn't hear me.

Jane Turpin, in a front desk, saw me, pointed me out to him.

Surprised, he stepped into the hall and shut the door behind him. "What's wrong?"

I blurted out the dilemma. "And you know he carves. You saw his statues in his basement."

Daddy pushed his glasses up and I could see the thunderclouds gathering in his gray eyes. "I'll see what I can do."

I hurried back to the cafeteria, just in time to get in line behind the fifth graders.

"Where were you?" asked one of the cafeteria aides suspiciously.

I hesitated. "I had to go," I muttered. I did a little dance in place to show her what I meant. "Really bad."

"Oh."

It wasn't a lie. I just didn't say where I had had to go.

As soon as the dismissal bell rang, I ran upstairs to Daddy's room. He was sitting on the edge of his desk, engaged in an animated discussion with Tina Lewis. Her arms were folded across her notebook.

"But who determines what is right?" she asked.

"Perhaps the question is 'What is right?'"

"How do we find that out?"

He shifted his weight on the desk. "That's where we must sift through the reasonable voices of the past and consider the challenges of the future. That's one of the reasons we're reading the classics."

She shifted her books into one hand and planted her other hand on one hip. "But how do you determine what is right?"

"Are you asking me personally?"

She lifted her chin, looking self-confident, maybe even defiant. "Yeah."

He took a deep breath. "If we're talking about accepting facts, it must pass the truth test. Did I see it? Or has someone reliable seen it? Is the witness's testimony valid? If it passes the truth test, then I accept it."

"Not all things are facts like that."

"Right. So, if I'm considering a philosophical system, like Emerson's, it must pass the practical test. Does it work? It must answer all of the important questions; otherwise, it fails to be true. For me, Christianity is the only belief system that passes both tests." He paused, rubbed his chin. "Does that make sense?"

She raised her eyebrows. "I guess so."

"Keep thinking. Maybe you should maintain a daily journal, write your questions down. Keep track of your thinking. Sometimes *seeing* what you think helps you to analyze *what* you think."

She smiled. "Maybe I will." She started to go, stopped. "You know, I have a second cousin in Hillcrest who did that. He even got his journal published."

"I'll have to read it."

I moved to the side as she passed me. "Hi, Angela," she smiled.

I fervently wished that I could someday be as smart and pretty as Tina.

Daddy saw me. "We were discussing the American Romantics," he explained.

"What about Tom? Did you hear anything?"

He stood, putting his hand on my shoulder. "I talked to Mr. Cranberry this afternoon and put my two cents in. He should've decided by now. Let's go and find out."

On the main floor, we found Tom walking sheepishly out of the high school office. Mr. Cranberry stood at his office door, arms folded across his chest, scowling.

I ran up to Tom, grabbed his arm. "What did he decide?"

He jerked his arm away, angry. "It doesn't matter," he mumbled.

Daddy approached Mr. Cranberry while Tom and I continued down the hall.

"Daddy told him you were just carving."

He refused to look at me. "I know. Old Prune told Cranberry, too."

He pushed furiously on the school's back door and stormed out. It shut behind him with a loud and final thud. I stood facing the closed door, frustrated and angry. I went through all that work to help him, and he never even said thanks. I marched back to the office. He was just a big jerk, I concluded.

Daddy was coming out of the main office. He patted me on the back. "You saved Tom from an extra two days of suspension."

"He didn't even say thanks."

Daddy stared down the empty hallway, his gray eyes showing no emotion. "Some people don't know how."

After school, we picked up the mail. Mr. Johanson saw us and waved us over to his newspaper office.

Mr. Johanson opened the door for us. "Jack, do you have a minute or two?"

"I guess so."

The office, which was really one large room decorated with cheap, warped paneling, had a desk that faced the large front window. In the far back of the room was an immense, obsolete printing press. On the right wall was a long, high counter for laying out the paper; on the opposite wall was a computer and printer.

He led us around the front desk to several tall stools by the layout counter. I perched on one and looked over the layout of this week's paper.

"How's school going? The attitudes of the students? The faculty?"

Daddy grinned, crossed his arms, and sat on a stool. "Is this an interview?"

Mr. Johanson lifted his hands in mock surrender. "If you'll answer."

Daddy laughed. "For Paradise's icon of literacy, all right." He then proceeded to tell him, without using names, about student shock, grief, and the ethical questions that had arisen. He described the somber faculty room, the quiet halls, administrative overreactions to apparent troublemakers, and the effect television coverage had on the school climate.

Mr. Johanson wrote down everything.

Meanwhile, quite fascinated with the layout sheets, I peeled up several waxed articles and set them down again. Mr. Johanson didn't seem to mind.

As they finished, Mrs. Johanson walked in. I hadn't met her before, but Daddy had told me that she wasn't a happy person. She was short, like Mr. Johanson, with a wide face, auburn hair, and a pale complexion.

"Afternoon, Mrs. Johanson," Daddy said.

"Is my husband playing junior reporter again?"

"Just getting information, dear," Mr. Johanson said quickly. He paled and seemed to visibly shrink.

"The only scoop Purgatory wants is who visited whom last week. They don't want to think. They just want to go about their lives believing that Purgatory is paradise."

I glanced at Daddy out of the corner of my eye. He was smiling politely at her.

"We all know that the town is going to change," Daddy said "It's just a question of how quickly. The paper helps them to understand that."

She glided to the desk and picked up some envelopes. "They buy the paper only because they've subscribed for so many years, and it's too much of an effort to change."

Mr. Johanson shrugged. "I'm afraid she may be right."

Daddy stood. "Perhaps. But you do your job well. What they do with it is up to them."

Mr. Johanson shrugged again, and I saw for myself that Daddy was right: Mr. Johanson was either unable or afraid to accept a compliment.

"What will you write about?" Daddy asked.

Mr. Johanson glanced at his copious notes. "I don't know. What I can. People don't always want the truth, just their illusions."

Mrs. Johanson snorted her agreement from the desk.

"That's true," Daddy said, "but you may be missing out on good stories if you hold back."

Mr. Johanson glanced at the paper that was laid out. He hesitated, as if he wanted to say more, but he didn't. Instead, he just nodded.

That evening after supper, Daddy worked on the train layout until bedtime. I spent the evening upstairs with my dolls.

"You don't like to help me anymore with the railroad," he said, tucking me into bed.

"Sometimes I do. I just wanted to play with my dolls tonight."

I didn't tell him that I didn't want to help him with his train layout when he seemed so determined, so bothered, that he didn't talk. He just added additional track or painted a car as one of his trains ran in circles.

I thought about Daddy's moodiness for some time before finally falling asleep.

The next morning, after I left Daddy's room and before I went to Mrs. Putnam's, I slipped into Mr. Manitou's classroom.

"Good morning, little lady."

I knew he liked Daddy and Daddy liked him. I also felt that I could trust him.

"Mr. Manitou, have you talked to Daddy lately?"

He folded his hands on his desk and answered cautiously: "Yes."

"Have you noticed anything different about him?"

He raised his dark eyebrows, seeming to understand my concern. "He is very quiet. Is that unusual?"

"Sometimes." I nervously twisted my backpack straps. I thought that if Robert needed to do it, maybe Daddy did too: "I was wondering if you could talk to him. Maybe he needs another man to talk to."

Mr. Manitou smiled. "I wish all children had your insight." He stood, towering over me. "I'll see what I can do."

I went to class, feeling better.

That next afternoon, for the second time that year, school was dismissed for a funeral. This one was held at a small country church a few miles out of town. The white church was quite narrow, had a tall wooden steeple, and a graveyard in the back by the parking lot.

The church was packed and many people had to stand in the back. The casket was open and I stared at the face. Without his breathing, without his usual sneer, Duane looked like a wax figure.

During the funeral service, the minister urged us to remember the good things about Duane, explaining that our memory of him would allow him to live in our hearts forever. The minister's message seemed hollow and he reminded me of Mrs. Hill. I didn't like it.

What the minister said contradicted everything I had been taught. Our memories have nothing to do with whether or not Duane lives forever, I thought. God determines that. If Duane had trusted God's Son with all his heart and soul and mind, then God had already accepted Duane. Eternal life has nothing to do with our memories of the deceased.

I recalled Tina's questions about truth and Daddy's reply about the two tests and I determined to ask Daddy about it.

"How do we know that we can believe God's promises?" I asked that night.

"Because of the resurrection," Daddy answered.

I turned onto my stomach, and he tucked me in. "And," he said, "we know that's true because of many reliable witnesses."

I twisted to look at him. "Does it pass your . . . what kind of test was it?"

"Do you mean my practical test?"

"Yeah."

Daddy raised his eyebrows, surprised at my question, I think, then he rubbed my back. "Christianity answers the questions of sin and evil. It gives us hope at the same time. It also passes the personal test: it works for me."

"Mommy knew Jesus, didn't she?"

"Without a doubt. That's how we know she's in heaven." His gaze drifted off toward my dolls.

"What's heaven like?"

"We don't know, except that we will be with God and those who love His Son. It will be great and never-ending and there won't be any tears. It will be a true paradise."

"Not like this town?"

He laughed. "Definitely not."

"When we lived in St. Paul, why didn't you go to church?"

Daddy didn't say anything for a few moments. I turned a bit, straining to see his face in the dim glow of my night-light. His gray eyes were in shadow.

He leaned over quickly and kissed me on the head. "Good night, Angel."

CHAPTER 19

*Thanks for writing a letter. I hate school. I like to find
quiet places and carve statues. Some I keep. I will carve one for
you if you want.*
　　—assigned pen pal letter from Tom Oatley to a senior

On Monday the snow fell and stayed. My grandparents moved
out of Minnesota because it snows in the winter. I thought they
were crazy. Snow is the best thing about living in the north. Just
about everyone in America endures summer's sweltering heat at
some time, but only the fortunate few have snow. A person can fall
in it, roll in it, shape it, throw it, eat it. And this first snow wasn't
the dry, airy snow, but it was the best kind: heavy snow that Daddy
hated to shovel but I dearly loved because I could make anything
out of it. Chelsea and I ran wild that afternoon—catching snowflakes
on our tongues, making snow angels, building snow forts.

Daddy wasn't happy when I came in soaked and shivering.

That evening, Mr. Manitou knocked on our front door. Daddy
had told me that he was coming, but Daddy uncharacteristically
ushered me to my room when Mr. Manitou arrived. Pouting, I
pulled back my window curtains and looked out. Fresh snow fell
quickly, but now it was lighter, drier, swirling down rooftops and
around trees and under cars. Behind the white flakes, the corner
streetlight shone like a hazy moon. Snow blanketed the ground,
making it impossible to tell where the sidewalk was.

I played with my dolls for almost an hour, then crept halfway
down the stairs. I didn't mean to eavesdrop, not really, but I felt
hurt and betrayed that I wasn't at least told something about what
was going on. After all, hadn't I asked Mr. Manitou to talk to
Daddy?

I hadn't planned to listen long, just long enough to know what they were talking about. I learned quickly.

Death.

I sat on the middle step, puzzled. What is there to talk about? I wondered. I started back upstairs, then stopped when I heard Mr. Manitou's deep voice ask about my mother.

I barely heard Daddy's reply, something about the long illness. I didn't remember much about her sickness. I had a picture in my mind of her crying in the bathroom after a visit to the doctor, and, later, of me standing by her hospital bed while Daddy gripped her hand over the white sheet.

I couldn't hear more and I was beginning to feel guilty. After all, I had told Mr. Manitou that Daddy needed to talk to another man. I quietly crept back upstairs.

I picked up the doll that looked like Mommy and gently brushed her hair.

Looking back, it's easy to see what was bothering Daddy. He always worked on the train set in the fall, around the time of my mother's death. But that year the two boys' deaths brought back painful memories. To cope, he continued to work on the train set longer than usual. His diligent tinkering kept his mind occupied.

Eventually I heard the front door open and close. I glanced out the window. Wind drove snowflakes against my window in thousands of whispering taps. Snow swirled around Mr. Manitou's departing car. His red taillights disappeared and the town lay quiet and still.

I turned, startled, as Daddy came into my room. He looked exhausted, as if he'd run farther than he'd ever run before.

The bed squeaked as he sat on the edge of it. He didn't move.

"Are you okay?" I asked.

"Just tired. It's one thing to look behind someone else's mask. It's an entirely different matter to pry your own off."

I sat beside him.

"Rick Manitou said that you asked him to talk to me. You said that I was acting differently."

My chin quivered. "Are you mad at me?"

His arm encircled me. "Not at all, Angel. I'm sorry."

"For what?"

"For holding things inside for years. I've been angry with God. I know I don't have any reason to be. Like Job, I have no right to open my mouth and complain. I know I don't deserve anything." He kissed my head. "But I can't help feeling that you deserved better."

I hugged him. "I still have you." I'd never seen Daddy like this: so vulnerable. The foundation of my world was shaking, cracking.

I bit my lip, holding back tears. "What did Mr. Manitou say?"

"We talked about justice and about suffering. He shared his own frustrations. He had a tough time growing up. There was alcohol abuse at home and ridicule at school. Can you believe that Joan's family wouldn't talk to her when she first dated Rick because he's a Native American? Her older brother even boycotted their wedding." He sighed. "I've tried so many different ways to deal with my anger. I know I'm not the only one who suffers. I know that others suffer far greater calamities, yet that never erased my anger. I even rationalized that if suffering did make sense, it wouldn't be suffering. That didn't help either."

At the time, I didn't know what Daddy was talking about; I just knew that he was hurting.

"You see, Angel, the two Paradise deaths not only brought back painful memories of your mother's death, but also rekindled my anger at God. Yes, I know that she's in heaven, that she's free of her pain, yet it doesn't ease my pain. Finally, Rick and I prayed."

Daddy took off his glasses and rubbed his eyes. "It's not death that's hard. It's life. I needed to surrender my hurt *and* anger to God. And I needed to give to Him what He had taken."

He held me tighter. "All I really know is that God cares, and that God weeps with us."

I couldn't help myself. I cried. He patted my head and didn't say anything for a long time.

School was canceled the next morning because of the heavy

snow. Daddy heard the announcement on the radio and didn't wake me up. When I finally did get out of bed, Daddy and I spent the morning shoveling our sidewalk as well as Mrs. Putnam's.

She invited us in for lunch.

She and Daddy discussed school. "The staff needs to work together to improve student morale," Daddy said.

She agreed. "With these deaths and the impending consolidation, the students are struggling. We need to be positive forces."

"But the administration needs to direct us, or at least give us time to work together."

"Mr. Cranberry is as good as gone. He won't be hired by the new district if they can help it."

"Why not? They might need a principal."

She rolled her eyes. "Mr. Cranberry's done what the Paradise board asked him to do—maintain the district at all costs. Those costs fell on the teachers and students. Lower salaries. Old books. Few computers. Hillcrest won't put up with that kind of administrator. They've always wanted leaders. Did you know that if I had taught in Hillcrest all these years, when I retire I would have—"

She remembered that I was there, stopped, and cleared her throat.

Daddy didn't ask any more questions in my presence.

I didn't know anything about salaries, but the next day I realized that Mrs. Putnam was sure right about attitudes in school. Everyone was going through the motions of school without really thinking. Everyone's behavior reminded me of what I think about when I brush my teeth or wash my face: during mundane routines like those, I think about anything other than what I'm actually doing. In school we might as well have been brushing our teeth. No one wanted to learn, no one seemed interested in being challenged, and no one wanted to face anything new. Even the usual excitement of next week's Christmas vacation seemed dulled, like an old ornament that had lost its shine.

Daddy took Miss O'Neil and me out to dinner that week.

They discussed school most of the time. I drew on the paper place mat.

"The esprit de corps is certainly low," Daddy said.

Miss O'Neil nodded. "This lack of motivation is driving me crazy. I'm afraid of next week's concert. There's no heart in their singing."

The next day, Daddy had a conference after school with Mrs. Oatley. I waited outside his room, sitting with my back to the lockers. Jane, Shelley, and Tina, talking heatedly, walked down the hall toward me in a tight cluster.

Tina spotted me sitting near Jane's locker and stopped talking. She grabbed the other girls' shoulders and nodded toward me. The others quit talking too. Jane cheerfully greeted me—too cheerfully, I thought—got her books, and they left.

So much for making me feel welcome.

Next, Tom Oatley sauntered down the hall, his backpack slung over one bony shoulder. He saw me, looked down, and then walked passed me, glancing guiltily into Daddy's room like a frightened dog.

"Your mother's in there," I said.

He shrugged as if he knew and didn't care. He hoisted his backpack higher on his shoulder. "So what?"

I guess his short size as a seventh grader made me brave. I grew sarcastic: "You're a regular Shawn Dixon, aren't you?"

His brown eyes darted to me and he looked wounded, then he turned away.

"Who cares?" he sneered, shuffling off.

Daddy and Mrs. Oatley were conferring a long time. I pulled out a book and started reading. When she emerged, she seemed, if not happy, at least relieved.

"I don't know how to thank you, Mr. Kiln, for bringing this up." She shook his hand. "You're a great teacher."

"Just doing my job. And," he added, "it's still 'Jack'."

After she'd left, I said, "You're just as bad as Mr. Johanson."

"What do you mean?"

"You can't accept a compliment."

He looked off for a moment, considering. "You're right. I better work on that."

I smiled. It was good seeing Daddy lighthearted again.

That night I awoke in the middle of the night. A driving sleet peppered the window. Before I fell back to sleep, I heard a noise downstairs.

At first I thought it was a mouse, then the thought popped into my head that it was a burglar. My heart pounded wildly and my mouth was instantly dry. I crept out of bed, slipping into Daddy's room to awaken him. I held my breath and reached over to shake him, but all I grabbed was blankets. My pulse rate shot up, faster than the pounding sleet.

I heard the refrigerator door close. I let out my breath, relieved: that meant Daddy was in the kitchen.

I slipped downstairs and found him in his bathrobe leaning against the kitchen counter, eating a cookie with a glass of milk.

Startled, he quickly put his glass down. "You're in your bare feet."

"What're you doing?"

"I couldn't sleep."

"May I have some?"

"Help yourself."

"Did you have a bad dream?" I asked as I dipped my cookie in the milk.

"No. Something woke me up, a dream about the shack and the depot. It was really strange, and I felt that my dream was trying to tell me something, something I was trying to remember."

"About the deaths?"

He rubbed his chin. "It had nothing to do with the deaths. Something else. But I couldn't quite grasp it in my dream." He reached up to adjust his glasses, then realized that he wasn't wearing them. "And I sure can't figure whatever it was out now."

I finished my milk.

He put the carton away and began herding me to the stairs. "Anything special you want to do over vacation?"

"You promised to take me shopping tomorrow after school."

"Oh. Certainly. I wouldn't forget that. And that reminds me: I do have two things I forgot to tell you about. The Hillcrest pastor called and asked if you'd play a carol on the piano for the Christmas Eve service."

I moaned.

"You've been practicing some carols with Miss O'Neil, and she said you were doing well, so I said you would."

I sighed quite dramatically. "Oh, all right. What's the second thing?"

"Would you like to visit the O'Neils on New Year's Day?"

Shocked, I stopped halfway up the stairs and turned to face him. "Miss O'Neil's family? You bet!" I flew the rest of the way upstairs, my feet barely touching the steps.

I jumped into bed, pulled the covers up, shouted "Good night!" before Daddy even had a chance to tuck me in again. I listened to the sleet hit the house. It was a great, almost musical, sound; a beautiful, almost magical, sound that suggested security and warmth and joy through any winter storm or rainy weather.

Daddy was happy again. My hair was looking better every day. Presents for Christmas. Linda O'Neil's for New Year's.

Except for the slight hurdle of having to play the piano at church, life was great.

CHAPTER 20

People need to be held accountable for their actions. Adults complain that young people lack values, yet where do we get values? As a teacher of mine says, values that are centered in self end up being self-centered.

—from an essay by Robert Oatley

Christmas vacation was wonderful. With the dismissal bell of the last class, Daddy put the Paradise deaths behind him, relaxed, worried about nothing, and had fun. He took me shopping in Rochester: I bought him a tie and a Bible with money that I had saved from my weekly allowance (which had miraculously doubled in November and December: "For selfish purposes," he said, winking.)

The next morning we bought a real tree that was so tall, it reached the ceiling.

"We don't have enough ornaments for a tree this big," I said.

"Yes, we do." He carried up a box from the basement that I had thought contained more model train stuff. Instead, it was packed full of lights and ornaments. While he strung the lights on the tree, I sorted the ornaments.

I held up a pink glass bell that actually tinkled. "Where did this come from?"

"If was a gift from a great aunt to your mother when she was about your age. That was her favorite."

We listened to carols while we decorated. I hung that fragile glass bell on a branch just my height.

When we finished, we sipped hot chocolate and sat together on the floor and looked at the colored lights and sparkling ornaments and glistening tinsel.

Moments like those are better than all the presents in the world.

The next few days I practiced my two songs for the Christmas Eve service. I practiced and practiced and practiced on that ugly painted piano until I thought my fingers would fall off. Even Daddy got tired of my playing.

On Christmas Eve day, we delivered some cookies that I'd baked to Mrs. Putnam. We also drove over to Hillcrest and delivered a dozen cookies to the Manitou family. They lived in an older farmhouse on the edge of Hillcrest. Mrs. Manitou ushered us into the family room that was filled with Native American art where Mr. Manitou was on the floor, wrestling all of his kids at the same time. He was losing badly, (the two boys holding his arms down and his daughter sitting on his chest) but I don't think he was trying very hard. Daddy and I laughed at the sight of him getting pinned.

That evening we attended the candlelight Christmas Eve service in Hillcrest. I smoothly played my way through "Silent Night" but lost my spot halfway through "Hark the Herald Angels Sing." After what seemed forever, I stumbled onto the correct notes.

I returned to the pew, embarrassed. Daddy put his arm around me, and lightly patted my shoulder. He leaned over and whispered, "Beautiful, Angel. I liked the pause in the second song. Nice emphasis."

Maybe my goof hadn't lasted as long as I'd thought.

On Christmas morning, we opened gifts. Daddy gave me a doll I'd never seen before, one with blonde hair and dressed in bib overalls and carrying a milk pail. He also gave me a set of paperback mystery books. I finally opened the gift (which had been sitting under the tree for a week!) that my grandparents in Florida had mailed. They gave me a nice blue sweater and a doll dress. Aunt Joan, who was traveling in Europe, had sent me a card and some money.

Daddy opened his gifts from me. The tie he suspected because he had caught me examining his one good suit a week before. When he opened the Bible, he said, "It's the new translation I wanted. Thanks!" Then he read my inscription to him: "Lots of things may change in life, but you'll always be my Daddy and I'll always try to be your Angel." He gave me a big, long hug.

Snow fell heavily the next few days, blanketing Paradise in two more feet of snow. Our maples' branches drooped with white mounds until I shook them, creating a mini-blizzard around me. Chelsea Turpin came over and we made two huge snow forts. Daddy joined us and shoveled snow into a massive mound that he then hollowed out, creating an igloo which Chelsea and I could both fit in at the same time.

Chelsea invited me to sleep at her house. Daddy said that I could. She lived in a small gray house across the street from the Oatleys, an older home like Mrs. Putnam's and ours, and she shared a bedroom with her sister.

Her mother, a tall, skinny blonde, met Daddy and me at the door and welcomed us with an adult version of a girlish squeal: "Oooh, it's so nice to meet you, Angela." The living room carpet had been freshly vacuumed and I caught the tacky pine scent of air freshener.

After I took my mittens off, Mrs. Turpin shook my hand. Her long hands were cold. She turned to Daddy and held out a bony arm and shook Daddy's hand while her eyes scanned him up and down.

"Hello," Daddy said. "I'm Jack Kiln."

"I think we met briefly at church in Hillcrest."

"Oh, yes." I don't think Daddy recalled it.

"Chelsea has talked so often about Angela. We're so glad she could stay over. My girls just got back from visiting their father in Minneapolis."

"Are you from the Cities?"

"Oh," she laughed, "how I sometimes wish that! But I'm a Paradise native. My relatives were some of the first settlers here."

I noticed that Daddy was struggling to come up with small talk.

"So, have you attended Hillcrest Community Church a long time?" he asked.

"We've just visited a few times. In fact, I haven't been there for a while. My parents threatened to disinherit me if I continued to go there."

"You're kidding, right?"

"The family roots run deep. My parents are Roman Catholic and I'd better remain Catholic."

"So, you've been attending St. Joseph's here?"

She rolled her eyes. "I haven't gone since I was confirmed."

"Yet your parents don't want you to attend a church in Hillcrest?"

"Only if it's a Catholic church. They're not happy about my not attending church, but at least in their eyes I'm still Catholic. So far, they don't know that Chelsea's been attending church with the Oatleys."

Daddy nodded sympathetically. "If you don't want to upset the relatives, maybe you should try St. John's Catholic Church in Hillcrest. People need to find a place where they can grow spiritually. I know from experience."

She laughed sarcastically. "In Paradise, it doesn't matter where you grow, just where you go."

They talked a little bit more, and then he gave me a hug before leaving. "If you need anything, just call."

Chelsea took me up the stairs to her bedroom. I pulled my paper doll collection from my backpack. Chelsea, having never seen so many paper dolls, having never even played with paper dolls, gave me free reign in all decisions. She was overjoyed at getting any paper doll to dress and left me the sole choice of which ones I wanted. With the dolls, we acted out wildly exotic adventures and mysteries in her bedroom. In the floor, she had a gravity heat vent and we could see into the kitchen. To the paper dolls, the vent was a deadly, bottomless pit that they had to avoid at all costs. Several inept paper dolls had to be rescued by our heroes.

After several hours, we eventually tired of self-made stories so she showed me a new video game on their TV. She reached level 4 while I never escaped level 1.

"That's okay," she encouraged, "I wasn't very good at first either."

I didn't tell her that we didn't have any video games for our TV. Daddy opposed them. "Read instead," he always told me. I resolved to tell Daddy that his prejudices were stifling my competitive edge.

I had brought my sleeping bag but discovered it wasn't needed. Jane insisted that I sleep in her upper bunk bed while she slept downstairs on the couch. Chelsea and I talked long into the night, all about our old friends, about Mrs. Putnam, our favorite songs, books, and TV shows until Jane finally shouted up through the gravity vent in the floor: "Be quiet up there and go to sleep!"

We giggled but did settle down.

In the morning, as we were finishing breakfast, I asked Jane when Chelsea and I would be old enough to join the Amazons.

"The what?" Chelsea asked, surprised.

Jane paled, looking as if I'd just spilled red punch on her best white dress.

"It's nothing," Jane said brusquely. She left the table and headed upstairs. "I hope my room's in good shape."

"What are the Amazons?" Chelsea asked.

"It's a club for girls. Tina and your sister are in it. Shelley Loone too. Don't you know about it?"

Looking hurt, Chelsea just shook her head and pushed her glasses up.

At that moment, Daddy came to the door, and Chelsea and I talked no more about it. If we had, the future might have been different.

The next unusual event of vacation was visiting the O'Neil family on Lake Minnetonka. Following Miss O'Neil's written directions, we drove down what seemed like an eternity of winding roads, then up a curving driveway to the top of a hill. The many-windowed, long, one-story home looked across the ice-covered lake.

We arrived in the late morning and walked up cement stairs set into the hill, up to the side porch where an entry led past the kitchen into the spacious living room where a fire roared in their brick fireplace.

While I took off my boots and coat, Linda O'Neil met us, wearing a dark green and red dress. She wore a sprig of holly in her hair. She led us to the very center of her relatives who were gathered near the fireplace, and I was introduced to many adults, too many to remember. The only one who stood out was Mr. O'Neil, Linda's tall, gray-haired father. He had a long face with a gray mustache, a barrel chest, and a deep voice. He didn't say much to me.

I looked out the picture window down the steep hill, past the swimming pool, toward the ice-covered lake. Down on the lake, a large square area had been shoveled clean of snow, creating a private skating rink.

I noticed movement just below the house. Out from the shed next to the snow-filled swimming pool, three children were pulling a long toboggan into view.

Miss O'Neil leaned over my shoulder and I smelled her light perfume. She whispered, "Those are my nieces and a young cousin. If you'd like, you can join them. They're getting ready for their first run down the hill."

I eagerly looked to Daddy, hoping for permission.

"Just pull your hat down tight," he winked.

Dashing into the entry and jamming on my boots, I threw my coat on and ran outside, pulling on my hat and mittens.

I glanced back to the house's long central picture window. Daddy stood next to Miss O'Neil, each of them holding a cup of eggnog. Her father stepped up to Daddy and began talking to him. Daddy glanced at me and waved. I waved back.

I ran through the snow, over to the other children. They were friendly, once they knew who I was. The oldest one, a fair-skinned, blond boy named Joshua didn't even wear a hat.

"And this is April and that's Sylvia," he said. He obligingly offered me the front seat in the toboggan.

I hesitated. "But I've never been on one. I can't steer."

"You don't steer a toboggan, at least not very well. Just hold on. If we start heading for a tree, we tip the toboggan over."

"What if we're going too fast to tip over?"

He laughed matter-of-factly. "Then we hit the tree. Hard."

It sounded like fun. They finished dragging the toboggan up near the house's foundation, and they helped me climb on. April's legs wrapped around my waist, then Sylvia's legs around her.

Joshua pushed, then leaped in back. We picked up speed. Before I knew it, we had whizzed past the swimming pool, narrowly missing a tall evergreen shrub.

Snow flew up on our sides and began pelting me in the face. My pulse raced. I couldn't catch my breath.

I blinked rapidly, trying to get the cold, biting snow out of my eyes. Reaching up with my mittens, I wiped my eyes. It didn't help. Powdery at first, then stinging and fiercely cold snow blew into my face, and I saw nothing but white. I began to panic, not knowing if we were heading for a tree. Behind me, the other children laughed and screamed joyfully. I didn't know if I was excited or afraid or both.

Not able to stand the onslaught of snow, I ducked my head and let April catch the brunt of the snow shower.

We went faster, seemingly faster than I'd ever gone before.

Suddenly we hit a jarring bump, flew through the air, and landed on the icy lake, skidding across the ice rink. I fell back against April who fell back against her cousin Sylvia who fell back against Joshua.

We slid to a stop and I could breathe again. We untangled our legs and looked at one another. Snow crusted our hats, our mittens, our coats, our faces.

"Ready for more?" Joshua asked.

I spit out small clumps of snow. "You bet!" I shouted.

Each time we went down the hill, we flew faster and less snow pelted us. I'm not sure which was better—more speed or more snow. Nothing beat that first ride for sheer excitement and sheer terror.

Later, we thawed before a roaring fireplace, just in time for dinner: a choice of roast turkey or duck.

At the adult table, the grown-ups discussed foreign affairs and the stock market. I was glad we kids sat at a separate table. We talked about school. April, Sylvia, and Joshua went to private schools and took pleasure in telling me about the advanced courses they were taking.

In the middle of the meal, Joshua looked at me in a calculating way and his tone became suddenly flippant, almost condescending. He raised his eyebrows. "And what special classes are you taking, Angela?"

"Special classes?"

"You know. Violin. Advanced math. Theater."

I blushed. I looked at their curious faces, at Joshua's supercilious smirk. He stabbed his meat with his fork. I swallowed, my mind suddenly a blur, then said: "Death."

Joshua stopped in mid-mouthful.

He quickly chewed, swallowed. "What do you mean?"

"We live in Paradise, remember?"

"So? Linda teaches there with your father. We know all about those suicides. We even discussed them in our values class."

"But," I said softly, leaning forward across the table, "I—" And here, I confess, I paused for emphasis. I know it was prideful, but I didn't like his haughtiness. "I was a witness. I saw both bodies."

I sat back and continued eating as the full implications of my knowledge swept over them. April and Sylvia immediately pestered me with questions. Through it all, Joshua smiled approvingly, realizing how I had turned the tables on him. He nodded in my direction, almost respectfully, acknowledging my feat.

I must say that I felt accepted as their equal for the rest of the day. After dinner, Joshua even let me ride in the back on the toboggan.

We had a light supper, and then I played my two Christmas carols. I didn't use any music, not having any, yet I wasn't nervous, and I played without making a mistake.

Some time later, as I was playing a card game with the other kids near the fireplace, I looked up from my cards and saw Miss O'Neil and Daddy standing near the mistletoe hanging from the kitchen archway. She and Daddy shifted under it and he gave her a kiss. She certainly didn't mind.

Suddenly I wanted to run up to them, press between them. I almost put my cards down and began to rise, a contradiction of emotions blazing within me, hotter than the fire. She was kissing my Daddy! He and I were a family, inseparable, immutable. I looked away quickly, back at my cards, embarrassed, confused. I had wanted to jump between them, yet Linda O'Neil had already jumped between Daddy and me.

I didn't understand what I was feeling. I wanted her for a mother, didn't I? Yet, how much would I lose Daddy?

"Your turn, Angela," Joshua said.

"What?"

"Your turn."

I blushed. "Sorry."

"Anything wrong? You don't look well."

"No, I'm fine. Too much eggnog."

I played my card, then glanced over at Daddy again. They were now talking with others. It would be all right, I told myself. Maybe I would have to share him a little. I would get used to it.

Linda O'Neil, laughing at some joke, moved near a corner lamp that elegantly highlighted her long, dark hair. Yes, I thought, I would get used to it. I would have a mother again.

A short time later we said our good-byes. I hated to leave. It had been a gloriously magical day.

On the way home, I fell asleep in the car.

"What did you think of the O'Neil family?" Daddy asked me over breakfast.

"I wish we lived there."

Daddy didn't say anything for some time.

"What did you think?" I asked.

"I have mixed feelings." He adjusted his glasses and looked off thoughtfully. "I'm afraid I don't mesh with their thinking, or with their prosperity."

"That doesn't matter. It's Linda you like, right?"

He nodded. "Yes, I like her. It's hard not to. But she's almost eight years younger than I am. And she's so attached to her family." He paused and his gray eyes looked directly at me. He was very serious. "When you marry someone, you also marry her family."

"What about Mommy?"

"That was true in her case too. She just happened to be an only child. If her parents weren't in Florida, you know we'd visit them regularly."

I quietly ate my cereal, not sure if I liked this turn in the discussion. I was confused: first I want Miss O'Neil for a mother, then I see them kissing and I'm not sure what I want, then I decide I'll take the risk, and now Daddy has misgivings.

That afternoon we played a game of Monopoly and I brought up Linda O'Neil's family again.

"They are all so nice," I said.

"Very much so. Yet their different values came out clearly at the dinner table. They are extremely interested in gathering material things. That's all they talked about: investing and remodeling."

"But they're Christians, aren't they?"

Daddy rolled the dice and landed in jail. "They would say they are."

"Miss O'Neil is, isn't she?"

"Without a doubt."

"Well?"

I rolled, landed on Chance, read the card, and joined him in jail.

"She doesn't realize how different it is raising a family on a teacher's salary. You and I manage just fine, but we buy most of our clothes at second-hand shops or discount stores. You know that I saved for half a year to buy you that Christmas doll. We make ends meet and don't complain, but I don't know if she's ready to give up all she is accustomed to having."

"She can learn."

He paid his way out of jail. "Yes, if she really wants to. But learning can be hard." He paused. "Being willing to let go can be hard."

He threw doubles, landed on Free Parking, collected the kitty, and then landed on Marvin Gardens with three houses.

I owned it.

I wiped him out.

"For us," he said, "money and the things that money buys aren't that important. It's fun to have some extra things now and then, but money isn't central to our lives. In the long run, the extravagant things—all material things—don't really matter. For Linda and her family, material things seem to be their driving force."

Later, Daddy and I wrote a thank you note to the O'Neil family for their hospitality. After we mailed it, we stopped in at the Paradise Thrift Shop. Miss Bloomsbury was sitting in her usual corner by the window. "Good afternoon. How is the famous teacher and his little princess?"

"I don't want to be known for things I'd rather have avoided," Daddy said.

She chuckled. "That's true of most people in Purgatory."

"I see you've picked up some slang from the kids."

"The name seems to fit, doesn't it? What can I do for you? Looking for warmer clothes? Last year's best seller?"

"I was wondering if you would take some model train cars and buildings. Do you take everything on consignment?"

"Yep. I write it in my big black book. If something sells, you get the money, less the 25% I keep. I write the checks twice a month. You can set the price or I can."

"Do you think model train cars will sell?"

"Hard to say what sells in Purgatory."

I'd been looking at some old toys under the window. She noticed.

"I've no new collector dolls for the little princess," she said. "I'm still meaning to fix up that old doll."

I smiled politely, but I dreaded seeing how that poor doll could be massacred further.

"If you don't mind, I'll look through some of my model train cars and bring them over," Daddy said. "I need to thin the collection."

"That's what I'm here for," she smiled. "As I always say, one man's trash is another man's treasure."

After supper that evening, before we were going to read together, I asked Daddy, "What's Purgatory?"

"Did you look it up?"

"The dictionary said it's a place where people 'expiate their sins.' What's that mean?"

"It's the belief that those who accept Christ have to be punished for their sins."

"But that would mean that Jesus didn't pay for our sins."

"I know. To my way of thinking, Purgatory doesn't make sense."

"Is Purgatory in the Bible?"

"I couldn't find it anywhere. Years ago I tried."

"Then why do some people believe in it?"

"That's hard to explain, Angel. I think that some people choose to believe that they'll suffer for their sins so that they'll behave better here on earth." He looked off thoughtfully. "Or maybe they want to make sure that the other person will pay for his."

"But Jesus did die for all our sins, didn't he?"

He put his arm around me. "Yes, Angel. 'Once for all.' And we can be glad of that."

"So there is no Purgatory, is there?"

He sighed. "If there is, Angel, it's this life, not the next."

I hugged him. "I'm glad. I can't think of Mommy any place other than in heaven."

"Neither can I, Angel. Neither can I."

CHAPTER 21

Scrawled inside the back cover of a battered copy of *Go Ask Alice* in the Paradise High School library:

> *people gotta take back this country.*
> *people gotta do what's right.*
> *people gotta kill the killers, if that's what it takes.*
> —Warren G.

Thursday of the next week, Daddy met me at my classroom door after school. He wouldn't tell me what was the matter until we were out of town and driving toward Hillcrest. The overcast sky made the snow-covered fields look gray.

"The investigator with the sheriff's department wants to ask me some questions. Evidently, something doesn't add up."

"I knew it!"

"Knew what?"

"Dirtball did it."

"Dirtball?"

"Warren Gallagher."

Daddy frowned: "We talked about that before."

When we arrived at the sheriff's office in Hillcrest, a tall deputy opened the door for us. It was Deputy Garrison. A man in a shirt and tie then came out of an office and shook Daddy's hand. He had a friendly smile and thinning hair like Daddy. He could have easily been mistaken for a teacher—except that he wore a gun and a badge on his hip.

"I would've been glad to come out to your home, Mr. Kiln."

"We've had enough unusual intrusions lately."

"Whatever makes you feel more comfortable," he said.

Daddy turned to me, introduced me to Mr. Jensen, the county investigator, then said: "You wait here, Angel."

While Daddy talked to him in his office, I waited in a brightly-lit hallway. Deputy Garrison brought me a can of root beer.

I soon became bored and started flipping through some worn magazines lying on a nearby table. Nothing for kids. I tossed the magazines back.

Finally, Daddy came out, looking tired.

Mr. Jensen put his hand on Daddy's shoulder. "Thanks for going over everything again, Mr. Kiln."

"I have one question before we go: do you still have the suicide notes? Something about them didn't seem right."

Mr. Jensen stepped back in his office for a moment, then returned and handed Daddy a copy of each. Daddy scrutinized the copies meticulously, then gave them back.

"Something wrong?" Mr. Jensen asked.

"Other than Duane's note is too eloquent, no, I don't think so. The only thing—" Daddy hesitated, then pointed to the copies in Mr. Jensen's hand. "Except the 't' in Chet's note. He always slanted them."

Mr. Jensen raised his eyebrows. "They've been thoroughly checked by the family, but thanks for the tip."

I took Daddy's hand and we headed for the door. "Did you learn who started the fire?"

Daddy stopped, looked down at me.

"What fire?" Mr. Jensen said, rushing up to us.

"The one in the shack."

Daddy knelt, facing me. "A fire in the shack?"

"Of course. Smoke was coming from the stove pipe."

"When was that?" Daddy asked.

"While I waited outside. I saw the smoke. When . . . you know."

Daddy put his hands on my shoulders. "Are you very sure about that, Angela?"

"Yes," I nodded. "I thought everyone knew it."

Daddy looked up at Mr. Jensen. "Maybe Duane lit it."

Or Dirtball, I thought.

"Could I ask you both to step into my office for a few minutes?" Mr. Jensen said. Daddy led me into the investigator's office. He had some soft big chairs for us and a long wooden desk for himself. He turned on a small tape recorder after Daddy gave his permission, then asked me to detail what I remembered. I told him what I recalled, which wasn't much. He asked me about the smoke again as well as a few more details.

Mr. Jensen thanked us, then ushered us to the lobby. I don't think he believed Daddy about the handwriting or me about the fire. On our way out, Deputy Garrison opened the door for us.

Daddy leaned over to me as we walked to our car. It was dark and cold outside. "Last night I had another nightmare, and this time I remembered it. I dreamt about those notes."

By that time, I was starving so Daddy drove to Hillcrest Pizza. The owner, a gray-haired, portly man with a slight accent, served us. After we ate, Daddy drove straight back to school. We entered the quiet building. A custodian was sweeping the halls. The third floor was dark.

Our footsteps echoed down the empty hallway. I ran my hand along a few lockers, flipping the locks. The rattling padlocks echoed eerily with our steps.

Daddy opened his door, turned on the switch. Warm light streamed into the dark hall.

He walked straight to his file cabinet, quickly searched the folders, and pulled out two—Duane's and Chet's. He laid the folders on his desk and opened them.

"See?" he said, pointing out one of Chet's papers.

I looked at Chet's handwriting. Every "t" of his did slant!

Daddy studied Duane's handwriting as well. His finger tapped the end of one of Duane's papers. "Look here." He pointed out the end of Duane's essay. "Duane never put a final period on anything he handed in. Yet he did in his suicide note."

"Maybe he wanted to finally do it right."

Daddy took the file folder. "Duane was never concerned about doing anything right. He always took the easiest road."

I knew from Daddy's excitement that he thought he had

discovered something important, but I thought that any small changes in handwriting could easily be explained by the fact that Dirtball had forced Duane and Chet to write those notes before killing them.

The next day at school, rumors were flying through the school like frenzied bats. Mr. Jensen had interviewed others in addition to us. Margie said that she had heard about a grand jury—but none of us knew what that was. A murder theory was quickly gaining credence in the popular imagination, and I wasn't the only one pointing a finger at the culprit: Dirtball was as good as convicted.

Saturday morning, I opened the living room drapes. The bright sun lit the clear morning sky and made the snow brilliantly white. As I stood in my nightgown looking out, Dirtball's truck pulled up outside our house and stopped. The murderer stepped out!

"Daddy!" I shouted, terrified.

Daddy walked in, tying his bathrobe around his waist.

I ran to him and clutched his hand. "Don't go to the door!"

"Nonsense."

I couldn't believe it! Daddy opened the door.

Dirtball stood, his hands in his pockets, looking down.

"Yes?" Daddy said.

He stammered. "I—I need your help."

I ran upstairs to hide.

Within moments, Daddy had him inside and sitting at our dining room table while I huddled at the top of the stairs. Dirtball unloaded his life story: his parents died when he was young; he had no friends in Paradise; he had an illegitimate baby and got married; his seizures began in Vietnam; he came home and his wife divorced him; he relied on his monthly veteran's disability check for food; he started taking drugs after his time in the military; he broke his drug habit over ten years ago.

"And I'm telling you," he concluded, "that the vandals have returned. I need your help. I don't know no one else. Least no one that would help. I need help to keep a watch through the night."

Daddy didn't deliberate; he didn't hesitate. He agreed.

Before I could do anything to prevent it, Dirtball, drug-dealer and murderer, had pulled Daddy into life-threatening danger.

As Dirtball drove away, I turned on Daddy furiously. "But he's a murderer!"

"I agreed to keep watch just one night."

My lower lip quivered. "I've gotta come too."

His gray eyes flashed angrily. "Listen, Angel, you can't always come with me. I wish you hadn't been with—" He stopped himself and his tone softened, seeing my tears. "Will it make you feel better if I find another adult to come with me?"

I nodded. I didn't fear that a vandal would hurt Daddy; I was afraid that Dirtball would.

Within seconds, Daddy was on the phone explaining the situation to Richard Manitou.

"Fine," Daddy concluded. "Six o'clock. We'll be there." He hung up and smiled at me. "Guess what? Not only will he come along, but they invited you to stay overnight."

I pouted. I crossed my arms. Then I thought about how much fun it would be to stay over there, but I wouldn't, I couldn't, give in too easily.

"I don't know—"

"Sure you do. You'll have fun. See what it's like to be surrounded by little brothers and a sister. And since Rick will help Warren Gallagher too, you don't have to worry."

After an early supper, Daddy put on his warmest clothing and we drove over to the Manitous' home.

"Someone else owns the farmland," Daddy explained as we got closer, "but they own the ten acres around the house."

We drove down their long lane. Mrs. Manitou greeted us at the door and ushered us in. The kids gathered around us, and

Gabrielle, the youngest, grabbed my hand and didn't let go until she'd given me the complete tour of the house. While Mr. Manitou gathered flashlights and changed into warmer clothes, Daddy joined Gabrielle and me on the tour.

Their home had high ceilings and dark woodwork. Like our home, it was old, and most walls were wallpapered which, upon close inspection, covered many imperfections in the plaster. The three bedrooms upstairs were drafty around the windows.

"This is my bedroom," Gabrielle said, indicating a pink and white decorated room. A sleeping bag lay on the floor with several stuffed animals beside it.

"I get to sleep on the floor," she said. "You get the bed."

I turned to Daddy, knowing I shouldn't accept the bed, especially when the floor seemed colder.

"Whatever Gabrielle wants," he said softly.

"That'll be fun," I told her. She grinned, quite pleased.

She brought us downstairs again and showed us a small bedroom turned into a study. History books lined the shelves. A large oak desk sat along the wall with some Indian art hanging above it. Mrs. Manitou joined us.

Daddy glanced over the books admiringly. "Rick should teach more history."

"He enjoys math, but history is his favorite subject," she said. "Maybe he'll get to teach more of it after the consolidation."

In the corner of the room, standing on a wood block, was a rough-surfaced, gray stone about three feet high. Above it, on the wall, hung a large rusted key.

"Why do you have a rock in your house?" I asked.

"Supposedly," Mrs. Manitou said, "if you stare at the stone just right, you can see a face. See these indentations here? Those are supposed to be the eyes. Here's the nose."

I tried to see the features, but couldn't.

"The stone was found centuries ago by Richard's ancestors. They called it the Spirit Stone. They hung corn on it, sort of like an offering. Sometimes they'd add pieces of meat from the hunt. About 1840, a missionary came to the tribe. When the chief accepted Jesus, he presented the stone to the missionary. The missionary, in return, gave the mission key to the chief.

"Years later, when the mission closed and the church was going to be demolished, Richard's great-grandfather discovered the stone in the church cellar. He knew what the stone was, having seen it as a child, and saved it from being buried along with the rubble. When Richard's father, a very strict Christian, later took possession of it, he buried it in their backyard. Later, Richard dug it up."

Just then, Mr. Manitou walked in, dressed in outdoor winter clothes.

"You may be wondering why I keep it," he said, pulling on heavy gloves. "Though it had been an idol, it is also part of my family's past. Unlike my ancestors, I don't worship it, and, unlike my father, I won't bury it. I believe we need to know our roots, so that we can fully appreciate what we've been grafted into—the family of God. I hope to pass that knowledge along to my children."

Just before leaving for Dirtball's, we all prayed together, then Daddy hugged me and kissed my cheek. I stood at the front window and watched them drive off. Dusk was falling. It looked as if it would be a clear, still night, perfect for their vigil. I had prayed for a heavy, blinding snow.

Mrs. Manitou laid her hand on my shoulder comfortingly. "They'll be fine. Neither Richard nor your father will take chances."

I nodded but didn't reply.

"Besides, vandals rarely strike twice in a row. If they do, their stupidity will make them easy to catch."

I nodded again, feeling even more afraid.

She knelt beside me. "Let's go outside for a minute before it gets too dark to see. I want to show you something."

Joan Manitou turned to Gabrielle. "I want to show Angela our land in the back." Gabrielle grinned and ran off to join the two boys who were now playing with toys in one of the upstairs bedrooms.

We put on our boots, coats and hats and stepped out the back door. Mrs. Manitou carried a large flashlight. The wind blew colder and the moon was out. Their yard light cast a silver brilliance across the snow. We hiked behind their house, our feet breaking through the crusted top layer of hard snow. It was getting colder every second. I held my mittens in front of my face and blew warm air onto my nose.

The land sloped down from the house toward a marshy area. Under her flashlight's harsh beam, dry cattail stalks stood like slender, fragile sentinels in the snow. The entire land glowed softly under the moonlight. A narrow, frozen creek wound through the fields and cut through the marsh. Near the marsh's edge, a small wooden bridge crossed the creek. On the other side stood a grove of oak trees. Past the trees, the snow undulated over several small hills.

"Many years ago this marsh was a lake's shoreline," Mrs. Manitou said, "but farmers tiled most of the water away. You must return in the spring, when the creek is running and the wildflowers are first blooming."

We trudged through the snow to the bridge.

"Those hills are ancient burial mounds. Richard's father bought this place when the farmer sold the house and the non-tillable land."

The wind gusted, blowing a light layer of fresh snow across the white crust. We walked onto the bridge. A thin sheet of ice made it slippery.

"I like to stand here in the summer and imagine all the people who have walked this land: the early nomadic hunting Indians, the later woodland Indians, the first trappers, the early settlers, the machine-wielding farmers. Like us, the land changes, but more slowly."

She paused and bent down to face me. "The only thing that doesn't come and go, that doesn't change with the seasons, is God. We can always count on Him." She smiled, patting my shoulder. "Don't worry about your father."

That night I had devotions with the Manitou children, but I couldn't help thinking that Joan Manitou and I had shared greater devotions on that icy bridge. I fell asleep, praying for Daddy and Rick Manitou, praying that Dirtball wouldn't get them.

The wind rattled the windows.

I awoke hearing Daddy's laughter. I jumped out of bed and ran to the kitchen. Daddy and Mr. Manitou were sitting at the table drinking coffee. Mrs. Manitou, in a sky blue bathrobe, leaned on the counter, arms crossed.

"Morning, Angel," Daddy said, seeing me in the doorway. He reached out his arms and I hopped onto his knee.

"Ooof," he groaned.

"We better start over," Richard Manitou said.

"After we got there," Daddy explained, shifting me onto both legs, "we decided to man our posts inside rather than outside, as Warren had originally suggested. It was just too cold. By the way, Warren was very glad that Rick was along. 'Your Indian blood will catch them fer sure,' he said. Our plan was simple. We took different rooms of the house: the back and two sides. Two of us were always to be awake while the third one slept.

"Around one o'clock, I heard footsteps crunching through the snow back by the garage. I hurried to the kitchen and found Warren, who was supposed to be awake, snoring on the floor. Before waking him I thought I'd verify that something indeed was happening.

"So I roused Rick who was stationed in an empty bedroom. The moon was out, so we kept our flashlights off as we sneaked out the front door and went different ways around the house toward the garage. We heard more noises—clumsy footsteps in snow banks, restrained giggling. The vandals were either very inept or very drunk or both.

"Since it was Warren's house, we both thought he'd want to be in on the catch, so Rick waited while I slipped back to the house to awaken Warren. I shook him several times. He was such a sound sleeper—I could see why he was an easy target.

"He finally stirred, then jumped up. Rubbing his eyes, he shook his head and grabbed his flashlight. I quickly explained what we'd heard so far.

"He nodded quickly, like an excited puppy, and then he

abruptly dashed out the front door, leaping down the steps and around the house like a madman."

"Meanwhile," Mr. Manitou said, "I'd crept to the right side of the garage on the corner by the alley. I heard someone spraying paint, and I could smell the aerosol on the wind, but before I could peer around the corner, Warren Gallagher came barreling through his backyard like a one-man tornado. I jumped around the corner, turning on my light just as Gallagher leaped around the other corner of the garage, shining his flashlight all around, and shouting some incoherent battle cry.

"They were facing his direction, so I could only see three backs. They wore thin jackets and gloves, but no hats or boots."

Daddy laughed. "I caught up with Warren as he lurched toward them. I fumbled for my flashlight, snapped it on and saw one vandal, a guy in his mid-twenties. Startled by my light, by the whole escapade perhaps, the vandal jerked his hand up before his eyes and tossed his can of spray paint into the snow bank."

"Weren't you scared?" I asked.

"Why?" Daddy replied. "Can you imagine them? Three drunk, incompetent vandals are standing in the middle of a narrow alley, flashlights shining on both sides of them and a screaming wild man leaping in front of them. They did the only possible thing: they ran right through the hedge across from the garage.

"Without hesitating, Dirtball leaped right after them. Rick and I split, running opposite ways around the hedge.

"As it turned out, they came my way. One pushed past me and I got a good look at the other two as they followed him. They headed off into Browner's Woods while Warren was shouting, 'Where's my gun? Where's my grenades?' They disappeared into the woods just as Rick ran up to me."

Mr. Manitou took over the narrative: "I suggested that Warren call the sheriff while Jack and I follow them. He swore, spit, and kicked some snow, but he liked my suggestion. 'Just don't kill them until I get there,' he said.

"Jack and I took off for the woods, not really expecting to find them. We stayed on the trail. A few times, we spotted a flickering light ahead. Evidently, they had a cigarette lighter with them. We realized how cold it was and we became more concerned about finding them for their own safety: three drunks were likely to get lost and freeze to death before morning.

"We came to three dead trees and followed a little path that led to a ravine. We saw the shack below us with yellow tape around the area."

Daddy hugged me tighter. We knew that place well.

"We saw there were no footprints going down there, so we retraced our way along the main path and spotted their footprints heading along a different path that headed south toward the depot.

"We followed that trail, but by then they must have made it to safety. We returned to Warren's and found that a deputy had arrived. It was the tall, young guy: John Garrison. Warren was screaming at him: 'This is the third time!'

"'We're working on it,' Deputy Garrison replied. He turned to us and asked if we got a good look at them."

Daddy took over the story: "I told him that I had. We then drove to school and rummaged through the library and found some past annuals. After some searching, I identified one picture that I was sure of.

"Deputy Garrison nodded as if he had expected it. 'That's Sam Morrison. His truck is still parked near Gallagher's house. That crew has been drinking and causing problems every weekend for over a year. They usually go to Joe Morrison's house west of town and sleep it off.'

"We asked Warren why they would single him out.

"He ground his teeth and said, 'Who knows?'

"Garrison asked if I could make a positive identification. I said I could if I saw the person again."

"After the deputy left," Mr. Manitou said, "we knew that Warren was hiding something, so we pressured him to tell us why they would vandalize his garage and not others. He finally told us that some years ago he had caught kids in the old shack using drugs and called the sheriff. It was some Morrisons. He guessed that they still carried a grudge."

"That's a long time to hold a grudge," Daddy said.

"Some people do all their lives," Richard Manitou said.

"By then it was almost morning," Daddy concluded. "We grabbed a few hours of sleep and came here."

Relieved, I hugged Daddy as hard as I could.

A few hours later we went to Sunday school and church with the Manitou family. At the beginning of the service, Pastor Jim announced that Mrs. Browning had delivered a baby boy. Daddy put his arm around me and whispered: "I was sure happy when you were born. I think I'll keep you."

"I think I'll keep you too," I replied.

Later I saw Daddy and Rick Manitou yawn quite a few times during the service, and I think Daddy fell asleep during the sermon. I nudged him and he jerked upright. I started to laugh but bit my cheek to stop. Afterward, Daddy and I went home and spent a quiet afternoon and evening.

By Monday, though, the whole town had heard some version of the chase. Evidently, Deputy Garrison had discovered all sorts of illegal activities at Joe Morrison's house when he drove out there early Sunday morning.

I thought Daddy and Mr. Manitou would be heroes. The next day, I learned differently.

CHAPTER 22

*I remember when dad took time from the farm, we went to
Yellowstone.*

I remember being picked last for kickball in first grade.

*I remember when Tina moved to Paradise and became my
friend.*

She didn't pick on me or hide from me like the others.

—poem by Shelley Loone

During morning recess, Chelsea and I sat on the swings, idly
kicking some fresh snow with our boots.

Margie strode over to us, put her hands on her hips, tipped
her head back, and sneered. "Why's your dad and Injun Joe goin'
after the Morrisons?"

I was shocked. I didn't know how to reply, what to reply.

Seeing my defenselessness, she pressed her advantage.
"Protecting Dirtball, are they?"

"Well, sort of. Uh. Um. He asked for help."

"A murderer like him?" She spun on her boot heels and marched
over the packed snow toward the other kids.

At lunch, an older student at the table behind me snidely
remarked, "Look, there's Kiln. The druggy lover's kid."

I blushed scarlet but didn't turn around.

Chelsea, sitting across from me, heard it too. She leaned forward,
her glasses sliding down her nose. "Don't feel bad. The Morrisons
are related to half the town."

After school, I found Daddy standing beside Mr. Manitou in
the parking lot. They stared at a flat tire on Mr. Manitou's car.

"Angel, someone slashed his tire."

"Well," Rick Manitou sighed, rubbing his gloves together, "it could've been worse."

"Be glad you live in Hillcrest," Daddy said.

"Are you worried?"

Daddy shrugged nonchalantly. "If this is the price I have to pay to help someone as miserable as Warren Gallagher, so be it. Besides, what do I have? A rented house and an old car with bald tires."

As they changed the tire, a stiff east wind began blowing across the parking lot.

"Snow's coming," Mr. Manitou observed, looking at the gray sky.

That evening, as a snowstorm started to whip through the county, Mrs. Putnam knocked on our back door.

"I just wanted to stop in for a minute," she said, stomping her feet free of snow as she stood on the top step.

"Come in and sit down," Daddy said.

She stepped inside. "I can't stay long. I need to get some papers corrected." She touched Daddy's shoulder and looked at him sternly. "Jack, be careful."

He grinned. "I always am."

"Many people here are related to the Morrisons, one way or another, and they've never taken kindly to teachers, much less teachers who help catch one of their own."

"What do they have against teachers?"

She crossed her arms. "A few hold grudges from when they were kids, but mostly because we're outsiders. We can't be controlled by the usual means."

Daddy took off his glasses and cleaned them with his handkerchief. "I hate to ask, but what are the usual means?"

"Intimidation. Threats. Malicious gossip. Vandalism. Andrew Johanson crossed them when he first came here. His paper's never been the same."

That night four inches of snow fell, but not enough to cancel school.

The Morrison comments subsided on Tuesday, only to have the other rumors ignite on Wednesday: kids were talking about more people being questioned by the sheriff's department.

Once we were home, Daddy read the paper and his gray eyes flashed with more indignation than I'd ever seen.

"Look at this!" he exclaimed angrily, throwing the paper down on the floor.

I quickly snatched up the paper as he stormed toward the phone. He had been reading a letter to the editor.

> It's a shame our justice system works so slowly. First, we suffer the grief of a death. Then a second death. Now some of us are hearing that the suicides weren't suicides after all. It's high time the sheriff and the county attorney earned their pay and got to the bottom of this.
>
> On top of this, the person most likely guilty gets involved with two outsiders and they get some fine young men in trouble with the law. Does the law wait to punish? No. Not this time. I ask, what's wrong with our county?
>
> Rebecca Madison.

Daddy was talking on the phone to Mr. Manitou.

"Of course I'm angry, Rick. Aren't you?"

Pause.

"Rebecca Madison is a Morrison, huh? Figures."

Daddy adjusted his glasses.

"But they'll tar and feather Gallagher."

Daddy's voice calmed. "You're right. Right. We'll keep praying. Thanks."

Daddy hung up, then reached for the phone and called Mr. Johanson.

He paced while talking, yet he made his voice sound calm, almost pleasant. He complimented Mr. Johanson on his news articles covering the county investigations.

"But," Daddy went on, "I think you're printing those letters prematurely. You're going to cause more problems. Yes, I know you're a journalist. Yes, I know you have the freedom to print those letters. No, I'm not asking you to censor, but you don't have to print them, and you certainly can edit potential libel. Where does responsible news end and inflammatory propaganda begin? We can't let the guy be lynched. Andy, just ask yourself if you are hiding behind the freedom of the press to increase your readership. Is your journalistic ethic selling out to the businessman in you?"

I never knew what Mr. Johanson replied, but Daddy accepted it, looking as if he'd done all he could.

"Be careful, Andy," he added. "You'll have to do what you feel is best."

An hour later, there was a knock on our back door. I answered it. Mr. Johanson stood there. "Is your dad home?"

I let him in, called for Daddy, then went into the living room, but I could still hear them. I pulled out *The Secret Garden* and tried to read, but my eyes just stared at the pages.

"Jack, I need to let you know why I can't take sides—or when I do, I need to stay on the Morrisons' side. When I first came here, I learned that one of the town elections was suspect—a Morrison running for county commissioner, Morrison relatives counting Paradise ballots, you know, the whole bit. I did my civic, journalistic duty and exposed it in my paper. The next day half my subscribers canceled their subscriptions and more than two-thirds of my advertisers dropped their ads."

"I see."

"I'm a businessman who can't afford to be a journalist. And because of that, I'm stuck in this community because I've nowhere else to go. I'm too old to start over."

I heard them go to the back door.

"Thanks for telling me. I'm sorry I wasn't more understanding."

"I admire your courage, Jack. I really do."

"It's not courage. I've had no other choices."

"I'm not so sure of that," Mr. Johanson said. "You just reject the alternatives."

The next day, new pieces of gossip floated through the school. About the Morrisons: were they involved with the twin murders? About Daddy and Mr. Manitou: why did they help Dirtball? Was there a drug connection? About the sheriff: what was he hiding? When was he up for reelection? And wasn't he distantly related to Gallagher?

After school, I went to Daddy's room and found him talking to Miss O'Neil. She stood in front of his desk with her arms crossed.

"I'm worried about you, Jack."

He leaned back. "Oh, I'll be fine. I only received one piece of hate mail, nothing like Rick's slashed tire."

Don't push off her sympathy, I wanted to tell Daddy. Accept it. She'd like that. I stepped back into the hall, not wanting to eavesdrop—at least, not noticeably.

"But you're involving yourself with this Gallagher I've heard about—"

"He's pretty harmless."

"But the Morrison family is very influential in this community. Did you know Larry Bates is married to a Morrison?"

"No, but that doesn't matter. Warren Gallagher needed help. Besides, Mrs. Putnam already cautioned me."

"I don't want to see your reputation dragged down, that's all."

I heard his chair squeak, so he must have stood up. "Don't worry, I'll be fine."

I held my breath. I hoped that I'd hear a kiss. Instead, they walked out of his room, but at least he had his arm around her waist.

Friday came. I couldn't wait for school to end. After the dismissal bell rang, I dashed upstairs to the third floor. Outside Daddy's closed door, I found Robert Oatley and Jane Turpin arguing in hushed voices. He seemed worried and she seemed angry.

I slipped past them, but stopped before opening the door:

through the narrow window I saw Daddy talking to Mr. Manitou and Miss O'Neil.

I waited by the door and dropped my backpack. Robert and Jane didn't seem to notice me.

"What's wrong?" Robert urged.

"Why should you care?" she snapped.

"I still want to be friends."

I didn't want to hear people arguing, so I left my backpack and escaped down the hall to the high school drinking fountain. Standing on my tiptoes, I could just reach the water.

Wiping my mouth, I turned and saw Mr. Hanson in the science room. His door was open and he was pacing near the classroom's long counter and gesturing wildly.

"What do you mean?" he shouted, then dropped his voice. I couldn't hear what he said next. I didn't want to.

I didn't know where to go. I was caught between two arguments.

I recognized Mrs. Walker' s voice. "It can't go on."

Mr. Hanson's hushed voice grew shrill, agitated. "But why? Your husband's a jerk—you've said so."

"Then so are you. You're only interested in the excitement. At least, if I stay with him, I'll have my children. They'll have me. And they'll respect me."

I found myself drawn into their quarrel. Yes, I thought, tell him off, Mrs. Walker. I stepped closer, moving to the side of the open door.

Suddenly Mr. Hanson came through the doorway and I jumped back, bumping the lockers.

He didn't see me.

He grabbed the knob, pulling the door shut on their conversation. The door's slam echoed down the nearly empty hall like a gunshot.

I looked back at Daddy's door just as Mr. Manitou came out and closed the door. He walked to his own classroom. At the same time, Jane was striding toward me. She marched past me while Robert trailed behind. They disappeared down the steps.

I walked back to Daddy's room and waited outside his door. Miss O'Neil was still talking to him. I wanted to go in, but they both looked quite intense, so I waited as patiently as I could, hoping that they wanted to be alone for a few minutes to talk over adult things.

I sat down with my back to some lockers. I thought about what I had overheard in Ted Hanson's room. Mrs. Walker was right. If Mr. Hanson cheated on his wife, he was a jerk. But she was too. Yet maybe she was going to try and make things right. I hoped so.

I pulled *The Secret Garden* from my backpack. Being an adult was hard work. But maybe they just made it harder than it had to be.

I found my bookmark and began reading.

I hadn't read far when I looked up, surprised to see Robert returning and walking toward Daddy's door.

He stopped right next to me, looked in the small window, and waited. He paced slightly, looking nervous.

He glanced down at me. "Will you tell your dad that I want to talk to him?"

I nodded and he left.

Daddy finally opened the door, looked down, surprised to see me. "Sorry, Angel, I didn't know you were waiting out here."

I rolled my eyes, disgusted: Where else would I be? I wanted to say, but I didn't in front of Miss O'Neil. I smiled politely, or at least I tried.

It wasn't like Daddy to not know exactly where I was at all times.

Miss O'Neil greeted me in passing and departed down the hall.

His gray eyes, looking somewhat wistful, watched her go, then he set his jaw and ran a hand through his hair. He was upset. She was upset. Everyone in Paradise was upset. I was the only one in the world who seemed not to be.

As Daddy gathered his papers, he told me what bothered him. "Mr. Jensen has been interviewing some people. I heard that the sheriff has been getting involved as well. There's talk of a grand jury." He read my puzzled expression. "That's a group of citizens who investigate to see if a crime was committed."

"Why do they think there was a crime?"

"Rumor has it that the autopsy report said that the bullet that killed Duane came from the wrong angle for him to have held the pistol."

"See?" I said triumphantly. "I told you."

"I showed Rick and Linda the handwriting samples and explained the differences with the suicide notes. I was sure that they'd agree with me, but they politely said that I should stick to teaching."

We headed out the door. "What are we having for supper?" I asked.

"Hot dogs," he said. "Sorry. No time to fix anything fancy."

I zipped my coat, put on my hat and mittens. "Did you and Miss O'Neil talk about anything special?"

He glanced down at me as he put on his hat. No doubt he was beginning to suspect my feelings.

"Yes, but don't get your hopes up."

That Saturday, I went over to Chelsea's house. The fresh snow was heavy and moist, just perfect for a snowman. We had just finished building the bottom two round sections when Tom Oatley came out of his house.

Hatless, mittenless, and wearing untied high-top tennis shoes, he kicked his way through a snow bank. He carried a small brown paper bag that he stuffed into his coat pocket, and then he shoved his hands into his pockets too. A rolled-up newspaper stuck out of his back pocket. He never looked up.

I noticed his stooped shoulders and shuffling gait, and I wanted to shout a "hello" or throw a snowball at him, anything to break his mood, but he didn't seem to know that we were there.

He stomped through a pile of heavy snow, no doubt thoroughly soaking his tennis shoes.

We finished rolling the snowman's head. Grunting, we hoisted the head and plopped it on top.

I turned to Chelsea. "Come on."

"Where?"

"On an adventure."

Giggling, she followed me as I followed Tom all the way to the eastern edge of town. The city plow hadn't cleared the streets there yet. Tom walked in the middle of the street, following tire treads. He passed Gallagher's house, still not looking up.

We stopped, looked at each other.

"Are you going past Dirtball's?" Chelsea asked.

"Why not?"

"But he's a murderer."

"Don't you think I know that? But it's daylight now. He won't do anything."

Tom, to our surprise, headed right into the woods. We waited a few minutes, wondering if we should follow. We've gone this far, I thought, we may as well see it through.

Chelsea sensed my decision. "We better not," she whined.

"He's up to something. Or something is bothering him."

"We shouldn't."

I wasn't worried. It was just Tom Oatley. He owed me. "You can wait, but I'm going." I ran after him into the woods, and Chelsea finally caught up.

His shuffling tracks in the snow were easy to spot. Chelsea cleared her throat nervously. Running as quickly and as quietly as we could, we followed the path and spotted him ahead. We saw him jump over the three dead trees, slip on the third one, and fall down. We jumped off the snowy path and ducked behind some trees until we were sure he had picked himself up and gone on.

We sneaked forward, climbing over the three dead trees. They were crusted with ice and snow.

Tom's tracks led down the embankment. He had gone into the shack, past the yellow tape that was stretched around it.

We waited. Nothing happened. Suddenly I remembered that

Robert had wanted to talk to Daddy. I had forgotten to deliver the message.

"Chelsea, remind me to tell my dad that Robert wanted to talk to him."

"What about?"

"I don't know—Look!" I whispered, pointing to the stovepipe.

Wispy fingers of smoke lifted into the cold air. Tom had lit a fire in the shack's stove. I shivered, vividly remembering the night Duane had died.

I wished we hadn't followed Tom.

Chelsea stomped her feet, beginning to get cold. "Shouldn't we go down to the shack and talk to him?"

"No. He can't know we were following him."

"Let's just say that we were exploring the woods. Our meeting him was just a . . . just a—"

"Coincidence. No."

"Then let's go back."

I was about to agree with her when we heard a noise on the other side of the shack, like someone walking through the woods.

Frightened, I ducked, pulling Chelsea down after me. We spied a figure trudging along the ridge of the old railroad bed through the snow, heading back toward town. It was Tom! He had left the shack, apparently through some back exit.

I stood. I was determined to find out how he had managed to get out the back. "Come on."

We slid down the embankment and slipped under the yellow tape. The shack was empty, cleared of every piece of dirt, wood shaving, candle, or pop can. The table was there, but moved to the side and cleared.

Snow had drifted in through the back wall, around the two sides of the old paneling. Walking to the base of the paneling, I pushed on it. It seemed solid. I looked up and saw that two small hinges held it to the ceiling. Grabbing the sheet of paneling, I pulled it toward me. It swung in easily and I lost my balance, tumbling backward to the cold ground. The paneled wall swung silently back against the snow embankment.

To my right, the stove crackled with a small fire.

I picked myself up and nervously pulled my mittens farther down my wrists. I went to the stove and opened the rusty door.

"Careful," Chelsea cautioned as she saw what I was about to do, "it's hot."

Inside, surrounded by burning newspaper and smoldering wood chips, lay a wood figure, its edges on fire.

I reached in quickly, grabbed the carving, and flung it behind me.

Stomping on the smoking figure, I quickly checked my mitten. It was only singed along the thumb.

We knelt by the carving. Though its edges were burned, we could see that the figure was a precise representation of Duane Johnson, one hand over his heart, the other at his side, his head slightly askew. Both hands were empty.

Chelsea pushed her glasses up and frowned, as puzzled as I. "What's the wood carving mean?"

"That's exactly how Duane looked when he was dead. Except that he held a gun. No one knows how Duane looked except the authorities, Daddy, Dirtball, and me."

Chelsea touched my shoulder lightly: "And the murderer."

CHAPTER 23

I like to swim
I like to play
I like to chase the girls all day
—poem by Duane Johnson

Chelsea and I rushed home, but we discovered Daddy gone. I shouted his name, then remembered that he had gone to buy groceries in Owatonna. "If you're going to spend the day at Chelsea's, it'll be a good time for me to go," he had said.

Chelsea and I paced around the house like nervous cats. I didn't like looking at the statue and so I shoved it under the sink. It seemed a safe place to stash it.

Chelsea called her mother and told her where we were. We paced some more.

"Should we call the sheriff?" she asked.

"I want to talk to my dad first."

Chelsea bit her fingernails. We watched cartoons for what seemed an eternity: about ten minutes.

"Maybe it isn't what we think it is," Chelsea said.

We retrieved the statue, set it on the kitchen counter, and inspected it from all sides.

Chelsea knelt, removed her glasses, stared at the wooden figure from a lower angle like a mechanic might look under a car. "It could be someone else."

"You know better than that."

She put on her glasses: "Well, maybe it is."

"Don't whine," I snapped. "Besides, you're right. It probably is a statue of someone else." I slid the statue back under the sink.

"Do you really think so?"

I know it wasn't right, but I lied to shut her up: "Yes."

She seemed relieved. She smiled: "Let's finish the snowman."

Frustrated, I muttered, "Fine." She had an amazing capacity for denying the obvious.

We returned to her house and the snowman. With renewed enthusiasm, she added larger cheeks to the snowman's face, and then, with a flourish, stuck on the finishing touch: twig arms. As for me, I kept my eye on the Oatley home.

When finished, we went inside and watched more cartoons. I sat by the window so that I could observe the Oatley house. In the middle of the afternoon, while Chelsea was watching an old movie, Daddy finally drove up.

I grabbed my coat and dashed to our car. "Bye!" I shouted back.

We were home in less than a minute, and Daddy was no doubt wondering why I was in such a hurry to leave a friend's home. Dashing into the kitchen (forgetting to wipe my feet, which Daddy reminded me of), I pulled out the statue and showed it to him. He took a sharp breath, didn't say anything, and examined the carving, turning it over and over in his hands. He frowned and his gray eyes began to smolder.

The phone rang.

"I'll get it," I said, not wanting to disturb his concentration.

It was Chelsea. "Angela, I remembered."

"Remembered what?"

"I was to remind you to tell your dad. Something about Robert."

"Oh yeah. Thanks."

"What's your dad think? About, you know?"

"I don't know yet. I'll call you later."

I hung up and told him that Robert had wanted to see him on Friday but I'd forgotten to deliver the message. He looked off thoughtfully and rubbed his jaw.

Suddenly, he grabbed his coat and headed to the front door. "Come on."

"Where? To the sheriff?"

"To the Oatley home."

Mrs. Oatley, wearing a sweater and jeans, answered the door. She looked surprised yet pleased to see us.

I glanced across the street, hoping Chelsea wouldn't notice our car.

"May we come in?" Daddy asked. "We need to talk to you."

She ushered us into the living room and took our coats. Daddy and I sat on the worn sofa. Flushed and slightly nervous, she perched on the edge of the chair and reminded me of a small and fragile sparrow, though she was neither small nor fragile.

Daddy explained the events of that morning, and then he pulled the charred statue from his coat pocket.

She gave a little gasp and took the statue slowly. Her blue eyes widened as she studied it. Her hands quivered.

"What does it all mean?"

Just then, Robert walked in from another room.

"Mom, I—" He saw us, stopped.

Mrs. Oatley stood. "Robert, do you know anything about this?"

Staring at the statue, he paled slightly. I wondered if he had seen it before.

He abruptly looked away and shrugged. "Looks like one of Tom's carvings." He shoved his hands indifferently into the pockets of his jeans.

Daddy shifted on the sofa and nervously cleared his throat. "Angela told me that you wanted to see me."

Embarrassed that I'd waited so long, I stared at the worn carpet.

"Oh, yeah," Robert said quickly, shrugging again. "I needed help with my assignment, but I figured it out."

No one said anything. The refrigerator hummed in the kitchen.

Daddy cleared his throat again. "Maybe Tom could help us understand his wood carving."

Leaving the statue beside the chair, Mrs. Oatley promptly went through the kitchen to the basement door and called for Tom.

Robert, meanwhile, sat in the chair, nervously rubbing his

hands together. "Well, um, good snowmobile weather, huh?" He smiled but didn't look happy.

"Yes," Daddy said but didn't smile.

Mrs. Oatley ushered Tom in. When he saw us, he stopped, becoming as stiff as his statue. He didn't say anything and looked down at his worn tennis shoes. Mrs. Oatley picked up the statue and showed it to him.

He crossed his arms, glaring defiantly. "So? I'm always carving things. If it's no good, I throw it away. You know that."

"But Angela saw you try to burn it in the shack where the—the—?"

He clenched his jaw, then pointed at me. "She had no business digging it out of the fire."

I flushed, suddenly feeling as if I were accused of wrongdoing.

Daddy, sensing my unease, put his arm around me. "Angela did what she thought best." It seemed that nothing good was going to come of this meeting. "We're all trying to do what's best."

Daddy rose. I jumped to my feet, wanting to get out of there.

"Mrs. Oatley," Daddy said, "I hope I haven't created a problem. I wanted you to know what I knew." His gray eyes regarded Tom kindly, and he added, "In case someone needed to talk."

Mrs. Oatley anxiously studied her two sons, then looked at Daddy. Her chin quivered and she blinked rapidly. "Thank you. I don't know what to do, what to say." She slowly, hesitantly, reached out her hand.

He took both her hands. "Maybe it's nothing after all." He turned to go. "Tom's quite an artist. We all grieve in different ways." He ushered me to the door where he turned, speaking softly. "I'm sorry if I made a mistake coming here. Our intentions were good."

Overcome with emotion, Mrs. Oatley rushed to Daddy, grabbed his shoulders, and kissed him on the cheek.

He blushed.

She stood back, her hands falling to her sides. "I know that. My sons do too. That's why they respect you so. I don't know what to do except pray."

"We'll pray for you too," Daddy said. "Sometimes that's all we can do, perhaps all that we need to do."

When we were in our car, I asked Daddy what was going on.

"We might have made a mistake. If Tom carved that as a way of coping with his grief, we erred by interfering." Daddy slid the key in the ignition. "But we would've erred worse by going to the sheriff." He started the car. "If, however, Tom knows something, then we haven't done enough."

"What do we do now?"

"We'll do what Mrs. Oatley's doing. Pray."

We did that right then, right there. But as Daddy drove home, I put the pieces of this mystery together. I knew, as well as I knew my own name, that Dirtball had killed Duane and Chet. Tom knew it also, but he was too afraid to tell. Perhaps he had been an actual witness. Carving the figure was his way of dealing with it.

The next few days flew by quickly, as if time itself sped up in a vain attempt to resolve the crisis quickly. On Sunday, we went to Sunday school and church. I was disappointed when we sat in the pew: Miss O'Neil wasn't there; Daddy saw my crestfallen look.

"She must be spending the weekend with her family," he whispered.

Mrs. Oatley and Robert arrived late to church and sat in the back. I didn't see Tom.

After church, Mrs. Oatley was friendly to us, perhaps too much so. Her hands fidgeted with her Bible and her lips quivered slightly.

Robert avoided us.

On Monday, Tom's name was on the school absentee list. After school, I saw Robert and Tina talking in the hall while Jane stood to one side, defensive.

On Tuesday after school, as soon as I got home, our phone rang. "I'll get it!" I shouted, beating Daddy to the phone.

It was Chelsea. "Come over right away." She sounded nervous or scared.

"What's wrong?"

"I only have a minute or two before she calls back. Hurry and you'll see."

Great, I thought. Chelsea's wild imagination is running loose in the world. I sighed. "I'll be right over."

Daddy set his briefcase on the kitchen table. "What is it?"

"Oh, Chelsea's excited about something. May I go over for a few minutes?"

"Sure. Supper's at 5:30."

I rushed over there as quickly as I could, climbing over a few snow banks on the way.

Chelsea met me at the front door, immediately grabbed my arm, and pulled me inside. "Hurry," she whispered. "She's on the phone again."

"Who?"

"Jane." I tossed my coat on the sofa and followed her upstairs. Since Chelsea was whispering, I did too. "What's going on?"

"I heard Jane on the phone talking about Duane and Chet."

"So?"

"She talked like she knew something." Chelsea gripped my wrist, squeezing it hard. "Angela, I'm scared, really scared."

"It's probably nothing."

She led me upstairs to her room that was directly over their kitchen. She pointed to the gravity heat vent. Bending over it, we looked down onto the top of Jane's head as she stood talking on the phone.

"Jane was off the phone for a few minutes, and that's when I called you."

"Where's your mom?"

"At work. Just listen."

We both knelt with our ears to the vent.

"Yeah. I know that," Jane was saying, her voice rising in pitch and sounding irritated. "But we can't hide it forever. You know that."

Pause.

"What do you mean?"

Pause.

"Shelley needs someone to talk to."

Pause.

"They're going to start a grand jury."

Pause.

"Things like this aren't suppose to happen in small towns."

I sat up. "This doesn't mean anything," I whispered.

Chelsea sat up too, but put her hand on the grate. "You didn't hear what I heard." The grate wiggled a bit and we both jumped at the noise.

From below Jane must have heard or seen us because she said, "I better go. Snoopy sister. Yeah. Maybe." She hung up and Chelsea and I looked at each other, panic catching us like a stiff wind ripping two flimsy kites.

We dashed to the door and down the steps.

Jane caught us halfway down, grabbing us by the arms. She was furious.

"What did you hear?"

I stammered for words, but couldn't say anything.

"N-nothing," Chelsea stuttered. She swallowed hard, her darting eyes looking to me for help.

"Yeah," I added.

"You know how I hate it when you listen to me on the phone," Jane snapped.

Her grip was hurting my arm. She dragged us into the living room and almost threw us onto the sofa. She turned her back to us and took a deep breath.

When she spun back to face us, she was biting her lower lip and looked close to tears. "Now what am I going to do?"

"I have to go home now," I said. "Supper's almost ready."

Jane glared at me. I didn't move. She turned away and ran both hands through her hair. Just then, the phone rang.

"You two stay here," she ordered.

We nodded obediently, too scared to do anything anyway. She left and we glanced at each other. I felt like crying. Chelsea began for both of us.

"Oh, she's just mad," I said. "Probably boyfriend trouble." I didn't believe me any more than Chelsea did.

We heard Jane pick up the phone and say "Okay" and hang up. In a second, she was back in the room, towering over us.

I swallowed hard.

"Angela, you better get your coat on. Didn't you say it was time for supper?"

"Okay," I promptly said, more than ready to get out of there. Jane led me to the front door as I put my coat on. I glanced back at Chelsea who attempted a weak smile.

Jane gripped my arm again, hard. "Don't say anything about this, okay? And it'll be all right for all of us. Understand?"

I nodded, but didn't understand. I stepped into the cold air. The streetlights were coming on.

I ran all the way home.

I dashed in the back door.

"Wipe your feet," Daddy shouted from the kitchen as I entered, breathless.

"Daddy!" I cried, finally finding my voice. He rushed to me, hugged me, and then I relayed what had happened.

He frowned and looked worried, really worried.

"Do we risk interfering again?" he spoke quietly, more to himself than to me. He walked back to the kitchen stove and stirred the stew for supper. I watched him, not knowing what to do, what to say. Everything had a crazy quality to it: I kept thinking these things couldn't be happening, shouldn't be happening. Nothing was making sense.

After a few minutes of stirring the stew, he sighed, then asked a second time if we should risk interfering again. I wasn't sure if he was talking to me, himself, or the stew. He abruptly shut the burner off, then, without saying anything else, grabbed his coat from the front entryway. "Come on."

I followed him to our car.

In a few minutes we were standing in front of the Turpin house, knocking. It took a least a minute for someone—Jane—to answer the door.

She looked surprised to see us, but, I thought, too surprised, as if she were acting in a play.

"Mr. Kiln," she gushed. "Come in."

We entered. We didn't remove our coats and she didn't ask to take them.

"Did I forget to hand in an assignment or something?"

Daddy was very businesslike: "Angela tells me of some unusual behavior over here."

Jane brushed her hand across her face as if swatting away a mosquito. "Oh, that. I was talking on the phone and kinda over-reacted. You know, pesky little sister and all that." She laughed slightly and called out to the kitchen: "Chelsea, come here and see Angela."

It took almost a half-minute for Chelsea to show up. She looked down most of the time. "Hi," she muttered. Her eyes were red.

"Chelsea, tell my dad what you told me," I blurted.

Jane interrupted, overly polite: "I can leave the room if you want me to," she said to Daddy.

Daddy didn't hesitate: "Thank you."

She looked surprised that Daddy agreed to her suggestion so quickly, yet left without even glancing at Chelsea.

Chelsea didn't sit down; she just stood there and sighed. "I shouldn't have called Angela."

Daddy knelt in front of her. "Why did you call her?"

"I heard some things that worried me. Um, that is, I thought I heard. I didn't hear. You know what I mean."

"What things?"

"Oh, my sister was just talking about boyfriends and stuff and I didn't understand it, I guess, and I got confused." She pushed up her glasses and looked directly at Daddy. "I get confused a lot, you know."

Daddy lowered his voice: "So, you didn't hear Jane talk about Chet and Duane?"

She shook her head quickly. "No."

Daddy rose and looked down at me. I knew that it wasn't true, but I knew there was nothing I could do. He laid his gloved hand gently on my shoulder.

"Let's go, Angel. Chelsea, I understand."

We went to the door. Daddy shouted back: "See you tomorrow, Jane. Sorry to bother you."

When we were outside, I exploded: "Daddy, it wasn't like that! Chelsea was all upset and I never got to hear everything and Jane was really angry and grabbed my arm—"

Daddy cut me off. "I know, Angel. I believe you. Something's going on, but we're not about to discover what it is. At least not now."

The next day in school, Chelsea wouldn't look at me when she came into the classroom. During recess, she avoided me.

On our way home from school, Daddy, as always, picked up the mail which included the weekly newspaper. When we got home, Daddy went through the paper and chuckled.

"What's so funny?" I asked.

"Listen to this." He read a letter to the editor:

> *"Paradise is at last showing its true colors. A murderer is rumored on the loose and the most important thing is family loyalty. Instead of the truth coming out, prejudice, just under the surface, is breaking out for the entire world to see. Instead of justice, Paradise closes ranks and throws mud on outsiders or those who are different. Wake up, Paradise. Grow up, Paradise. What we need is the truth. It's the only way to heal."*

"Who wrote it?"

"It says the name was withheld by request, but I suspect that Mr. Johanson himself wrote it." He chuckled: "A true journalist comes through in the end."

The next day at school, Chelsea still avoided me. Near the end of recess I had had enough, so I walked up to her and asked what had really happened the other day.

Tears brimmed her eyes. "They said I couldn't say anything."

"Who said that?"

She looked down. "I can't say."

I didn't push it any further. Nothing was making sense to me. I didn't get a chance to talk to Daddy about it again because after school, when I entered his room, Shawn Dixon was sitting in the back of the room, quietly working on a math assignment. Detention again. I hoped, with everything else going on, that we wouldn't have a return visit from Mr. Dixon.

My boots clumped along the floor. I slipped into a front desk on the other side of the classroom, as far as possible from Shawn Dixon. I laid my coat on the desk behind me.

Daddy came in, saw us both at work, and began to finish his paperwork. I could hear the clock ticking.

Suddenly Jane Turpin ran into the room.

"Mr. Kiln!" she said breathlessly. "You gotta come. Robert needs help!"

Daddy jumped up. "Is he hurt?"

"No. Please come. We need your help."

Daddy dashed to his closet, grabbed his coat. He didn't put his boots on. I quickly slipped my coat on.

Daddy rushed to the door, then stopped and looked back at Shawn. "Under the circumstances, you can leave early, Shawn. Consider your time complete. Please turn off the lights on your way out."

Shawn grinned smugly, already getting up.

I ran down the hall after Daddy as he hurried after Jane. My clumping boots slowed me up.

"Your car," she called back to us, "We don't have much time!"

We ran down the stairs and out the building.

Daddy and Jane reached the car first. She opened the back seat for me and jumped in the front seat. Daddy started the car as I hopped in.

Shawn was already slipping out the building and zipping up his coat, a big grin across his freckled face.

Daddy turned to me. "Angel, I better drop you at home." He glanced at Jane. "Where to?"

"Back in the woods. The shack."

Daddy paused, a sense of foreboding coming over both of us.

"Hurry!" Jane pointed wildly at the steering wheel. "Don't stop at your house. I'll watch her."

Daddy stepped on the accelerator, almost spinning the car in the parking lot.

Jane began to cry. "I should've told you the other day. I almost did, but couldn't. I just couldn't. I'm sorry, so sorry. But Robert figured everything out. He knew I had a key, but he trusted me and didn't want to get me into trouble. But he kept prying, kept pushing. I never should've mentioned it to Tina. It's all my fault! She is meeting him at the shack, she said, and explaining everything to him. He never should've gone!"

Daddy sped to the edge of town, parked by the path. "Go ahead. I'll catch up," Daddy said.

Jane took my hand and we headed down the snowy path. Quickly slipping on his old boots from the trunk, Daddy then followed Jane and me into the woods.

We ran along, following two sets of footprints in the snow. A short distance into the woods, I stopped, suddenly very scared. Fallen branches, broken by snow and ice build-up, littered the snow-covered underbrush. Above us, bare tree branches stretched like a canopy, but many of the branches were twisted, gnarled, intertwined. I shivered. The sun was setting and long shadows stretched throughout the woods. Then Jane grabbed my hand, pulling me onward and the trees became a blur.

We came to the three dead trees. I remembered the other times I'd been here, and I thought: three dead trees—we've had two deaths already.

Jane stepped over the fallen trees and stood at the edge of the slope, pointing to the shack. The yellow tape had been ripped and some of it had blown away.

Daddy leaped past me, over the trees, and almost lost his footing in the snow. I took a deep breath of cold air and followed.

Heedless of his own safety, Daddy slid down the embankment, snow and gravel mixing behind him.

Jane and I followed more carefully and caught up with him. He was standing just inside the doorway; he was completely still.

We peered past him into the small shack. Tina, wearing a wool scarf and coat, sat at the table, facing Robert, facing Daddy, facing us.

In her gloved hands, Tina had a pistol pointed our way.

Daddy's breaths came in short, heavy gasps, and he didn't say anything for a moment.

Tina looked surprised to see us, yet her gun never wavered.

"Getting a little crowded in here, don't you think?" Daddy said.

No one laughed.

"Should we go outside?" he asked.

No one moved.

Behind his back, he gestured for Jane and me to back up. We didn't move. His hand gestured more urgently, wildly.

"I'm not leaving," Jane stated, sliding past Daddy.

I stepped forward, grabbed Daddy's hand, but stayed half-hidden behind him. I peered past his elbow.

Jane walked to Robert's side and said, "Tina, it's gone far enough." Jane's back blocked my view and I couldn't see Tina anymore.

"It's already gone far beyond any of our intentions," Tina said coolly, "but I have no choice."

"There are always choices," Daddy said. He pushed me back, forcing me behind him. He pushed me again, trying to move me further back, but I stuck to him. There was no way that I was leaving.

"Mr. Kiln, you're the only one in Paradise who would understand what we did and why we did it. We were true to ourselves and to our beliefs."

"Murder? That's hardly a high calling."

What? Tina? She can't be the murderer, I thought. Dirtball killed Chet and Duane. I know it. Tom knows it. And the town knows it too.

Robert spoke, his voice quivering: "The more I thought about it, the more I knew that Duane would never have killed himself. But since I had no other explanation, I had to accept it. Then I noticed how Tom began acting weird, really weird, after Duane's death. When I saw the statue he carved, I knew that Tom knew the truth." Past Daddy's elbow, I saw Robert glance at Daddy. "I'm sorry I didn't say anything then."

"Did Tom witness the murder?" Daddy asked.

"I didn't know he was hiding in the side room," Tina said. "I didn't know anyone ever used this shack anymore. But I don't have to worry about little Tommy. He's too scared to say anything."

"That's true," Daddy added quickly. "And you can trust us to be quiet as well."

She laughed, a slightly sad laugh, yet chilling all the same. I felt cold all over. "Mr. Kiln, you're the only adult I know who understands me, and the one I definitely can't trust to be quiet." I heard her chair slide. She must have stood. "I wish you wouldn't have come."

"I had to bring him," Jane wept. "Someone had to stop you."

"Wait a minute," Daddy said. "Let's not be hasty."

I nodded my agreement though no one saw me. I began to pray urgently, fervently.

"So what exactly happened?" Daddy asked. "Tina, it seems that you killed Chet and Duane. But why?"

"Chet was an accident, sort of. I had meant to kill Duane that night in the depot. I lured him there with a suggestion. But instead of Duane, Chet showed up. I guess Chet wanted to get his points. Though I hadn't planned it, justice was served after all."

"Points?"

"Their Pound and Beauty Club. A girl's weight times her beauty rating. The boy with the highest points wins."

I shivered, recalling the gantlet of boys that I'd seen.

"Everybody's happy. Everybody wins." Tina's voice grew colder, angrier. "Except the girls."

"So you lured Duane that night but got Chet. Didn't Duane realize what had happened?"

"He was drunk when I made the offer at his party. Panting like a rabid dog, he wanted to do it then, any place in his house. He didn't care. Though I had already stolen his father's pistol, I wouldn't do it then. I would've been caught for sure. I told him that I wanted him when he wasn't drunk. I wanted some place special, somewhere quiet, like the depot the next night. It was the perfect place, I told him, nicely secluded. But I knew that it was the perfect place for justice to be served. Getting in wasn't a problem: Jane still had a key that she'd gotten from Robert during the summer."

"Why single out Duane?"

"Duane was the ringleader, their point leader, the one who had to go. Not only had he started his club in Paradise, but Oak Center girls told me that Duane was going over there and starting the same stuff with those guys. With Duane out of the way, maybe some sanity would return to dating. Anyway, at the party that same night, in his drunken generosity, Duane must have passed me off to Chet, but was even too drunk to remember that."

"And you had to cover your tracks."

"I had a note ready for Duane. It wasn't hard to write a new one for Chet on the remaining half sheet of paper. In small classes like ours, we all know each other's handwriting. My only mistake was forgetting to leave the key on Chet's body. That kept the authorities snooping."

"Yet justice hadn't been served. You still had to get Duane."

"Exactly. But I had to wait for another opportunity. Duane wasn't interested in girls for a while. He said he couldn't, that he was feeling bad about Chet." She laughed briefly, sardonically, and I shivered. "His so-called grief didn't last long—a few days. Soon he was back to his old habits. He had another party. It was easy to get into his bedroom, steal a pistol from the gun case."

"But you didn't know you'd have a witness this time."

"No. I didn't count on Tommy hiding in this shack."

I heard a girl sobbing behind the curtain to the other room.

"Shelley, it'll be over in a minute," Tina called.

"So, what do you do with us?" Daddy asked.

I peered around Daddy's elbow.

I could now see Tina as she moved to the center of the room, her back to the paneling. With her free hand, she brushed her blonde hair from her forehead, and her voice softened. "I don't want to do this. Please believe me."

"You don't have to," Daddy said calmly.

She gripped the pistol with both gloved hands. "The Amazons must be protected."

I looked up at Daddy and was shocked, for he was nodding understandingly!

"I can see that. But what will you do? How can you explain our deaths?"

She gestured with the gun in her hands. "After Robert confronted me with his suspicions yesterday, I thought of how Dirtball's house is always unlocked. I slipped into his house and got this gun. The town already believes he killed the other two. The Morrisons will be glad to get him."

"Convenient."

"Believe me, Mr. Kiln, I wish it wasn't necessary. Especially you. But there are always civilian casualties in a war."

"Are you planning to murder the entire Pound and Beauty Club?"

"I will do whatever is necessary." She pointed the gun at Robert. "You're not one of them, but you understand, don't you, Robert?"

"Are you going to kill my daughter too?"

"What?" Tina gasped. "She's here?"

"You'll have to kill me, too," Jane shouted.

Trembling, I grabbed Daddy's waist and closed my eyes. My whole body was shaking from fear and I was as cold as if I'd been tossed unprotected into a January blizzard.

Suddenly the gun went off. My whole body jerked. Daddy moved forward and I fell to the cold ground.

Terrified that he was hit, I screamed: "Daddy!"

Daddy was still standing and his back blocked my view of Tina. To my right, I saw Shelley peering out from behind the ragged curtain. Robert and Jane cringed in the corner near Shelley.

I jumped up, toward Robert, and saw the back panel-piece swinging. Daddy stepped back, holding Tina's gun. I then saw Shawn Dixon crouching over the fallen Tina. Dust filtered down onto my head. The darkening sky could be seen through the bullet hole in the tin roof.

"I was never one to miss a fight," Shawn said proudly, standing up. He looked across at Daddy, his hands on his hips. "Hey, Mr. Kiln, is this extra credit?"

CHAPTER 24

The American judicial system must be overhauled. Not only does it take far too long to bring a case to trial—a deliberate miscarriage of justice for both accused and victim, but then justice is not always carried out. Procedure has greater weight than people, technicalities greater weight than truth.

—from an essay by Tina Lewis

The media's third wave that rolled through Paradise was the biggest yet. The television networks even showed up for an hour.

I don't remember how many people we talked to—attorneys, deputies, and even reporters. Yes, reporters. Daddy let down his anonymity for a little bit after Shawn Dixon stood before the cameras and told the reporters fantastic tales of his phenomenal exploits. Daddy talked to reporters only long enough to let them know that Shawn was not Sherlock Rambo Holmes.

Reporters wandered along Main Street, quadrupling the usual traffic, as they searched for Paradise residents to interview. If I had been a reporter, I thought it would be fun to pose as a Paradise native and give an interview to another reporter. Looking back, maybe Shawn Dixon and I were more alike at that age than I had thought.

Surprisingly, not a single reporter to my knowledge contacted Mr. Johanson, yet he continued plodding along, printing the facts as they became available. He was a changed journalist, looking for news and human feature articles regardless of whether or not it hurt—or helped—his business.

"I'd forgotten why I originally wanted to be a journalist in a small town," he later told Daddy. "I started out wanting to write what I felt was important, not what an omnipotent editor wanted to read. I'm only sorry it took me years to remember the relative freedom one can have with a small paper."

As the full details of the Amazons' actions were published, shock and indignation erupted in town. Older people heard the Amazon name and were convinced that a new cult had invaded southern Minnesota. Home schoolers shook their collective heads at their gatherings and said that this just showed the decadence of public schools while they patted themselves on the back for not having their children tainted by such an environment.

Initially, since the story trickled out in tidbits, sometimes entwined with rumor and speculation, most people linked Dirtball Gallagher with the Amazons. In Paradise's collective imagination, he became the wild-eyed, sex-crazed, drug-dealing ringleader. I'm sure the Morrison clan—with all its many tentacles—added to that rumor as it ran rampant through Ironwood County. After all, if the rumors were accepted as fact, then the Morrison boys charged with vandalism could be portrayed as valiant defenders of virtue.

A resentful anger, usually reserved for big government, simmered through Paradise residents, looking for a focal point. They were angry that their countywide reputation for peace and security had been shattered. When the authorities cleared Dirtball Gallagher of any connection to the Amazons, that anger descended upon Tina.

She was ridiculed and reviled in any and all conversations. Whenever Paradise residents talked about the case, they distinctly pointed out that Tina wasn't born in Paradise but had only recently moved in. No one clarified that "recent" meant the first grade.

The consensus in town was that she should be tried as an adult. The courts eventually agreed. Talk spread about an insanity plea. When Daddy heard that rumor, he said that Tina would never allow it. As usual, Daddy was right. Tina had known precisely what she was doing. Even after caught, she didn't repent.

Everyone quickly learned that Duane's date rape of Shelley had set Tina on her murder course, but no one in Paradise ever tried to justify her motivation, at least not in my hearing. The two murdered boys, Paradise residents seemed to feel, were just boys.

The St. Paul and Minneapolis papers mentioned the Pound and Beauty Club, but it didn't get the space that the Amazons did. There was also a passing reference to the Pound and Beauty Club on one of the Twin Cities news broadcasts, but the reporter talked about the Amazons more, making it sound as if most of the girls in school were part of a new feminist cult. No one ever brought up the fact that Chet and Duane had died with high levels of alcohol in their blood.

Of course, Mrs. Hill returned to school for the third time. She was determined to find all the girls who were Amazons, but she quickly learned that the group had been limited to Tina, Jane, and Shelley. Mrs. Hill had mistakenly believed the media.

No charges, by the way, were ever brought against Jane and Shelley. The defense could easily have put Shelley on the witness stand, and the last thing the prosecution wanted was to raise the specter of Duane's vicious treatment of girls.

Because of the time we spent with the authorities and with lawyers, we saw the Oatleys more than ever. Daddy seemed to enjoy talking with Mrs. Oatley and he even took her out for dinner once. As I got to know her better, I learned that she was extremely caring and had a very good sense of humor.

One night I had a nightmare and woke up screaming.

Daddy was at my side even before I was fully awake. He hoisted me onto his lap.

"Do you want to talk about the dream?" he asked.

"I don't know," I mumbled.

"That's not like my little Angel not to say what's on her mind."

"I dreamt that you didn't know me anymore." I searched his face in the amber glow of my night-light.

"Something must be worrying you. Do you know what it is?"

"What happens if you find someone else?"

"You mean a new wife?"

I nodded and my chin quivered. "Am I still your 'little Angel'?"

"You'll always be. No matter what happens to me or to us, or how old and feeble I get, or if you get married and have ten kids, you will always be my Angel."

I impulsively leaned against his chest and he stroked my hair.

"If you had one wish," he asked, "what would it be?"

"For nothing to change."

He sighed. "Many times when I stood over your crib while you slept with your special pink blanket hugged tightly against your chest, I wished that you wouldn't grow any older. But time moved on anyway. Then the night before the first day of kindergarten—do you remember?—you were so afraid, I rubbed your back until you fell asleep. I thought then how I wished that I could freeze time and keep you little forever. But because the present is only a fragile moment that will soon be gone, we treasure it. And we treasure each other."

He hugged me tighter. "I learned that when your mother was sick."

I pulled away a bit so that I could see his face. "Daddy, do you still love Mommy?"

"Yes, Angel, I do. Sometimes the pain I felt when she died comes back and hurts me almost as if it were yesterday."

"Yet you've dated Miss O'Neil and Mrs. Oatley."

Daddy paused, searching for the right words. "I still love your mother. If your mother had lived, no other woman would've been anything to me. But now, with your mother gone, an occasional date helps the pain go away." He stroked my hair again. "You'll always be my little Angel. Your mother will always be Mommy to you."

I hugged Daddy tightly, and I wanted to freeze time, but I couldn't.

After the publicity storm passed and the slow gears of justice began to grind, we visited the Oatleys to see how Tom was getting along. Mrs. Oatley insisted that we stay for supper.

"I won't tolerate any excuses." She blocked our exit and crossed her arms. A smile crossed her lips. She was a strong-willed lady.

Daddy acquiesced. I sure didn't mind: Mrs. Oatley was an excellent cook, and it had been my evening to make supper.

As we ate, Tom seemed more like himself, more like the boy I'd seen carving in Mrs. Putnam's class.

"Tom's been meeting with Pastor Jim Thorsen weekly," Mrs. Oatley said. "You like him, don't you, Tom?"

Tom grinned self-consciously and rolled his pale blue eyes. "He's better than Mrs. Hill."

I laughed, glad that someone else shared my assessment.

Robert was extremely quiet for most of the evening, but as we stood near the door to leave, he stepped forward, impulsively grabbed Daddy's hand, and shook it vigorously. "Thanks, Mr. Kiln, for everything."

Daddy was quite reserved in the face of Robert's blatant emotion. "Er, just part of my job," he muttered.

Irritated by his mild response, I poked him in the side. He glanced down at me and blushed as emotion broke through his diffident manner. He grinned, knowing he was caught. He gripped Robert's hand tightly. "You're welcome."

Robert then turned to me, bent over, and kissed me on the cheek. "Thank you, Angela, for helping too."

I felt my face blush a deep scarlet.

After that, Robert and Daddy spent several evenings together at our house, finishing the improvements on Daddy's train set before retiring it for the spring. Actually, I think their work sessions allowed them, unofficially, to discuss the events, although they usually didn't talk much. Men are sometimes like that. If they just do something together, it's as if they said all they need to.

On a few occasions I joined them before becoming bored and wandering off to read. One time Robert asked Daddy, "What would've happened if Shawn hadn't come?"

Daddy listed the possibilities as if it were a multiple-choice test.

Personally, I didn't like to think about those possibilities.

As for Shawn, he was a local hero for a few days. In the television interviews, he portrayed himself as being involved with the mystery from the beginning, cleverly staying after school to gather information, artfully eavesdropping on hallway conversations, adroitly slipping behind the shack in Browner's Woods, boldly attacking Tina at just the right moment. Of course, he wasn't capable of using any of those adverbs without the prior help of Daddy's thesaurus. It was the one time I saw him willingly seek out a book.

Daddy, watching the edited interview on television, laughed. "They bought everything he said."

I was angry. "He just happened to be in detention when you ran off. He was nosey."

"Aren't we glad he was? By the way, I did offer him extra-credit if he would write about it."

"Did he?"

"No. Talking to reporters was more fun."

CHAPTER 25

Spring is watching the last icicle melt.
Spring is running through puddles.
Spring is a tulip pointing to the sun.
Spring is a new beginning.
                    —poem by Angela Kiln, fourth grade

Daddy and I continued to attend the Hillcrest Community Church and we eventually became members. We staked out the fourth pew on the left, and the Oatleys began sitting near us.

Tom never did say much to me about the events surrounding the murder; he never said much to anyone actually, yet I felt that we were friends again, or at least that we were on the road to becoming better friends.

I felt far more comfortable with Robert because he always took time to talk to me. It was almost as if I finally had an older brother. He and Daddy started to create a new train layout and I became the design consultant. Their new layout created a town around a model of the old Paradise Valley trestle, and they dubbed the model town Emmaus: "A fresh beginning for us," Daddy explained, "just like in the New Testament." Tom even got involved, making benches, sidewalks, street lamps; whatever I said that I needed he'd try making.

Daddy and Mrs. Oatley always seemed to find or make opportunities to talk. I did begin to like her more and more, and her cooking was the best.

It bothered me that we didn't see much of Miss O'Neil. Of course, I saw her in music class and for piano lessons, but we didn't socialize beyond the school walls. I first noticed her distancing herself from us after a piano lesson during the height of the media blitz. I was just finishing my final song when Daddy walked into the music room.

"Sounds wonderful, Angel."

While I gathered my piano music and backpack, he sat beside Miss O'Neil on the piano bench. He talked softly, so softly that I couldn't hear him, but I think he asked her out for dinner.

She shook her head. "Sorry, I can't." She looked down at her polished fingernails. "Jack, I'm worried about you and Rick. Many people are saying some awfully mean things about you two."

Daddy's back stiffened and he spoke louder. "We did what needed doing. The whole story will eventually come out—about Tina, about Warren, about the Morrisons."

"Many people support the Morrisons." She lifted her chin pertly and her large blue eyes looked at Daddy as if she were reprimanding a small child. "A Christian has to watch his testimony."

Daddy paled and his mouth dropped open, almost as if she'd slapped him.

Then his gray eyes began to smolder and he removed his glasses. "Linda, there's a time to worry about reputations and a time not. We want to avoid getting soiled by the world, but there's a time to reach down and pick someone out of the mud."

She shook her head slightly, almost imperceptibly, as though afraid to consider whether he was right or not, and she stared at the piano keys and didn't say anything. She didn't need to. The set of her jaw said it all.

Daddy stood, slipped his glasses back on, and looked down at her dark and shining hair. He turned to me and we left. We didn't talk much during supper that evening.

Though the distance between Miss O'Neil and us widened after Tina was caught, in looking back, I think the friendship started to become strained after we visited her family on New Year's. At that point, she began to recognize the contrasting priorities between Daddy and her, priorities that Daddy had seen too, a contrast as clear as the difference between her car and ours. Their friendship could've continued and blossomed, but Daddy was right—change is difficult. Some people aren't ready for it.

They hold onto yesterday's manna.

One evening a few weeks later, Daddy sat at the kitchen table, paying bills. I was reading on the sofa. I heard him sigh, so I came over to him and leaned on his shoulder.

"Can I help?"

"*May* I?" he corrected, grinning.

I groaned. "May I help?"

"You can stamp these envelopes."

"Don't you mean *may?*"

He laughed and hugged me.

I stamped the electric and the phone bills, and then I came to an envelope addressed to the Lewis family. It was square, like a card.

"A note to Tina's family," he explained. "I sent them some money."

"Why?"

"They're hurting financially as well as emotionally. Their legal expenses will consume whatever surplus Mrs. Lewis has, and I doubt Paradise residents will have a fund drive for them."

"Won't Mrs. Lewis think it's odd coming from you?"

He opened the gas bill. "I sent cash. I didn't sign my name. It's ironic: Paradise is upset over the Amazons because the name smells of the occult, but I've yet to hear anyone condemn the Pound and Beauty Club for harassing and abusing girls. The boys sought their own pleasure at the expense of others. Tina, though misguided, sought to create her own justice system."

"You really feel sorry for Tina, don't you?"

Daddy laid his pen down and leaned on his elbows. "I liked her from the beginning. She was fun in class, so bright, so quick."

"But she almost killed us."

"She said she was going to. I don't know if she would have followed through on her threat." He rubbed his chin thoughtfully.

"She felt trapped. She started the Amazons in response to evil. She murdered because of Shelley's deep hurt, perhaps a deep hurt in herself as well. She desired justice." He leaned back, his gray eyes looking thoughtfully at the ceiling. "And she tried to fight injustice with more injustice."

"How do you fight injustice?"

"Each war against evil is unique. All I know is that we must also use the only weapon that heals—compassion." He grabbed his pen, signing a check for the gas bill. "When it comes to how *we* want to be treated, who wants justice? Don't we really want mercy?"

I put the stamp on the Lewis card, pressing it down firmly.

In March, Daddy started the spring play and we were busier than ever. He wanted to direct a more challenging play than the slapstick comedy Mr. Cranberry had suggested, but when Daddy approached him with a different idea, Mr. Cranberry set his jaw and vigorously shook his head, his jowls trembling. "Paradise wants laughs. Stick to hillbilly comedies. They always work."

Daddy reluctantly agreed. "If I ever have to do this again," he later said to me, "I'll have experience and be able to say that I know what I'm doing. Then I'll choose what's right." He smiled. "Now I understand Andrew Johanson's dilemma all these years. It's not easy balancing a profit with what's best for others."

Because of Daddy's full schedule, we were forced to eat out more than ever. Some days it was our only opportunity to sit and talk. Surprisingly, after a few too many consecutive evenings of greasy french fries, I even tried different menu items. They weren't too bad, either.

At those relaxing meal times, I had time to reflect on my contradictory feelings toward Linda O'Neil or any other future mother. I knew that I might have to share him with other kids and certainly with an adult (adults always seeming to take up more time); yet, after mulling it over, I still came to the conclusion that I wanted a new mother. Though I would be losing some of Daddy's time, I would gain some of hers. And a mother would be more helpful as I got older. In some areas, Daddy was a bit inept. He still put stripes and plaids together and was of absolutely no value in helping me fix my hair.

I just wanted veto power over any woman Daddy chose.

One particular evening, after the grand jury had indicted Tina Lewis, we sat at the Paradise Café near the back, our usual spot.

Two older men sat in the booth next to ours.

"George was saying that Channel 10 talked about the Amazon cult last night," one of the men said. "Did you happen to catch it?"

We perked up our ears.

"Naw, I missed it too," the other said, "but I was told it was nothin' new. That female cult come from the Cities. I hear tell it involved Indian voodoo."

"Is that why that Indian teacher helped Dirtball?"

"Sure. I hear the Lewis girl's got a hot-shot lawyer from the Cities now."

"Where'd they get the money?"

"Some lawyer firm from Minneapolis is helpin' them out. They figure it'll be good publicity."

"The county attorney'll botch it for sure."

"You bet. He charged the Morrison boys, after all. How's he gonna do right this time?"

"A real shame those Amazons killed two of our best boys."

Daddy and I looked at each other, shocked: Best boys? I started to say something sarcastic about the gossiping men to Daddy, but he laid his hand gently on mine.

"Real good football players," one said.

"Real good."

"Some game wasn't it? Nearly won."

Daddy leaned toward me and whispered, "Isn't it amazing that people are so loyal to their hometowns?"

"Becky's the same way. She thinks St. Paul is the only place to live."

Daddy ran a hand through his ever-thinning hair and glanced

at a "Home Sweet Home" plaque on the wall: "I suppose that people who identify with New York think it's the best place to live, and people who claim no allegiance, like Mrs. Johanson, think their way is right. I wonder if believing in the righteousness of a town—or no town—is just a reflection of the need for us to believe in our own righteousness."

"What's 'righteousness' mean again?"

"It's like not sinning."

"That's not possible."

"We all have an amazing ability to deceive ourselves, to think that we are better than others. We like to view ourselves in the best possible light. And when it comes time for me to make rules, I will write rules that favor me, not the other person."

"But that's setting up the rules of a game so that you can win."

Daddy grinned. "Exactly."

"Didn't the Fair—." I struggled to recall the word.

"Pharisees?"

"Didn't they do that in the Bible?"

"Yes, Angel, but Pharisees aren't only in the Bible."

A week later we were eating again in the Paradise Café. After Robert took our order, Larry Bates walked in and headed for the center table. Noticing us, he sauntered over to Daddy.

"Well, Kiln, you're a regular celebrity these days."

Grinning, Daddy lifted his hands in mock surrender. "What can I say? Unfortunate timing."

"I'd call it fortunate for you," he grumbled. "You got press coverage just as the consolidation committee was working on staff. Seems an English teacher of theirs, a Mrs. Monroe, is pregnant and wants the year off. Because you got all this publicity, Hillcrest wants you on their staff."

Daddy's reply was slow in coming and cautiously phrased. "I hope they want me because they desire a competent English teacher."

Bates looked at the wall. "I don't have to tell you how this

black eye hurt Paradise in the consolidation. Hillcrest is now callin'
all the shots."

"When I first came to town, you told me then that they were
calling the shots."

"Well," Bates snorted, "almost. Now they call *all* the shots.
Take away the school and you take away the town."

"I'm glad you think education is important."

He glared at Daddy as if Daddy were a complete dunce.
"Education? I said the school."

Daddy looked at me and I almost burst out laughing. He bit
his cheek and I covered my mouth, turning red. Fortunately, Larry
Bates didn't notice.

"It'll be a new beginning for Paradise and for Hillcrest," Daddy
said. "I heard that Dodge County is doing some consolidating as
well: three schools merging. Starting something new isn't always a
bad thing."

"I wouldn't be too sure of that." Grumbling to himself, Larry
Bates turned and sat at the center table and ordered the special.

Robert brought our food.

"So, did I hear that you'll teach at Hillcrest next year?" Robert
asked.

"Sounds that way, though I've heard nothing official."

Robert nodded his head toward the center table. "If Larry
Bates says it, it's official. I'm glad you'll be at Hillcrest: I'll know
two teachers over there—you and Mr. Browning."

"I often wonder," Daddy said, glancing at the back of Bate's
crew-cut head, "if we never see the thing that's born until we let
go of the thing that's died."

Most spring evenings found me at the back of the gym while
Daddy directed play rehearsals. On one particular evening, after
he had turned off the gym lights and I saw students acting on the
lit stage, I leaned against the wall and decided to write my own
book. I pulled my pink notebook and pen out of my backpack.
There was just enough light for me to write.

I won't be able to freeze time, I thought, but I can capture a few moments with words. It won't be good enough for others to read, but that doesn't matter. This is for me. And for Daddy. Maybe someday, when I'm a lot older, I'll look back at these moments I've captured. Maybe then, I'll be able to write good—er, well—enough for others. And maybe then, our time in Paradise will make sense.

In early April, as the legal battles began, Dirtball knocked on our door one last time. Most of the snow had melted, and only dirty islands of snow remained under trees or on the north side of buildings. The tulips, in fact, were already pushing through the moist soil of Mrs. Putnam's flowerbed.

Daddy asked Dirtball in, but he shook his head. "I just came by to say thanks," he mumbled through the screen door. He turned and left.

I've never seen him since. We moved that summer to Hillcrest to be closer to Daddy's new teaching job, but every December we exchange Christmas cards with him. He just signs his name "Warren G."

One Friday, after all the other students had marched out for recess, I lingered and approached Mrs. Putnam's desk, the desk that always seemed so foreboding. There was something that I needed to do, but I was scared to do it. I reminded myself that she was also my neighbor, the one who had shown concern for my father, the one who at times looked at me wistfully from her back door, the one who compassionately came to my rescue at Dirtball's house. Daddy had told me on more than one occasion that she really liked me. I had a hard time believing it. Nevertheless, I knew that I needed to clear my conscience.

She was looking toward the windows and seemed lost in her thoughts.

"Mrs. Putnam?"

She turned, surprised to see me still there. "Angela? I'm sorry I didn't know you were here."

"I wanted to apologize."

She took off her glasses, looking very concerned. "For what, dear?"

"For what I said."

She frowned, confused. "What did you say?"

"For what I said to you before school started, about you being old and everything. I didn't know that what they said was about you, I mean, not you personally, I mean, I didn't know anything really, I was just talking, and—"

She interrupted my babbling. "Angela, I knew that last fall. Until you brought it up just now, I had completely forgotten it."

"You had?"

"Of course. Teachers don't take those sorts of comments personally. You know, if anyone should apologize, I should. Do you remember when I gave you that list of books to read?"

I nodded.

"I knew that you didn't want to read most of those books."

"You did?"

"Of course. But I knew that you had the ability to read them and I thought you'd like them, once you started them. So, maybe we can just call the apologies even."

I smiled. "I'd like that."

I started to go.

"Angela—"

I stopped and turned.

"You have liked those books, haven't you?"

"Yes."

"Good. They say that all is fair in teaching."

"But I've heard Daddy say that all is fair in love and war."

"Angela, teaching *is* love and war."

I started to leave again, then stopped one last time. "Mrs. Putnam, as long as you don't think I'm trying to butter you up for a better grade or anything, I have learned a lot in your class. And I do like you for a neighbor."

She smiled warmly and for a split-second looked as if she might cry. "Thank you, dear."

On a Saturday afternoon, when spring was firmly established, Daddy called me up to my bedroom. He sounded angry. I entered my room. He had pulled my bed away from the wall, and he *was* angry. Very.

"Angel, what's this?"

On the floor where my bed had been lay a small pile of old Halloween candy, its color obscured by the colony of ants crawling over it.

I had totally forgotten about it. It seemed ages ago that Chelsea and I had run around town collecting Halloween candy.

"I'm sorry," I apologized lamely.

He didn't let me off the hook. "You should be. I've been wondering where these ants were coming from. You should know that you can't keep candy around."

As I stared at the scurrying ants, I knew that he didn't have to tell me twice.

A few days later I found a present on the kitchen table. It wasn't my birthday and there was no label.

"Where did this come from?" I asked.

"Just a little something I picked up for you," Daddy said.

I ripped into it. It was a beautiful doll with short dark hair. She wore a pinafore and a navy blue dress with tiny flowers.

"Where did you find it?"

"At the Paradise Thrift Shop."

I was surprised that he had found anything there of value, but as I studied the doll's face, I finally recognized the eyes. "But this doll was a total wreck!"

"I know. Miss Bloomsbury restored it."

"She fixed this herself?"

"So she said. And sewed the dress too."

"But this doll used to be so . . . so ugly."

Daddy shrugged, grinned. "Just shows you what a little love and kindness can do."

The next day I visited the Paradise Thrift Shop. Miss Bloomsbury was sitting in the corner, as usual, reading a science fiction paperback book, as usual. She hadn't lost any weight.

I thanked her for fixing up the doll so nicely.

She smiled and her wide face dimpled as she leaned back and rested her hands on her large stomach. "She was a joy to work on, honey. And the more I fixed her up, the more I fell in love with her. I never played with dolls when I was little, but now I see the fascination." Behind her glasses, her green eyes sparkled. "Dolls don't change, do they?"

"No," I said. "They're always beautiful."

"So many things in life turn rotten."

"It's like the Israelites and manna," I said. "Did you know that if they kept manna overnight, it was full of worms the next morning?" Of course, I had no experience with manna, but I did know what happened to old Halloween candy left under beds.

Her gaze drifted off toward the window. "I like what Robert Frost wrote: 'Nothing gold can stay.'"

"I've heard my father say that. And he always adds that sometimes the beauty is in the changing."

She looked at me for a long moment with her green eyes that suddenly misted over. She took off her glasses and nodded to no one in particular.

I then realized what Daddy had meant about people wearing masks. Disguises come in all sorts and, in Miss Bloomsbury's case, all sizes. Behind her mask, I believe, lay the real treasure. She was just afraid to let people see it.

In school, I remained the hero of my class. I had become the established authority on all matters of consequence, the arbitrator of all recess games. Margie was, quite literally, forced to the sidelines.

One day during lunch recess, after a cool spring rain in early

May, I spied Margie sitting on the first tier of the tire house. Her back was to me. She was hunched over.

We were playing Poison with the boys, getting quite mud-splattered in the process.

The action slowed and I skipped over to Margie. I felt happy and quite magnanimous—that was a word I'd just learned from one of my books.

"You can join us," I called, hopping over a puddle.

She spun and faced me and forced back tears. "Angela Kiln, you are the most wicked person who ever lived."

I stopped, stunned, baffled.

Not moving, I stammered. "What did I do?"

"Everything."

She turned away, her shoulders trembling.

Chelsea ran up, breathless. "Come on, Angela, we're starting another round."

"In a minute," I said, and Chelsea skipped back to the others.

I wanted to return to the game, in fact, I did—for a few moments—but then I realized that Daddy would have tried to help her. I walked back to Margie. How would Daddy handle this? I asked myself, while part of me just wanted to leave her alone.

I spoke softly. "Is there anything I can do?"

"You've done plenty," she snapped.

I blushed, beginning to feel guilty, but about what, I wasn't sure.

She turned away, looked past me toward the school building.

"I haven't done anything to you," I stated, sure of myself.

"You've stolen all my friends." Her venomous glare, like a snake's bite, struck me instantly.

I planted my hands on my hips. "I've a right to friends too."

"They've been my friends since forever."

I didn't know what to say. This wasn't going well.

"So?"

"You're an outsider and you stole my friends. You already have everything."

"What do you mean?"

"You have all those dolls—"

"You make fun of them."

"So? You still have them. And you have a nice house—"

My stubborn streak erupted, forcing me to argue. "It's just rented."

"And you have a dad around every day."

I didn't say anything. I didn't have a reply this time. I decided to listen. That's what Daddy would do.

"My dad's gone. I see him once a year, at Christmas. Your dad is always here and you see him every day after school. Sometimes he even visits you during lunch. And you've been on television. You're a big hero. And now you have all my friends."

She wiped her eyes with the back of her hand. "They're all I got." She bent forward and covered her face with her hands.

I didn't reply. I didn't move. I stared at the top of her head. Her shoulders quivered.

I couldn't make her understand anything, not really. I couldn't explain how we frugally saved for dolls. Telling her that we rented the house made no difference, nor would it help to point out to her the fact that I had no mother. Nothing I said would matter.

She didn't care.

I didn't care.

I began to walk away, back to the other kids, then reconsidered. I looked down at a tuft of grass just starting to grow between cracks in the asphalt. Life coming out of tar and rock. Then I thought of the doll from the thrift shop and how Miss Bloomsbury had restored it.

What could kindness do to Margie? I didn't know, but it couldn't hurt. Sighing, I came back.

"I'm going to rest for a bit," I said. "Go play with your friends."

I hopped up on a tire, sitting down near her. She glanced at me, at first disbelieving, and then she wiped her eyes again, sniffled, and jumped off.

She didn't say anything. Maybe she felt she had proven herself to be right, maybe she felt I was giving her a gift, maybe she didn't think at all. She left.

"Come on," she shouted jubilantly to the other kids, "let's play a new game."

Hesitating at first, they stopped playing their game and clustered around her.

I didn't watch. I stared at the dark brick school building. I looked up to the second floor, to Mrs. Putnam's window. Tom sat by the window, carving.

I looked higher, to the third floor. Daddy's room faced the other direction, but I could see the stairway window. It was comforting to know where Daddy was. Just then, Miss O'Neil passed by the window. She was wearing a new, sky blue spring dress, and her long, dark hair glistened as it flowed down to her shoulders. Below her, in the second floor stairway window, I saw the sixth grade rushing down the stairs. Their dismissal meant that in three minutes Mrs. Fisher would call us in.

I reached back and felt my hair that was finally long enough for a ponytail.

I think I'll cut it.

~ The beginning of
Life on the Fly,
the third novel in
the *Ironwood County Chronicles* ~

Every so often you get an invitation to a place where you don't want to go, and you make up excuses quicker than a collegiate star athlete who is caught plagiarizing, but sometimes you should tell your mind to shut up, put your feet in motion, and go. When that happens, you need to go. Or it might be too late.

For years I kept putting off David Browning. Each spring he'd invite me down to his favorite trout stream. He wanted to teach me how to fly fish, he said, fully knowing that I already knew how. Or at least I once did, when we were kids.

I last picked up a fly rod a little over fifteen years ago.

When I was eight years old, I found two bamboo fly rods in my grandfather's house—down in a pile of boxes my parents were setting aside for the estate sale. I grabbed the rods partly as a fond reminder of my grandfather and partly because the bamboo rods looked intriguing. I have always been drawn to gadgets, especially gadgets involving sports. The rods were in perfect shape, each with a simple reel and spooled line.

When I got home, I gave one of the rods to Davy, my best friend who lived in the white house next to my white house. We rode our bikes over to the nearby football field and practiced casting those rods for hours on end, trying to master the art of sailing line through the air.

I remember fishing together a few times on a muddy creek near Hillcrest and catching a few chubs. Once I hooked a two-pound carp that took a good fifteen minutes to land. But we weren't interested in chubs and carp—the rough fish that anyone could catch with a hook, minnow, and bobber. We wanted to catch trout, those colorful fish that need cold, pure water to survive. However, most good trout streams were too far away for young boys without cars to reach.

So, instead, we enjoyed the vicarious thrill of casting the line on the football field. We would set up coffee can lids as targets for the small pieces of yarn that we would use as flies. Two points if the yarn landed on the lid; one point if the yarn landed within a foot of the lid. I could cast my line farther, but Davy had the greater accuracy. He could land the line anywhere he wanted, if the target was within forty feet. But move the target farther out, and only I had a chance of reaching it.

When we were older and finally able to drive, Davy—or David, as he then wanted to be called—went fishing almost every Saturday. He invited me each time he went. I sometimes went with him to Prince Creek, a clear spring-fed stream usually loaded with small brook trout and a few larger browns. But I had my license too. I had places to drive. Rochester was far more inviting. People—well, certain people—wanted me to drive them. Girls were far more enticing than fish. Life seemed full of possibilities, and I didn't want those possibilities limited to a narrow stream.

But that was years ago. Several lifetimes ago. Before either of us started teaching. Before California. Before my marriage crumbled. Before my long dance with alcohol.

Each Christmas he was faithful to send me a card, sometimes with a picture of his family. Some years I returned a card of my own. A few years I was too drunk to know. Or care.

When we both got e-mail addresses, he sent me regular updates. On his children. On their family trips. On his fishing.

That was before my forced departure from the teaching profession. Before my move back to Minnesota. Before my aborted career as a restaurant manager.

He still sent me letters. I rarely replied.

Then I turned down one invitation from David too many.

A few weeks after I left the restaurant business, I got a phone call from David. I was shocked to hear from him. I hadn't heard his voice in years. He told me that he really wanted to talk to me about something important. He needed, he said, to talk to me in person. Not an e-mail message. Not over the phone.

I put him off. I told him that I could come down in a week or so, fully intending to delay that meeting as well. I didn't want to see him, to let him see me, to see how far I had fallen.

It hadn't been that long since I had left the treatment center in Minneapolis. Though I was thoroughly dried out, I had aged a lot. I was a recovered. Recovering. Always a process.

A few days after his phone call, I saw it on the news.

David Browning, Hillcrest English teacher, had been shot— apparently a hunting accident.

Shot while fly fishing. A wild turkey hunter, the authorities were surmising. Shot in the back. David fell forward into the stream. Drowned. An accident. The hunter didn't even know David had been there.

Maybe.

David Browning wanted to tell me something. Now it is too late.

Too late for him.

Perhaps for me as well.